PHILIP ('Pip') YOUNGMAN CARTER was born in Watford in 1904. He met his future wife, Margery Allingham, when they were both 17. They were married in 1927 and from 1935 lived in north-east Essex. Whilst his wife established herself as one of the 'Queens of the Golden Age' of English crime writing, Youngman Carter followed a varied career as a journalist, a soldier, an artist, a prolific designer of book jackets, a wine writer, magazine editor, a travel writer, novelist and writer of short stories, all distinctly 'on the off-beat'. He died in 1969.

BARRY PIKE is the Chairman of the Margery Allingham Society, the editor of its journal The Bottle Street Gazette and the author of Campion's Career: A Study of the Novels of Margery Allingham.

MIKE RIPLEY is an award-winning crime writer, the author of more than twenty novels and a dozen short stories. He has edited over sixty books for Ostara, including the two Youngman Carter 'Mr Campion' novels. He completed Carter's third novel, left unfinished on his death, which was published as Mr Campion's Farewell in 2014, and has gone on to write two more.

Also by Youngman Carter and published by Ostara Publishing

Mr Campion's Farthing
ISBN 9781906288983

Mr Campion's Falcon
ISBN 9781906288990

Tales on the Off-Beat

Youngman Carter

Ostara Publishing

Ostara Publishing 2015.

This collection © Joyce Allingham Trust 2015

Introduction © B A Pike 2015

Paperback edition   ISBN 9781909619258
Hardback edition   ISBN 9781909619272

A CIP reference is available from the British Library

Printed and Bound in the United Kingdom

Ostara Publishing
13 King Coel Road
Colchester
CO3 9AG
www.ostarapublishing.co.uk

Foreword

That this anthology can be compiled at all, 45 years after the death of the author, is due in no small part to the sterling work done at the Margery Allingham Archive in the Albert Sloman Library at Essex University, whose staff are duly thanked for their courtesy and tolerance during 2014 and 2015.

The stories here are not listed chronologically, but in three sections: *Crimes, Crooks and Con-Men; Army Stories* (reflecting the author's experiences during World War II) and finally *Tales of the Unease*. Hopefully, these arbitrary delineations reflect the main themes of Youngman Carter's short fiction. If they do not, the fault is entirely that of the editor.

Details of previous publishing (where known) and a few explanatory notes appear in the **Editorial Notes** and the end of the book.

M.R.

CONTENTS

Introduction

Youngman Carter was married to a famous writer, Margery Allingham, by whom some considered him overshadowed. Be that as it may, he too had considerable creative powers and the body of work he left is impressive. His contribution to crime fiction was fourfold. As his wife repeatedly acknowledged, he helped her plan her books, particularly those written early in her career. He designed the dust wrappers for many crime novels, notably for his wife's Albert Campion series, but also for titles by Carter Dickson, Gladys Mitchell, Henry Wade, John Rhode, Leo Bruce, Raymond Chandler and Georges Simenon. He completed his wife's last book, *Cargo of Eagles*, left unfinished at her death in 1966, going on to write two poised and idiomatic Campion sequels. He also wrote some fifty short stories, most of them mysteries of one kind or another, though they are decidedly 'on the off-beat' and acknowledge no convention beyond the need to entertain and satisfy the reader.

His full name was Philip Youngman Carter and he was always known as 'Pip'. He was born in Watford in 1904, the son of the headmaster of the local grammar school who died when he was ten. He was educated at Christ's Hospital, the Bluecoat School, where his gifts as an artist showed strongly. He remained deeply loyal to the school and its men throughout his life.

He trained in art at the Regent Street Polytechnic in London, where Margery Allingham was studying drama and elocution. When her verse play *Dido and Aeneas* was staged in 1922, he was designer for the production. Through the advocacy of his former English teacher R.C. Woodthorpe, later himself a crime writer, he became a paid artist, contributing cartoon drawings to the *Daily Herald*. He became an accomplished etcher, with work exhibited at the Royal Academy, and for a time hoped to make an enduring reputation as an artist. Eventually, however, in his wife's words, he 'sold his soul to commerce', disappointing her expectations and, probably, his own.

He became a prolific designer of dust-wrappers, claiming, ultimately, to have produced more than two thousand of them.

His first such design was for *Blackkerchief Dick*, his wife's first novel published in 1923, when both were still in their teens. By 1930, he was designing for Heinemann, with Somerset Maugham, Graham Greene, J.B. Priestley and Daphne du Maurier in his sights. Many of his wrappers are keenly sought by collectors, who value them now more highly than the books they adorn.

He was commissioned to illustrate one book only, *The Casanova Fable* by William Gerhardi and Hugh Kingsmill. Whatever the merits of the text, the illustrations make it exceptional, and the wonder is that there were no more commissions.

He became a writer during his war service with the R.A.S.C., in North Africa and the Middle East. By 1943, he was in Baghdad, the newly-appointed Editor-in-Chief of Army publications. He was co-founder and editor of *Soldier* magazine, and his early stories were written for another service journal, *Gen.* The earliest title known is *You Know How It Is*, published in *Gen* in January 1943. *Kane's Doll*, in this collection, was also written at this time.

After the war, Pip Carter worked briefly for the *Daily Express* and began to find a market for his stories, which appeared in the *Strand Magazine, Argosy* (UK), *John Bull* and *Ellery Queen's Mystery Magazine.* For ten years he was with *The Tatler*, first as Assistant Editor and then, until his resignation in 1957, as Editor. For *The Tatler* he made many portrait drawings of current celebrities, an invaluable pictorial record of those then in the public eye.

After his premature retirement from Fleet Street he devoted his energies to freelance activity. He returned to dust-wrapper design, producing a long run for Simenon and a set of covers for Dorothy L. Sayers' Wimsey novels in paperback. He wrote a series of books on wine and wrote and illustrated a travel book, *On To Andorra*, published in 1963. He created a new magazine and a complicated game, but neither was taken up. He wrote more of his highly individual stories, his 'tales on the off-beat', as he called them. When Margery Allingham died, he completed *Cargo of Eagles*, so skillfully that the join is not apparent (though Edmund Crispin, in his review, claimed to have seen it).

By the time of his own death in 1969, he had published *Mr Campion's Farthing* and *Mr Campion's Falcon*, two elegant sequels to his wife's work, most cunningly contrived. Thanks to an enterprising publisher, they continue to command an audience. A planned third novel remained a fragment until recently, when Mike Ripley made it the basis of *Mr Campion's Farewell*, a lively, clever story, set impeccably in the ambience Margery Allingham created.

Youngman Carter's stories have much to commend them and thoroughly deserve to be brought to a wider audience. They have a high degree of finish and are meticulously composed in a variety of styles. Invariably they include much pleasing detail. *One for the Record* maintains the pompous formality of a rat-catcher's official report, even when routine procedure no longer meets the case. *Old Soldiers Never Lie* is a sober account of a true-crime investigation, marshalling facts and references in a scrupulous, scholarly way. *The Trouble with Locksmiths* is narrated in short bursts, each recording scandalised reaction to a phenomenon beyond official control. Several stories have first person narrators, more or less bemused, recalling odd experiences they have encountered, in the time-honoured way.

These tales are startlingly imaginative, moving beyond the usual, but so confidently achieved that we are persuaded of their truth. It is impossible to predict how a Carter story will end, so the reader is always surprised and usually gratified. *Alias Mr Manchester* sets at odds an imposing array of villains, all seen very clearly. Their joint confounding is a model of how to put one over on the opposition. *The Seeds of Time* encompasses the narrator's schooldays and his attendance years later at a school reunion. An oblique narrative assembles the evidence of Beaky Foster's uniqueness, displayed both in life and what appears to be death. The final revelation and the closing sentence are equally remarkable. *Grand Seigneur* takes the breath away, so powerfully is it imagined, so grandly achieved. Its amazing climax recalls that of Margery Allingham's *Look To The Lady*. Both entail the violent death of an arrogant intruder whose presumption is cut down by an elemental force.

The eponymous invention in *Humble's Box* was revived for the final Carter novel, existing only as a fragment until Mike Ripley took up its challenge. It serves its purpose admirably in this sly, unsettling story in which a clever young student of meteorology exploits his teacher and sets his nerves on edge. *The Second Saint* combines meticulous detection with dust in the eyes, for the narrator as well as the reader. Mr Widgeon leads us by the nose in a most engaging manner. In *The Evil Eye of Brother Polidor*, the final revelation leaves the reader with a sense of irretrievable loss. All that has gone before it, alive with dark suggestion, suddenly falls catastrophically into place.

Kane's Doll, is an early story, an eerie invention, swiftly and obliquely told, achieving strong effects with great economy of means. The doll, a voluptuous woman, obscenely lifelike, dances for two men, one of whom dies in consequence. In *Peter the Blind*, set during the Blitz on London, the narrator describes himself as 'firmly gripped by the lapels of my mind', an intense experience which the reader shares. This extraordinary story is one of

9

Youngman Carter's triumphs redolent, even, of Margery Allingham in its creation of a legend. Postillion Street might well be hers and the roll-call of murder victims; likewise the portrait by Pryde, 'a fine piece of subdued bravura' and 'little Louis Bidon' with his 'delicious childlike chuckles'. Every detail tells, as two distinct worlds are evoked, the fantastic past and the bomb-blasted present.

Two stories buck the trend of unpredictability. In *The Last of General Trotter* the old soldier travels in the opposite direction to Orwell's Napoleon and his cohorts, and the tale records his progress. Ovid would have enjoyed this one. *Dead Ringer* demands to be taken on its own terms but the reader may find that a tall order. The pivotal impossibility remains just that and the narrative evades it by shifting to another tack. The end is unpredictable but also equivocal.

Youngman Carter's stories are, to quote his wife from another context, 'a discovery for the civilised reader'. They are intelligent, erudite, fanciful, exuberant. Despite variations in manner and tone, all have the same wry, distinctive, 'off-beat' quality their author himself recognised and aimed for. We are fortunate to have them brought together at last, with a chance to find an appreciative new audience. This collection is an act of reparation and homage, richly deserved.

B.A. Pike

CRIME, CROOKS and CON-MEN

Humble's Box

The most shocking student I ever had in my care was a boy called Jeremy Fox. You may have heard the name already and if not I fear you certainly will within a very few years, for he has a most immoral brilliance.

He came sharply under my eye when he was studying for the science degree he never bothered to take, since I am the lecturer on Meteorology to the college. I first noticed that thin sly-shy face with its narrow taunting eyes and shock of carefully wind-swept yellow hair when he stood up at the back of the class to ask the very question I had hoped would not be asked. I had brought the wrong notes and was speaking extempore and trying to conceal the fact. Fox, as I knew immediately he opened his mouth, shared my secret. He did not expose me but played me gently like a good fisherman and then deliberately gave me the right answer in a careful re-iteration of what I had half said.

"You mean, sir, that the Buchan Chart variations from the norm in 1869 were....." I will not bother you with details, but I made a very careful note of the young man's name in my diary and his personality was etched permanently on my otherwise erratic memory.

He continued his tactics throughout that spring, but he never caught me again. On the contrary, I found myself taking a private pleasure in glossing over a point, almost implying ignorance, in the hope that he would rise to the bait and I myself would hook him.

Twice I scored over him, a couple of pedagogic triumphs on the lines of 'as every schoolboy knows' and on a third occasion I got as far as "Perhaps if Mr Fox had been following more closely he would have appreciated that...."

It was undignified and disturbing, for the young devil always conveyed by his diffident smile that he knew precisely my whole thought process and was several leaps ahead of me.

The college is not quite like those of the older universities. There is very little personal contact between student and lecturer.

I avoid the bars and coffee shops in the neighbourhood and despise those colleagues who openly hobnob with students in pursuit of popularity rather than hard learning.

But one gusty March evening just after a whipping hailstorm, a subject on which I had been expounding, young Fox caught me in the street close to my own club.

The meeting had all the quality of inevitability that had marked so many of our encounters.

"Why, sir," he said, "This is a piece of luck for me, you are the very man I wanted to see. You can do me a particular favour, sir - I'm sure you will. Would it be bloody impertinent if I were to ask you to have a drink with me? Barrons - a very nice little hole in the wall, sir - is just round the corner."

I did not wish to go into Barrons, which is next to my club, but I perceived that for once young Fox was impeccably dressed. He was hatless, but his suit had clearly been cut, and very badly, by his own old school tailor. His linen was clean and his tie showed discreetly that he was a member of another illustrious body. It was almost as if the meeting had been pre-arranged.

I took him into my own establishment and offered a drink. He took a dry sherry, a point in gamesmanship above my pink gin.

"To come to the point, sir," he said, "Now I've trapped you, if you'll forgive me saying so, I wonder if you would mind frightfully if you came and had a look at an antique I've just invested in?"

This was the last thing I had expected. Some hint about the line a question paper might take, or a request for an introduction to a foreign government perhaps, but....antiques?

When I had agreed he went on. "Of course it's rather a peculiar kind of a job, sir. In fact I wouldn't be surprised if you'd never heard of it - though with a chap like you it's quite on the cards you know all about it." He paused and eyed me with that quiz in his smile half way between a fencer's and a poker player's.

"It's a Humble Box," he said.

Now as it happens I know a great deal about my subject, meteorology, in its modern scientific application and quite a lot about the byways of its history. Josiah Humble (circa 1790) comes into this last category. He was of the type who advertised his so-called invention to the nobility, the gentry and the credulous in the personal columns of public prints of the day.

Mr Josiah Humble having perfected his miraculous device for the foretelling of storms, floods, droughts and every description of weather to be experienced within this kingdom will demonstrate the machine to the general public at twelve noon in his commodious premises.....

13

I could almost recite the paragraph and I had in fact once inspected an example in a great house in Northumberland when it was housed icily in the east sculpture gallery.

"I wouldn't have suspected you of collecting curios, Fox," I said, and began to relax with a second gin. "This is a new facet of your character. I would very much like to see this ancient piece of phonus bolonus at close quarters. Where is it?"

"It's in my rooms," he said. "Quite near - in Gower Street. But please don't write it off as a joke. I'm frightfully serious about it. You see, I think I'm on to something with it and it might make a hell of a difference to me if you happened to see my point of view."

This flabbergasted me. Josiah Humble and his box have nothing to do with science and in fact the old scoundrel was exposed within a few years of his first appearance. I said as much to Fox in the taxi on the way to his rooms.

He lived in one of those student apartment houses which abound about that other London centre of learning, in greater comfort and better taste than I had supposed. He had some good paintings, one of which might have been a Stubbs, a Sheraton sideboard and an original Mervin nephoscope in one corner. But the centerpiece was an undoubted Humble Box.

Perhaps I had better describe it. It is a large and handsome affair, as big as a coffin or a spinet and constructed in pale mahogany, inlaid very tastefully with bone. It stands about three feet high on six legs and on the top are an assortment of glass covered dials each resembling the face of a standard barometer. These are marked 'Rainfall', 'Wind', 'Earthquakes', 'Temperature', 'Pestilence' and so on.

The dials are not in themselves remarkable. The oddity lies in Mr Humble's claim that his invention foretells the future, for whatever period may be desired, according to the handsetting device beside each of them. I was delighted to see the monstrosity again, for they are virtually forgotten curios and were they not so large would probably be very valuable as furnishing pieces for decoration, like early celestial globes.

"Before you mess about with it," said young Fox, "I must tell you something. I set all these dials for nightfall to-day, as you see. But the point is, I set the dials four days ago - on Sunday in fact. Now you see. 'Hail - very severe', 'Wind - gale force', 'Temperature - 35°'. All dead right. How do you like that?"

I saw the joke, for it was dead against me, and laughed with him. Yet there was an undercurrent which I could not grasp. I felt once more that I was hooked and being carefully played.

"This damned thing," I said, "has just about as much virtue,

14

scientifically speaking, as Joanna Southcott's box. Inside this fine cabinet is a collection of crude barometers, all hopelessly inaccurate, and divination hocus pocus ranging from damp sea weed to the mummified toe of a gouty chinese mandarin."

"Oh sir," he said and his face became completely dead pan. "Do you really think so? Look what it has prophesied for today. I have a feeling old Josiah was not dumb as they say."

Now I really knew there was something in the wind, a joke or a scheme of some sort that I could not fathom. He was twenty-three, I reflected: too old for a pointless private leg-pull.

But my dignity was at stake. "Now listen, young Fox," I said. "You're not balmy, so don't pretend to be. Humble's Box was a fraud in its own day and never deceived anyone except a few wealthy country bumpkins. As an antique curio it might be worth a ten pound note to a collector and this looks to me like a genuine specimen which has not been interfered with. But you're a student of meteorology, an important and precise science. If you're fetched me half across London simply to find out if you can pull my leg and make a students' canteen story then you must think again. This isn't my idea of humour."

He did have the grace to lower his eyes and I thought for a moment he was going to blush, but he did not go as far as that.

After quite a pause he said, measuring his words. "I was afraid you might feel that way, sir. But I do assure you that I'm not joking. In fact I'm in deadly earnest. Do you think you will remember my exact words, sir, if I say I believe in this box completely? I think Josiah Humble had grasped a principle which has escaped others and I'm proposing to do some research into his box with a view to improving and perfecting it."

There was something in his carefully chosen phrases which ought to have given me a clue, but I missed my chance because I was getting irritated. The mockery had returned to the corners of his eyes and it was making me hot under the collar.

"Listen yourself, young man," I said. "You're making me very angry indeed. You're a second year student in a very important subject. I don't believe for one moment that you are mad. Nor are you deceiving me about a charlatan who had no claim to serious consideration even 170 years ago. The box as you very well know is a box of tricks. It always was and always will be. Don't waste any more of my time. Your whole future may depend on my good opinion of your work. You remember that before you start playing the fool with me again."

With that I stormed out and slammed the door, a silly gesture which left me with an uncomfortable feeling that in some mysterious way he had not only won the encounter but had achieved precisely the effect which he had reckoned upon all along.

I did not see him again, except in the lecture rooms and laboratories, for a couple of months. He worked hard and well, and in his queer magnetic way managed to convey that he was on my side for once, and even mildly grateful for anything I could teach him. He asked questions, but they were probes for answers and the mockery had left his smile.

Then one evening he returned to the attack. He came sidling up to me after a session and murmured almost respectfully, "Can I offer you a coffee, sir? I have something I'd like to show you."

We went to one of those Kensington cafes which are decorated like Brazilian jungles furnished in chromium. We sat on high stools in a corner. He had a brief case with him and he placed it on the counter.

"I don't quite know how to express this," he said. "Because I'm asking a favour and for once I'm not trying to be impertinent. Perhaps, sir, you'll try to think of me not as one of your students but as a man consulting an expert about a business proposition. Will you try, sir? I mean - well, the truth is that I want a certain statement from you with your signature on it - an absolutely accurate statement of course, sir - and I'm prepared to pay for it. Just as if I were consulting a barrister or something. I'm prepared to pay fifty guineas."

I asked him what the devil he meant and before he answered he opened his case and pulled out a printed pamphlet. I glanced at it and felt my wrath kindling again.

"Humble's Box Reconsidered," it said. *"A treatise by Jeremy Fox in which the principles of the work of Josiah Humble as incorporated in the instruments known as Humble's Box of 1790, are examined in the light of present knowledge. With appended suggestions for modernisation and improvement."*

"Now understand this, Master Jeremy," I said. "Your behaviour has all the hall marks of a confidence trick. You must realise quite clearly once and for all that I am having no part in it. You are deliberately prejudicing yourself in my eyes. I can't understand why, but stop this tomfoolery here and now."

He looked at me for the first time straight in the face. "Fifty guineas is nearly all the money I have in the world. I've written the cheque and I assure you it's not rubber. All I ask is that you read my pamphlet and write me your opinion of it as an expert meteorologist, stating your qualifications, in the presence of some witnesses whom I nominate."

16

The infernal boy always managed to catch me on the wrong foot. Fifty guineas is a good fee for anything I may do, yet there was clearly a catch in it. I could stand on my dignity or quarrel with him and fall off my stool of pedagogery. Or I could give in. Finally, for the influence of his personality was remarkable, I gave in with what grace I could find.

"I'll study it," I said, "I'll give you my opinion, which I suspect will be unflattering, and I will not budge one milimetre from it. I'll sign a statement and you can tear up your damned cheque."

This was sheer arrogance, but despite temptation I felt I must keep a shred of adult scientific dignity or I'd be lost.

Suddenly he became as excited as a schoolboy. "This is terrific of you, sir. You're a sportsman whatever they say. I really am frightfully grateful and I promise you I'm not letting you in for anything you'll reproach yourself for - even in your nightmares. Now I've got it all worked out......"

It was that hook again. Despite myself I felt the invisible line tightening. Young Fox continued to play me with an expert touch.

"I - er - well, what I've done on the off chance that you'd accept my offer, is to hire a car for you, sir. I'm afraid it's a fearfully ancient Daimler, but it's very comfortable, I believe, and we're only going as far as Seven Sisters Road, if you don't mind. Would tomorrow evening be any good?"

This was a yes-or-no question. I said yes.

Master Fox, as solicitous as a nannie, collected me at the time appointed and ushered me into a very elegant motor, the sort of thing one uses for funerals or for expeditions to remote weather bureau outposts where they conduct experiments in fog analysis or the incidence of tides.

The chauffeur, I remember, even went to the length of putting a rug over my legs, though it was a mild and muggy evening.

As we settled down and drove through the squalid streets of Camden Town, past Hilldrop Crescent where the late Dr Crippen practised, hard by Holloway prison, I made my final effort on behalf of my own self respect.

"I've read your pamphlet," I said. "The box is nonsense, simply hocus-pocus for credulous nitwits as you very well know. Your suggested alterations simply turn the thing into a slightly less inferior series of barometers, all very inaccurate. You're just modernising Merlin for Tony Lumpkins and I warn you I'm determined to say so, if I'm asked."

"That's perfect, sir," he said, "I'm only asking for a simple declaration. Sorry about this scruffy neighbourhood. We're nearly there."

We got out at a point almost under a railway bridge, in an area

17

of shoddy little shops. Between a cut-price confectioners and a second-hand dress store there was a doorway to which I was beckoned. Beside the entrance was a tarnished brass plate which bore a legend.

The Humble Society - Offices.

Up the linoleum stairway the atmosphere cleared and I walked into a rather pleasant Victorian room on the first floor. There was a round table in the centre with a faded red cloth on it, fringed with bobbles, some nice staffordshire pottery, a couple of oils by W. B. Leader and engravings of Q. W. Orchardson, all a little self conscious, but very comfortable and undemanding of criticism.

A large toad of a man with warts on his pouchy chops and thick pebble glasses greeted us wheesily.

"My name is Porteus," he said, "I am the President of the Humble Society. I happen to be a pharmaceutical chemist if the matter interests you, but I am retired. This is my house. May I present Mr James Entwhistle, our secretary, who is also our legal adviser and the senior partner of Entwhistle, Entwhistle and....I forget how many there are?.....Robinson Sons and Baxter of Gray's Inn."

I bowed to a dim and frigid man who clearly wished no personal part of the proceedings and was determined to remain a necessary cipher.

"And this is my housekeeper, Mrs Bond, who will witness any document we may wish to draw up. She will sign as the last remaining subscriber and member of the Society."

Mrs Bond said nothing. She looked as if her entire career had been devoted to the straightening of hassocks in a rather cold church.

We all sat down round the table and I half expected sherry and seed cake to be produced. But Mr Porteus was clearly in charge and he was conducting a ceremony the form of which he had obviously decided very precisely.

"This," he said, clearing an imaginary forelock from his polished head, "Is an extraordinary meeting of the Humble Society established in 1794. All members are present and we have with us an expert of the Royal Meteorological Society. We are here to consider the work of Mr Jeremy Fox, a respected student of Meteorology and in particular his treatise upon certain improvements to the Humble Box. If we find it, upon advice, to be satisfactory, then this will conclude our business."

His rheumy eyes were like parboiled sago and he turned them to me.

"Now, sir," he said. "You have considered this young man's treatise, I hope. What have you to tell us?"

Before I could answer young Jeremy intervened.

"I must explain to everyone," he said, "that the professor is a most reputable modernist. He is an expert, probably the greatest living authority on his subject to-day (you don't mind my saying that, sir, do you?) It follows from this, I'm sorry to say, that he is, so far as the Society is concerned, an unbeliever. I have only asked him here to answer one simple question, which is strictly proper, according to his own conscience. I shall abide by his answer."

I still did not see where this fantasy was leading, but the line was becoming taut and I was determined now to know the secret of the whole farrago of nonsense. The room was lit by gas under cosy little shades and an odour of cooking scented the place with a benign homeliness..

I said as primly as I might. "Just what is the question?"

Young Jeremy placed a sheet of paper in front of me, typewritten in capital letters. "I hope this is fair, sir," he said, "I've tried to make it sound legal and Mr Entwhistle here agrees that it's quite proper as far as he's concerned. I've even tried to imagine the sort of thing you'd write yourself, so as to save you the trouble."

They were all looking at me like goldfish, coldly and solemnly. I spent a moment polishing my glasses before I began to read.

"I have read the treatise by Jeremy Fox," it said, "Relating to the apparatus known as Humble's Box. I expose no opinion whatsoever about the series of devices contained therein, but insofar as they relate in any way to meteorology as it is understood today then the amendments suggested in the said pamphlet will tend to improve the instrument if incorporated in the general design. I am a Fellow of the Royal Meteorological Society and a lecturer on that subject to the College."

So far as it went it was true. Jeremy had removed the seaweed, the gall bladders of oxen and the acoustic wind pipe substituting columns of mercury and genuine instruments. A small improvement could not be denied. Mr Entwhistle handed me a thin steel pen ready inked.

I was deep in the mystery now, too late for wriggling. Exactly as I signed the paper, adding my credentials in full, Mr Porteus passed me an envelope which clearly contained the fee I had so brashly spurned.

"Now, sir," he said. "This is in some respects a melancholy occasion. You are entitled to an explanation and I make it after very considerable forethought, for this may prove to be the final meeting of our Society." He pulled his glasses forward on his nose and studied some notes.

"The Humble Society was founded in 1794 by supporters of

19

Josiah Humble of Clerkenwell, subsequent upon certain scurrulous attacks upon his scientific reputation. In that year his many admirers rallied to his defence under the chairmanship of Lord Redcar, a nobleman much given to the championing of forlorn causes. He was supported by Lord Dinwiddie, Mr Ephraim Bamforth, the Honourable George Merryweather and several other philanthropic enthusiasts. These gentlemen subscribed certain modest sums for an association under the name "The Union for the Furtherance of the scientific principles of Josiah Humble", a title changed in 1862 to "The Humble Society". Its object has remained the same. It is to promote the good name of The Box and to improve it by grant of cash where that is shown to be possible."

He paused and tweaked his nose as if he were taking snuff.

"Our husbandry has not been negligible, indeed every investment we have made of the original capital in our trust has been highly profitable. Yet the fact must be faced that we have never until this moment been able to achieve our object. One must recall regretfully that changing fashions in philosophy and science and Humble's death from apoplexy in 1796 have driven our little group into almost total obscurity. What has remained to us is our solemn duty to our founders.

At last, at very long last, so to speak, a suitable candidate has come forward properly qualified to make a claim on us. The acceptance of that claim will enable the society to fulfill its single duty and to consider its usefulness at an honourable end. Can you confirm this, Mr Entwhistle?"

The solicitor answered in a rumbling tone as if his voice were recorded far back in his throat.

"Your statement is perfectly accurate, Mr Porteus. The funds of the Society have always been held in trust for the improvement of the device. There has never before been a claimant. Now we have one in the shape of Mr Jeremy Fox, whose treatise is by expert testimony precisely what we have been charged to find. A grant quite properly authorised by the president and agreed to by the surviving member and the secretary - a legal quorum - will enable us to close our books and to disband this archaic and, if I may say so, hitherto utterly useless body, for good and all. I hope I make myself clear?"

No one replied and finally Mr Porteus rose very slowly to his feet. There was a certain dignity about him, for at that moment he was a minute footnote to history.

"Mr Fox," he said, "It is my duty to hand into your keeping the sum we have held in trust for one hundred and sixty five years. Your claim is perfectly in order and I must congratulate you upon

20

your industry, your devotion and your scholarship. The Humble Society is proud of its final and only choice."

With that he made a formal bow to the wretched boy, passed him an envelope and sat down heavily. For once in his life young Jeremy found himself without a suitable response.

In the funeral motor car on our way back to the west end he still sat next me in silence for half the journey.

Then he opened the envelope and held out the cheque in front of me, still without comment. The bright lights of a cinema illuminated its aimable pink face.

It was made out to Jeremy Fox Esquire for the sum of thirty four thousand pounds seven shillings and tenpence.

I looked at him over my glasses and he returned my stare. The fish had been landed.

"Well. I understand it all now," I said at last.

"I'm so glad about that, sir," he said. "You were a tremendous help and I feel you honestly do deserve to be right in the picture. Let me give you the last detail. Old Porteus is my maternal uncle, a very wise and astute sort of chap, sir, in his unscientific way."

The Trivial Round

The writing on the card did not say at all what it should have done.

Simpson read it twice to make sure, before looking up across the counter at the man who was holding it out towards him. In the ordinary way of business a traveller's card carries a simple message such as 'John Wilkinson: representing Ramsbotham Products Ltd.' but this one was quite different. It had nothing on it but a number.

Simpson took a long breath before he raised his head. "The war's over," he said. "Finished fifteen years ago. I'm a grocer and I mean to stay that way."

"This is quite important," said the stranger softly. "I wouldn't have come otherwise."

He was a young man, with ruffled fair hair and a friendly smile that managed to be nothing but a mask. His mackintosh windcheater was nondescript but the oil on it suggested tinkering with motors and Simpson could see what looked like a very speedy job standing outside the little shop which was now the centre of his world.

Slowly he shook his head.

"It's nothing to do with me any longer. I've retired - just like I told them all at the time. Can I interest you in soap flakes? Special offer this week."

"This is very serious," said the young man in the same even undertone. "And we don't think it's funny to dig you out like this. We know it's naughty, in fact. Could I, please Mr Simpson, sir, have a word in your office?" More audibly he added, for the vicar was moving down the counters: "It's a rather special line. I'm sure you'll be interested."

A decision was being forced. Reluctantly Simpson said, "Well, O.K. Come into the back." To the girl who was selling sweets in a far corner he added, "Carry on, Beryl, will you? Shan't be half a tick."

The little back room was scented even more strongly than the shop itself, a pleasant mixture of soap, cheese, newsprint and country herbs. There was barely room for the two men beside the table with its order books and catalogues.

Neither man sat down, for Simpson was in no mind to prolong conversation. He was a grizzled figure, square of jaw and chest, a stranger might have guessed that he was an ex-chief petty officer, though they would have been very wrong.

"Now before you start," he said to the younger man, "Let me tell you something. I spent fifteen years in the Department and I had a bucketful of it. When I came out I came out for good and all, and I told the Old Man just that. I meant it."

"But, sir...."

Simpson swept him aside. "Do you know why I came here - why I bought this very shop in this very village? I'll tell you. This is Benham St. Mary - Balmy Benham, they call it. The place where nothing ever happened and nothing is ever going to happen. They like it that way and by Heck, so do I. The road leads nowhere, the parson doesn't quarrel with his parish, we have no trippers, no ghosts, no ancient monuments. We mind our business and the less work the policeman and the postman have to do the better they're pleased. Now be a good chap and leave me in peace, will you? I've got plenty on my hands and it's the girl's half day."

The visitor made no move. Instead he seemed to be weighing chances, or perhaps making a diagnosis.

"The Old Man's retired," he said at last. "Bill Mason's the boss now. You'd remember him?"

"Good Lord," said Simpson, involuntarily. "Bill, of all people. What happened to Macduff then?"

"Mac had an accident in Berlin two years ago. I'll tell you about it if you're interested. You knew him pretty well?"

Too late Simpson saw that he had taken the bait: he struggled for escape.

"Look here, I don't want to talk about that sort of thing. It's not for me any longer. I run this little store and nobody gives a damn about the Department - which they've never heard of - or wars - or -"

"Bill Mason sent you a message," said the young man. "He said you'd read it for Mac's sake if not for his. May I give it to you?" He fumbled in an inner pocket and produced a plain envelope which contained a typewritten single sheet. It was unsigned and had no heading.

'This is Jason's corner for me. You are the only man in the world, quite literally, who can get me round it.'

A sudden ancient reflex made Simpson burn it and crush the twisted ashes among cigarette ends in a tray.

"I don't know why we have to be so damn theatrical," said the

23

young man. "That gibberish didn't mean anything to me. Something before my time perhaps?"

"Yes," agreed Simpson absently. "As you say, before your time. But urgent all the same. Cry for help, so to speak."

"Then you'll come?"

"Oh, damn and blast everything," said Simpson. "The department in general and you in particular coupled with the name of Bill Mason. How long will it take, this job?"

The young man looked at his watch. "I'll run you to Town," he said. "We'll be there in two hours at the outside. Job itself might take an hour - five minutes with luck. You should be back by this evening and no one a penny the wiser. I'll brief you in the car. Shall we go?"

The car was long, low, rackety and very fast, making conversation impossible. As they approached Eastern Avenue the young man swung abruptly into a lay-by and switched off the engine.

"This is the gen," he said. "I'm going to drop you off at the first likely tube station. You go to Tottenham. Court Road - no changing, if I remember - then to Postillion Street, just by the British Museum. Know it? Good. The pub on the corner is called the Welsh Harp, God knows why. It has two bars, the Private looks straight across to the classy one, but has an entrance in the other street. No one can go in or out of the main bar without being seen, which is useful. There are little glass partitions - sort of windows - in yours, so that you are pretty well hidden. Got that?"

"I know the pub, I know the bar. I even know the landlord if he's still there," said Simpson. "What then?"

"You watch. You stay there till closing time, if necessary. But as soon as you see a familiar face the job is done. Yon just pass the information on to a man who'll be standing around drinking. A little man, shiny blue suit, flat 'at, white neckerchief, drinking port. You call him Bert. You say 'I bet that bloke grows roses' and point out the character in question. Then you buy Bert a drink and you can go home. It's as simple as that. Unwise to know any more in fact."

Simpson frowned. "It's not quite good enough," he said "I don't like working in the dark and never did. Ask Bill Mason. Now just why does it have to be me?"

"I'd have thought that was obvious," said the young man and paused. He lit a cigarette and pulled hard at it, considering two courses, just as he had done in the shop. "O.K. then, I'll come clean - as clean as I can, that is. You are the only person, probably literally the only person in the world, who can make the identification. It's this-a-way. We've picked up some short-wave stuff which is pretty important this side of the curtain. Part of it concerns a rendezvous and we've only just got it deciphered. It's for half past one today at the Welsh Harp. Now do you get it?"

"Not entirely." Simpson was obstinate. "Give a little more."

"What we don't know," said the young man, "is either of the two people who are to meet. If we had one we'd have t'other, you see. But one of them, and this is the big if, one of them might be Charleyboy himself. You see it's important? If the matter interests you it was Charleyboy who fixed poor old Mac in Berlin, that's for certain."

Simpson whistled. "Charleyboy," he said. "That bastard. I knew he was a killer, but weren't we all? The difference was that Charleyboy liked it. He disappeared towards the end of my time. I'd hoped he was dead."

"Somewhere in gaol more likely. Absent from the scene for six years, which suggests a sentence, somewhere or other. The trouble is we don't know where. You realise of course that there's no picture of him in our little gallery and that no one - except you - has ever seen him. That's why you're vital this afternoon."

Simpson was casting his mind back. Autumn 1945; a bombed-out cellar in Hamburg which was hardly credible as a hide-out beneath so much rubble. A rat-hole cafe for black marketers, displaced persons who wished no identification, half starved tarts and the unsavoury jetsam of international traitors.

He remembered the stink and the terrible home-brewed German gin and Charleyboy selling the hiding places of war criminals for thirty pieces of silver. He remembered the yellow puffy face, the pale blue chin, the codfish eyes and the greasy but primly respectable suit that looked as if it might cover the filth of a life time.

"Yes," he said at last. "I think I'd know him again, even after fifteen years. I'd know him by the pricking of my thumbs if by nothing else. Drive on."

* * * * * *

The Welsh Harp is the most predictable of London hostelries. The private bar has taxi drivers, elderly locals and manual workers from the Museum as its clientele. They are discreetly hidden from the parlour lounge by a cut glass screen which hinges coyly at intervals to permit of orders and to hide the customers from the superior eyes of the students, the reading room men, the publishers and the secondhand book salesmen who patronise the main bar. It was going to be just like falling off a log, he decided.

In the far corner there was the clearly identifiable Bert, with whom he exchanged a cautious wink. Armed with a pint and a racing edition Simpson found himself the perfect station by a small pivoted window which was permanently open. At twenty five past one the insignificant figure in the cloth cap sidled up to him, belching lightly over a fresh glass of port.

At half past one precisely the double-doors of the bar parlour swung back and a man pushed unhurriedly through them. He edged through the crowd, caught a barmaid's eye with remarkable speed and called for two gins. As the girl presented the glasses he changed the order.

"I asked for whisky, Miss," he said. "This is gin."

The girl made no particular fuss and very soon a drab woman with a shopping basket turned towards him and picked up the second glass, without acknowledgment.

She's the contact, thought Simpson, and that, after all these years is Charleyboy. Charleyboy in person, the biggest dealer in all the small change of international dirty washing and traitory since Judas. He was not greatly changed, a little heavier, a little cleaner and very much more wealthy, but the same bland cold smile which had pure evil in the recipe.

At one thirty two Simpson turned to Bert. "I bet that bloke grows roses," he remarked and found his observation well received.

"The same again, eh?"

At one thirty three the landlord opened all the available windows to deliver the port and exclaimed with a shout of professional pleasure.

"Well! Well! Well! If it isn't Mr Simpson. Ted Simpson in person after all these years. Now what on earth brings you here?"

*   *   *   *   *   *

At the corner of Tottenham Court Road Simpson knew almost by instinct that he was being followed. The information brought an exhilaration which surprised him; this was a day off from the real business of life, a visit to the old school but without its threat of discipline.

At the White Horse on the corner he waited until his shadow had placed himself at the bar and then took a malicious delight in leaving before the grey unremarkable man could consume the drink he had been forced to order. He called a taxi and shouted 'Paddington' to the driver, changed the instructions five minutes later and dropped off in a traffic jam so that he could dive conveniently into the rabbit warren of Piccadilly Circus. An exit brought him directly to a cinema where he bought a ticket before any other customer had crossed the quilted foyer.

At five fifteen he walked out by a side exit, just before the main picture was over and took coffee in an expresso bar. The proper course would be to ring the Department and tell them of his little adventure, but he was in no mood for liaison. This was a holiday - he had done all that was required in loyalty and he was free, white and enjoying middle age.

But by the time he had reached lower Haymarket two men were on his tail, heavy purposeful figures who knew at least as much about the game as he did himself.

He was still in the mood. He wandered among the evening office workers, took a tube and changed twice almost at random. At Sloane Square he remembered a small drinking club off the King's Road where there would be no strangers.

There is no longer a railway line to Benham St. Mary for it was pulled up two years ago to advance modern transport. Travellers to that pleasant haven get off at Cursitor Junction and make their own way. The last bus leaves an hour before the last train arrived and the solitary taxi driver keeps to his own early hours.

Thus Simpson found himself walking the five miles through the low mist of the warm spring night. The road bends and twists in accordance with the feudal centuries, but the country is flat.

The mist lay in stray inert pockets across his way, giving a floating effect to trees and fences. At Little Benham, the next village to home he became aware that a car was pottering quietly behind him, using only its sidelights. He dodged into a dry ditch and it passed him, a small tradesman's van with two men inside.

He gave them ten minutes and trudged on, until the outlines above the mist became reassuringly familiar - the long barn of Rigg's Farm, the three great fuddy-duddy elms and the gothic roof of the vicarage with its foot warmer of respectable laurels. Only four hundred yards to go before the King's Head, the forge, and the shop. Thank God for Benham St. Mary, Balmy Benham, on the road to nowhere, the unassailable sanctuary where nothing made even a guidebook paragraph.

By the Vicarage drive with its white five barred gate perpetually open he paused for a moment to see if a light still burned, but everything was still and black, a paper silhouette embedded in cotton wool.

He heard the sound, a "phut" as if a cane had struck a pillow sharply and felt a stinging pain in his left arm. The mist was almost waist high and he dropped into it on the grass verge.

For a long time, a five full minutes, he lay completely still, his ears picking up every granule of silence, until he located the sound he was expecting.

Footsteps were approaching, slowly and cautiously, a hunter on padded feet closing for the kill.

The pain in his arm was acute but not agonising, a vicious scratch enough to make him very angry indeed. His opponent loomed suddenly, very close, within a hand's touch. He reached toward with his good arm and brought him to the ground beside him, sprawling. Even in his fury Simpson received a shock. His adversary stank like a pole cat, a sickening blend of all the personal affronts to civilised man.

They fought viciously, without rules, but unlike animals, in complete silence.

Neither man was young and neither in any sort of condition for sustained effort but Simpson's blinding anger had wiped the years away for a few vital moments. His arm was now giving him a fierce ecstasy of pain and he was remembering every dirty trick in the book.

Gradually he reached the essential grip and beat his attacker's head savagely back on to the tarmac.

The man screamed, a high pitched inhuman sound and lay quite still. Simpson stood up and shook himself: his left arm had resigned and was completely numb.

Out the mist two figures came running with torches and a headlight brought a white blanket of confusion to the scene.

"Simpson, isn't it?" said a voice. "Bill Mason here. Are you O.K.? We couldn't spot you in all this fog even though we were just behind you. Now, just who is our pal?" He knelt down. "It's Charleyboy, isn't it?" There was a long pause before he straightened his back and muttered.

"You're a very rough and careless fellow, Ted Simpson, when you're roused and you always were. Between you and me and the gatepost I rather think you've killed him. That gives us all a delicate little problem, to which there is only one solution.

"You get the hell out of here. Go home to bed and remember that the whole thing never happened - it was nice seeing you. By the way don't worry your pretty head about Charleyboy's chum - he's been looked after. You can sleep tight."

*　*　*　*　*　*

The shop at Benham St. Mary is not well lit at the best of times. Piles of soap flakes, tins, mops and bargain offers blot out the little windows and provide discreet shadows. Simpson managed a painful morning's work and kept to the darker corners where the bruise on his cheek was unnoticed and his one good arm could do duty without remark.

The vicar however was in garrulous mood. He settled himself on a pile of biscuit tins and was prepared to gossip.

"A remarkable thing - a most extraordinary thing, I may say - happened last night, he said. "There was quite a disturbance outside the house. A fight or a quarrel of some sort, and a couple of cars. I heard it distinctly."

"Teddy boys from Cursitor, after a dance," suggested Simpson.

"Not quite, I think," said the vicar. "This is what I found in the vicarage drive this morning."

He opened his hand and displayed his trophy.

"Of course you weren't in the war, were you? But even I as a padré recognise this. It's a spent round from a .38 revolver. See?"

"It seems a very little one," said Simpson mendaciously. "Best to forget it. It couldn't have done much harm."

"Couldn't it?" said the vicar laughing. "Many a good man has lost his life through one of these let me tell you. Still, it looks harmless enough. How it came to be lying on my path though, I don't know and I certainly shan't ask! The 'trivial round' one might call it and that's all we ask for at Benham St. Mary, isn't it?"

"Very wise," said Simpson. "When one's found a bit of peace hang on to it, that's what I say!"

Means of Escape

Dr Forsdyke, Senior Research Assistant at the Evans and Layton Laboratories, flicked the tiny glass capsule with his cuff and it rolled along the bench for a full yard. It was pure chance, the lightest touch, for he was not a clumsy man, but the beginning of a considerable journey. One of the dozen juniors in the laboratory, who happened to be standing next him, since he was also taking material from the safe, did not see the incident, but ten minutes later he swept the capsule into a batch of his own which were almost identical in appearance, parcelled them carefully and handed them to the boy from the dispatch office.

This was at half past twelve on the morning of the 15th of April, a Friday. The capsule was not missed until six in the evening, which is the wrong hour at which to start a hue and cry. Dr Forsdyke knew precisely how important the loss might be, but he was in an impossible and frustrating position. It was after nine before he deduced, accurately, what had happened to the capsule and near midnight before its sixty possible destinations had been unearthed. By then he was grey with terror.

In the small hours he explained the situation at Scotland Yard to a weary official who had been dragged from his bed to deal with the problem, for this was a matter for experts.

"Now this drug...." said the official.

"It is not a drug at all." Forsdyke was explaining his troubles for the twentieth time. "It is a virus culture - the disease in person - do you understand? It is part of a collection sent from Hong Kong, the isolated brute itself, sealed in a glass tube about four centimeters long. You break the top to get at the contents. We at Evans and Layton are trying to discover the anti-toxin, so far without success. This germ has come down from God knows where in China or Mongolia where it's killing thousands, possibly millions, if we did but know. It's a very hardy specimen, bred out of a lot of half-witted experiments behind the Iron Curtain where they've been playing around with cholera antibiotics for years. The only result we know of is this entirely new virus which nature has developed for herself to beat us all. It is as infectious and as contagious as 'flu, a killer within a few hours and at the moment there's nothing we can do to stop it."

"I see," said the official. "Then if someone takes it by mistake for something else, he's a dead man."

Forsdyke sighed. "If anyone injects himself with that quantity he will be dead within minutes. He'll be found dead. Someone will touch him, fumble with his clothes, probably two or three people. Then a doctor, ambulance men, mortuary assistants - say a couple of dozen people. Within twenty four hours they'll all be carriers, even if they're still alive. Now do you see what I'm driving at?"

* * * *

At the Home Office the Assistant Commissioner explained his problems on Monday morning to a whitefaced group. "As far as we can tell," he said slowly, "this damned virus was confused, God knows how, with a perfectly normal drug sent out to dispensing chemists, hospitals and so on, in the usual way of business. They're all recorded of course, very strictly. It isn't a very usual drug, thank God. Out of the sixty batches sent out we've recovered fifty three intact, which narrows the field to seven lots. The rest are safe, only these seven have reached the public.

"Six of these have been traced and the poor wretches are under observation. There have been no results so far, which is a very good sign, because this thing works like the wind. Practically speaking, we can be sure it's not one of them. Number seven is our headache."

The group looked at him silently and he plodded on as if reading a prepared statement.

"This drug is used, as an injection - the chap can do it for himself - to alleviate pain of a particular kind. It is given to victims of one of the off-shoots of polio. It gets them in the legs generally and hurts, I'm told, like the very devil. A shot of this cools it off and may keep them quiet for days.

"It needs a doctor's prescription, which helps us quite a bit.

"You see, Number Seven, whoever he is, is carrying six - probably five now - capsules round with him and he may not use the vital one for a long time. We can't count on that of course. He may have done it already."

"I thought," suggested a Home Office man, "that you said there was a record of these things. If the search is so narrow now, why can't your last man - your number seven - be traced?"

The Commissioner referred again to his mental notes.

"The vital capsule," he said, "was almost certainly given out

31

yesterday at an all-night chemist in Baker Street. That is to say it is one of the six little tubes - six separate injections - which are issued on a single prescription. Unfortunately the prescription was forged and whoever obtained it gave a false address and almost certainly a false name."

There was a general murmur of concern.

"Then we're back where we started. The B.B.C. must send out a message....the press......"

"That is not quite the end of our enquiries," said the Commissioner. "We have a fairly shrewd idea who the man is, or at least a reasonable supposition. Last week, on Sunday night to be precise, a man escaped from Wakefield Prison. Henry Musgrave Saunders, 43, doing time for mail van robbery. He's thought to be in London and he's been having treatment for this particular trouble. There's more than a chance that he's the chap. A very intelligent criminal and possibly dangerous. He's been a free man for a week, so he must have money or friends. The chances are that he's reached the Smoke by now - he's a Londoner - and he fits the chemist's description to a 'T'."

He looked up from his invisible notes and surveyed his audience individually.

"Now we have several choices before us. We can broadcast a detailed description and explain both to him and the public why he is wanted. That sounds very fine and practical but it has objections. The first is that this man is the type who might prefer suicide to arrest. If he does, the epidemic will start from there. The second is that if anything is explained to the public about this danger there may be considerable alarm, to put it mildly. The third is that if we merely say he has a dangerous and lethal drug in his possession he may very well decide to use it as a weapon without realising just how powerful that weapon is.

"If he knew precisely what he was carrying about with him he might decide to blackmail the entire nation - and he'd possibly get away with it. And of course there is another important factor. Evans and Layton, as you probably know, is part of W.C.C. - World Chemical Combine - and very strong pressure is being put on us to settle this out of public sight. Bad for prestige. They're powerfully (I use the word advisedly) against any loss of face at this particular moment.

"As we see it at the Yard there is only one possible course, since we feel it most unwise to enlist the public. That is, we must set off the biggest undercover man-hurt that can be contrived. The facts don't give us a lot of time."

*   *   *   *

32

It was five hours before Henry Musgrave Saunders, late of Wakefield, received some of the impact of that morning's decisions, but before that the day had not been easy. He was carrying too much money for health in his circle of acquaintance, even though his escape had been costly and nearly half his share of loot had gone to procure it. There remained, however, just over a thousand pounds in beautiful, dirty assorted notes - a very dangerous cargo for a man in his social position. He was at the mercy of every informer or blackmailer who could recognise him and was utterly unprotected. Then there was the added problem of pain. Finally, the question of the girl: everyone in the business would be watching her. Phones would be tapped, letters scrutinised and she would be shadowed night and day.

Better than most, he could spot a plainclothes man at a reasonable distance. This afternoon he was a little late because his leg was blunting his reflexes.

The officer facing him was middle-aged but mercifully slow: his reactions were those of a bad actor doing an underlined double-take.

This was on the corner of Piccadilly Circus, just outside Swan & Edgars. It was five o'clock and the afternoon sunless and chilly.

The older man had seen him first, by a few seconds. By the time Saunders realised what had happened the watcher had taken a paper from his pocket, checked on it and started to move.

Saunders reacted automatically, shifting behind a group of walkers so that he was unsighted and then turning to the first shop window which reflected the enemy. He saw the man hesitate and then turn back to the police call-box in the circus.

This meant that he was registered as being in the area and danger was imminent. He turned into Air Street and paused for a moment in the shadow of the Regent Street arch. A uniformed policeman standing magnificently back towards him made it necessary to hesitate.

He thought almost with detachment about the men who would soon be searching the neighbourhood for him. How much had they memorised about him, how much did they know? Six foot two, sallow complexion, dark hair and of course a heavy limp.

This last was the vital item.

It was a difficult intensely painful business, smothering that limp, an acrobatic feat accompanied by torture but if he took it slowly it could be done.

Under the arch he took off his trench coat, in case it had now been added to his identification, folded it over to show the tartan lining, and flung it over his shoulder. He ruffled his hair, put on his glasses and doubled agonisingly back into Piccadilly.

Almost opposite was a man's outfitters, a palatial establishment of several floors, comfortably full of late shoppers. Once inside he felt it safe to straighten up, limp freely and gain a few minutes before any plain clothes man got on to him. He made a couple purchases from a bored and busy young man; two caps which could be folded into the pocket, a sporting check and a modest green.

To these he added a muffler, reversible in a different colour and a pair of sunglasses. The tobacco kiosk also provided inspiration in the form of a large cherry wood pipe, mercifully out of his normal character.

In green cap, yellow muffler and puffing jauntily he made for the Jermyn Street exit. No one had remarked him, he decided. In the unruffled calm of an artists' colourman store he bought a large indiarubber, some sable brushes and a tube of gum.

By now a drink was essential to dull the pain from his leg and provide a pause to consider strategy. He settled for a small expensive hostelry towards St. James - an establishment with several advantages, including a respectable washroom and exists on two streets. He was, he decided over his first gin, to be a sporting type, probably ex R.A.F. and he began to think himself into the role as an actor might.

He had a second gin but the pain still lowered at him.

The real problem was to reach the girl and to get some money to her, to pierce the cordon. Once it was in her hands she could time her own getaway and he could lie low until the worst of the hue and cry was past.

In the washroom he filled out his cheeks with the indiarubber which gave a satisfactorily pouchy look, though it was hardly comfortable. A shot of the drug - only four now remained - restored his balance.

In his absence a man, obviously a plain clothes policeman had come into the bar and was looking around. Freedom from pain gave him the courage to eye danger casually and to order another drink. It was time to move.

The suburbs, he had decided, were the safest hideout for the night. A taxi immediately outside the bar took him to the Edgeware Road where he collected a bag from the tube luggage office. Watford seemed the furthest point. It was going as well as could be expected.

* * * *

At half past six the Assistant Commissioner held a conference. The day's reports were before him. Saunders had been seen in

34

Beaconsfield, Truro, Goole, Bradford, Lowestoft, Newhaven and in Central London.

"The Piccadilly report seems the most likely," said his aide. "He was noticed by a reliable man there, who's used to this sort of thing. This chap says he's pretty sure, their eyes met and that Saunders, if it was he, disappeared into thin air. Wearing a trenchcoat, he says. Otherwise he can't add much.

"But there's some confirmation for the story. Our chaps went round all the pubs in the area within the hour. At the Craven, that's in Jermyn Street, a barman says a man came in limping heavily and went off after a couple of drinks as fit as a flea. He thought it odd."

"Well, assuming this is the chap, where do we go from here? If he was limping, maybe he was in pain and gave himself a shot. It can't have been the right one or we'd know by now. How are you following up?"

"Every which way, sir. If he was spotted in London and knows it, he may go to earth if he's got friends. This we doubt, because they may be as keen to meet him as we are, for different reasons. No, he'll not go far, because of his girl, we think. He might step out to the suburbs - Hendon or Kingston or Colindale, somewhere like that - anywhere on a tube line where he could nip off smartish. They're all altered of course."

"I see. Now about the girl?"

"She works at a hairdressers in Pimlico. A quite little kid, by all accounts. We've got men on her twenty four hours a day."

* * * *

The next day's conference was a meeting of angry men. They were rattled and unhappy too, for at that level there was no buck-passing to be hoped for.

Commander Rayne of the C.I.D. made his report in person to the Assistant Commissioner.

"He's slipped us," he admitted. "We can disregard all the out-of-town stories - there's no doubt now that he was the man in the West End yesterday.

"This morning there was information from Watford - just the sort of place we expected. A man booked in at a Commercial hotel just by the station, last night. The local police had made their check up just before he arrived, and he didn't altogether fit the bill anyhow. He does seem to have had a bit of a limp however when he left this morning. What put them on to it was the fact that he had a fight in his room sometime during the night. A man was picked up by the landlord this morning trying to sneak out of the pub and he'd clearly been badly beaten up in the suspect's bedroom. The place was a wreck.

"This chap's name is Hicks, Charles Arthur, a small time con man with a long record; he's even been an informer in his day. Pretty clear what happened. He must have spotted Saunders somewhere along the line and gone into his bedroom to put the black on him.

"Hicks hasn't sung to us yet but he evidently got the worst of it and spent part of the night either knocked out cold, or tied up with a gag in his mouth, probably both. The sheets were in ribbons and our bird had flown.

"We've got a bit more descriptions. Saunders is now a sporting type, big pipe, yellow muffler and green cap. He's discarded the trenchcoat - left it in the tube. If he's got money he may switch his outfit quite a bit.

"But that's not all, unfortunately. It looks as if he'd reached the girl right under our noses. Very neatly done, really - you have to take your hat off to him."

"I'm not in the mood," said the A.C. gloomily. "What happened?"

"At half past twelve this morning," recited the Commander, "A man arrived in Ember Street, Pimlico, which contains the back door of the Maison Henriette where the girl works. He was on a Gambetta, one of those little scooter jobs. Stolen in Watford. Completely typical, our may says. Bowler hat, duffle coat and R.A.F. moustache - hundreds of 'em about. Our chaps didn't give him a second thought. He was carrying a box of chocolates and some flowers wrapped in cellphone. A couple of the lady assistants came out of the shop on their way to lunch - not his girl, Jessie Dale, but two friends. Saunders, if it was he, went up to them, gave them the stuff and they took it back inside, evidently at his request. Our chap says he thought nothing of it until little Jessie took her lunch, or rather should have done. In fact she nipped out earlier than usual, caught a taxi and vanished. There was a squad car up the street but she managed to get lost all the same. The other two girls say a nice gentleman asked them to take the flowers and chocs in to Jessie because it was her birthday. She read the card on the bunch, took the lot into their washroom and when she came out, shared the chocs with the girls, left the flowers in a vase and set off for outer space without saying goodbye. Our guess is that Saunders sent her the best part of a thousand quid in that box of chocolates and told her just where to go. She knew perfectly well we were tailing her - in fact she was co-operating very nicely until just that moment."

A telephone bell had begun to murmur discreetly in the room

and from the habit of importance, the A.C. waited for Rayne to finish before answering.

He listened in silence for a full minute, said, "Yes, well, keep at it," and hung up. "Your man Hicks," he explained. "He's sung, as you envisaged. Admits everything. One new detail. After the fight in the bedroom Saunders tied him up and gagged him. But he could still see. Saunders gave himself another shot just before he left. That leaves him, according to our reckoning, just two to go."

*　*　*　*

At that precise moment the man called Henry Musgrave Saunders was speeding along a line somewhere between Much Hadham and Bishop's Stortford. His little machine was running easily and his plan was clear. He would leave it at a garage on a pretext of repairs and take a Cambridge train. He had discarded his duffle coat and returned to his sporting check cap and muffler.

A sudden flash of pain as violent as a repair stab in a nerve threw him, and the Gambetta, completely off balance.

They swerved together, struck the side of the ditch and the man was flung forward into the knotty bank of the hedge like a sack of turnips.

He lay there for an hour and a half.

*　*　*　*

Towards midnight Commander Rayne and the A.C. spoke again.

"This beats everything," Rayne was shouting with fury. "We had him, had him stone cold, in our hands - only just got to pick him up - and he walks out into thin air."

"What happened?"

"Found lying by his motor cycle in a ditch in Hertfordshire. Both of them smashed up. Good Samaritan took him into Bishop's Stortford Hospital." He sighed heavily. "He was there for an hour - a full hour - eight stitches in his forehead. Then they let him go. Just ten minutes before the local people identified the bike as the one he's lifted in Watford. I ask you! Ten minutes, and he's vanished."

The A.C. stood up.

"Well it's something," he said. "Now listen. I want some action. Cordon off the area, get every available man in Herts and Essex on the job. Vans - loudspeakers - specials - dogs - the full treatment. We're looking for a limping man with a heavily bandaged head. Even you ought to be able to spot him from a hole in the ground."

"Precisely so," said Rayne, adding heavily, "Sir." He paused for a moment and continued. "Those orders were issued an hour ago. So far we've pulled in twenty out-patients with bandaged heads - none of them right. I came to ask you for any extra ideas you might have."

By Thursday afternoon nearly four hundred bandaged persons had been questioned, searched and reduced to varying stages of fury. Saunders had been reported, bandaged and unbandaged, in Newmarket, Colchester, Northampton and King's Lynn.

Yet the net did not produce the right fish.

At six in the evening every senior policeman in East Anglia was exhausted and all over five counties grim men were tramping fields, combing woods and waiting wearily at four hundred road blocks. Traffic over a quarter of England came virtually to a standstill.

On Saturday evening at precisely seven fifteen a turbanned Indian wearing a dirty white robe which might well have been a sheet and carrying two cheap rugs over his shoulder arrived on a ladies bicycle at the police station at Gurney St. Mary in Suffolk. After some delay he was admitted to the distinguished presence of Inspector Duncannon, who was in no mood to discuss the problems of itinerant rug sellers.

"Well?" he enquired, cooking a ferocious eyebrow at the placid figure now seated before him.

"My name is Saunders," said the stranger. "Get a doctor." Then he collapsed.

Inspector Duncannon was a prudent man. He had been fully warned about the dangers of the infection or of touching any corpse that might appear suddenly in his vicinity.

He rang for the Police Doctor, a courageous soul named Bartlett, who had fewer scruples and sufficient forethought to call at the hospital on the way and provide himself with the vital drug.

Saunders, relieved of the torment which had driven him senseless, was trying to pull himself together. He sat before them, his turban making an untidy heap on the floor.

His bandaged head gave him the air of a tired hero of a melodrama.

"Well," he said. "Here I am. I had a run for my money, but you beat me to it. Had to give up, you know. Too many of your chaps looking for me. I shouldn't have thought I was worth all that trouble."

Doctor and Inspector exchanged glances. It dawned on them that he was completely ignorant of his own importance. Duncannon, as was his habit, approached the subject like the elderly crab he largely resembled.

"You've caused a deal of brother," he began severely. "You and your girl friend. A verra considerable dance as you probably know full well. And what precisely did you do with the wee Jessie Dale?"

Saunders rubbed his wounded forehead. He made quite a romantic figure with his stained brown face, the trace of blood on his brow and fatigue in every line of his body.

"My girl friend Jessie, as you call her? By now I hope she's in Switzerland. Incidentally, your police work isn't always so good. If you haven't laid your hands on her already you never will, so there's no harm in telling you. She's my daughter - got a touch on one lung. A year or so out there is just what she needs. Anything else you want to know? Oh yes, I beat a man up - half killed him, I'm afraid - but he was a smalltime crook, so you won't be bothering about him. I pinched a motor scooter and wrecked it - you know that, no doubt. I've broken and entered one or two houses for food, sheets, rugs and oddments, including a bicycle. I've lived pretty rough, mostly in ditches. Damned uncomfortable. I'll make a full statement when I've slept a bit."

"Now, not so fast my friend," said the Inspector. "Not so fast. We ken a thing or two about you that maybe you don't know yourself."

Saunders eyed the two men quizzically. Even in his weariness the reception was puzzling him.

"The doctor will tell you. You see, for the best part of a week you've been the most wanted man in the world. You didna ken that?"

Dr Bartlett held out his hand and it was shaking.

"I want your injection syringe, the one you carry with you, and any capsules you may have left. It's very important."

Their prisoner fumbled with agonising slowness in the recesses of his sheeted robes. Finally he laid the syringe and a little glass capsule on the table.

For a time nobody spoke. The Inspector mopped his brow and the doctor rubbed his spectacles and then his hands with a handkerchief. He examined the little glass object minutely without touching it. Then he sighed heavily.

"That's it alright." To the bandaged man he said: "It's a miracle you're alive."

By gritting his teeth Saunders managed a smile.

"Nice of you to care about me," he said. "Not that it's important now. I've shot my bolt, I've done what I set out to do and I'm dead beat. Nothing in the world matters a damn to me any longer. Tell me something interesting if you want to keep me awake."

The Inspector stood up, towering above the drooping figure by the table.

"Maybe I will," he said. "You're a remarkable man, perhaps the most remarkable man on earth. It's a miracle you're alive as the Doctor says. What may interest you is this, if you can spare us the time. An order came through from the Home Office ten minutes before you had the good sense to walk in here. 'If Henry Musgrave Saunders will surrender to the police together with a medical supply which he is believed to be carrying no further charges will be made against him and his present conviction quashed.' You're a free man, ye ken, or will be by the morning. What do you say to that?"

"Wake me late, Inspector," said Saunders and bowed his head in his arms over the table. With a final effort he raised himself again. "By the way Doctor, that capsule of yours - I'd never have used it. The colour was wrong - too dark an amber altogether. Mine are as yellow as cheap lemonade. People sometimes make damn silly mistakes and I don't believe in luck. Goodnight."

Old Soldier's Never Lie

After the mystery of the *Marie Celeste* and the identity of Jack the Ripper the world holds no more remarkable minor problem than that of Dr Robert Gabbitas who walked unseen out of the condemned cell of Islington Gaol ("The Felons' Hole") on a Sunday evening in December 1899 and was never seen again.

The Police, the Home Office and the Prison Commissioners have always maintained a bland and complete silence on the subject. The Governor of Islington, the late Colonel Sir James Cox-Codrington V.C., never even mentions the incident in his memoirs. It is true that he also omits the battle of Rorkes Drift: perhaps he disapproved of both events.

Nor do the newspapers of the day shed much light, for their attention was elsewhere. The old Queen was dying, there was war in South Africa, Mafeking was beseiged by the Boers. The new century was about to be born. *The Times* however, was in proper form. It produced the story with masterly brevity:-

Condemned Man Escapes
(London, Tuesday)

A condemned man escaped from Islington Prison on Sunday last at about 6 p.m. He is described as Robert Gabbitas, a Doctor of Medicine. The Police are making enquiries.

(From a Correspondent)

The Morning Post repeated the story the following day, adding that Gabbitas had been convicted at the Central Criminal Court by a jury before Mr Justice Entwhistle for the murder by poison of two women, his wife and his housekeeper. The poison was Antimony. This is one of the last examples of its use for criminal purposes, since it is easier to detect than arsenic, which was then becoming widely known. He had been in practice in Hendon, then a village outside London. Interested readers were invited to refer to back numbers for reports of the trial.

This, fantastic as it may seem, is virtually all there is in the way of contemporary material. Yet there is no parallel for it since the days of Jack Shepherd.

After the closing of Newgate Gaol before its demolition in 1903, Islington had a brief spell of gloomy notoriety. It was old, hideous, dangerously unhygienic and miserably cold. Its surrounding wall was five feet thick and between the condemned cell and the outer world were four locked doors that would have defied a siege. Dr Gabbitas walked, it seems, through all of them, into a vacuum which has surrounded him ever since.

The Piccadilly Magazine of 1901 was the first to realise the possibilities of the story. It published what purported to be a full account of the affair by a retired warder who claimed to have been one of the two officials on duty in the cell at the time. The writer bore the unfortunate name of George Watchit and it is a matter of history that he was not using a pseudonymn.

According to Mr Watchit, the doctor was not only a man of enormous physical strength but a mesmerist into the bargain. In his presence victims passed into a coma and iron bars bent like licorice in his hands. If this were even in part true it makes one wonder how the doctor ever came to be arrested. Mr Watchit also endowed his charge with a third attribute: he could, he said, leap or scale a twenty foot wall with all the facility of the mythical Spring Heeled Jack himself. Reduced to plain terms it would appear that Mr Watchit and his colleague were overcome by supernatural forces whilst their prisoner gathered up his strength and leapt into space.

It is probably because of this implausible and high coloured nonsense that there was no great revivial of interest in the story.

A more authentic contribution comes a year later from an American author Carl Vandenberg in his *Remarkable Escapes and Deliverances from Peril*. It is full of beautiful verbosity for connoisseurs only, but says quite a lot about the doctor and makes one vital point. Gabbitas was a little man, balding and pop-eyed, with a formidable black moustache. The book includes the only known photograph. It shows him, part of a formal group, surrounded by the fading shoulders, knees and elbows of members of a fraternal society, the Ancient Order of Flintcrackers, perhaps. His face is completely expressionless and he wears a wide sash to which insignia are pinned.

Vandenberg adds that he was born in Hounslow in 1860, the son of a grocer, educated in Twickenham after his parents moved, qualified in medicine in Edinburgh, followed his profession for some years overseas notably in the China station and on Tea Trade ships, and married, briefly, an English lady in Calcutta, a well-to-do widow. She survived only eighteen months, dying 'of a fever' and leaving him £15,000.

His second wife, née Millicent Dawson, was also fairly wealthy for she was the daughter of a speculative builder. She brought him £10,000 in bonds and securities and some unspecified property 'overseas'.

If we may leave Mr Vandenberg for a moment, it was this property which later provided an important clue.

The author's theory of the escape itself is less rewarding. He inclines to a good part of Warden Watchit's account, but adds, as a deduction, an accomplice.

"The iron bars of the cell itself were undoubtedly smashed apart by what superhuman force no man can guess, and the two guards were overpowered. Perhaps the dread terror of the noose, due so soon to end a life of unrepentant sin, endowed this wretched man with strength beyond our ken. The occult powers of the East may have been known to him. Suffice it to say....."

He continues: "Certain it is that the final wall was scaled by the aid of a rope and grappling irons, for its vast and forbidding height offered no foothold. Who can doubt that some unknown accomplice, in response to a prearranged signal, flung the fugitive the very object which should have ended his days - a rope?"

Who indeed? Vandenberg's speculations only underline the mystery. They ignore, for example, every other warder on duty, and at least three locked doors.

The next factual reference to the affair occurs in the autumn of that year and is one of those legal oddities which the law occasionally looks straight in the face and ignores.

A Dr Frederick Amber, once the junior partner of Gabbitas and his only heir - for the will was clear and concise - applied for leave in the Courts to presume Gabbitas dead and to be granted probate. After some deliberation Lord Mulligan himself, a forensic giant of his day, held that if Gabbitas were not physically dead then he certainly was morally and should be legally. Dr Amber was granted probate, though precisely upon what grounds was not made clear. Perhaps taking all the circumstances into consideration the learned judge may have thought it unlikely that he was creating a popular precedent.

The young doctor, thirty one at the time, therefore removed himself from English gossip and opened a practice at Davos in Switzerland, establishing a very successful clinic in the hotel he had so curiously inherited from his senior partner.

No journalist seems to have asked him for his story or perhaps they did and were rebuffed for their trouble.

What remains? It is true there is no reference in the Governor's memoirs to the escape itself but there is this odd paragraph for those who care to read between the lines of *Shikari: A Soldier's Life and Adventures,* published in 1904.

"At this time (1898) I was offered the curious and interesting appointment of Governor of Islington Gaol, one of two or three very old prisons still in use after the abolition of Newgate.

"I took with me on to the prison staff several old members of my regiment. These included the faithful Sgt. Percival, my batman and later my butler; Colour Sgt. Thomasson and Corporal Watchit, the last two becoming senior wardens despite some local protestations which I had not the slightest hesitation in suppressing. My house was cold and insanitary and made very uncomfortable quartering...."

"Watchit was in poor shape at the time and attributed his decline very largely to the conditions. He did not, alas, survive long. He was soon pensioned and the African sun took its toll some two years later....a faithful and honest servant to Her Majesty and the Empire. Would that there were more like him, for he had been at my side in many a danger."

Here for the first time we find the name Thomasson: he is of interest since he was the second of the two warders in the condemned cell. A picture of him survives, shewing a faded shrunken old warrior much be-medalled, dressed in pathetic finery for a wedding or a burial, boasting a shaggy walrus fringe which clearly had once been stiff and pointed with wax.

The Piccadilly Magazine revived the story in an aside, in its issue for January 1906. "Our Vanishing Prisons" was the title for a pictorial feature. It dealt in some detail with Islington Gaol, then in the process of demolition. It had several old prints of its more famous inhabitants, and the buildings themselves were recorded for the last time, already in the hands of the housebreakers. The condemned cell of course is among them, and there are two photographs of it. The first shows the outside of the block, a solitary one storey affair of stone standing isolated in a grim yard, a morgue or a slaughterhouse without doubt. Executions, it was explained, were carried out in the room adjoining the cell itself, built above a cellar, part of an even more ancient dungeon.

The second photograph, remarkably clear for its time, is of greater interest. It shows a small window high up in a stone wall, from which several thick bars have been smashed or removed. The remains of them are still embedded in the sides and the air space is boarded over from the outside. A caption runs: "The condemned cell, or 'Felons' Hole', showing the bars broken by Dr Gabbitas in his astounding escape in 1899. No further executions

44

ever took place here, since it was felt to be unsafe."

It is hard to see how anyone could have reached this tiny aperture, let alone scramble through it. It stands over seven feet from the ground and would appear to be at best eighteen inches wide even if the remains of the bars are discounted. Dr Gabbitas was a short man, about five foot six. There is no easy explanation here. Yet somebody broke those bars.

So the student must try elsewhere if he is to solve this problem.

He should look perhaps into the mood of the time, into the history and psychology of the four men most closely involved.

First there is the Doctor himself. We know that he was cunning and resourceful: the reports of the trial show that he was as able in his defence as his own counsel. But the evidence was against him: there were too many damning facts capable of proof once suspicion was afoot. Of the four he was easily the most intelligent. It is not reasonable to look for collusion since all the officials were total strangers to him.

Sgt. Thomasson and Cpl. Watchit may be considered together. They were new men on the job, having been introduced by the Governor himself, which probably made them unpopular with their fellows. The 'death watch' was at that time an extra duty in prisons and carried some small additional pay and certain privileges in food and leave.

Both men were elderly for the task and due for retirement within a few years. Both had expectations of a small pension if they completed their term.

Watchit was suffering from the after effects of campaigns in Central Africa, possibly malaria. The poor heating of the prison provided the worst possible conditions for him.

Sir James, the Governor, was an entirely different character. He was tall, big boned, arrogant, dictatorial and utterly without fear. His V.C. was gained in unarmed combat and his memoirs reveal him as a loyal friend, if a remarkably dull one. He was clearly a typical specimen of his period, comic in this day and age, but magnificently beyond caricature.

The only other detail to emerge on research is that the night of December 12th 1899 was bitterly cold and there was a heavy fog, a 'London Particular', which had lasted for forty-eight hours.

Armed with these curiously assorted scraps, a mixture of fact and colour, it is possible to evolve three theories:-

(1) The guards were drugged or mesmerised according to Foster Williams writing in 1912, and robbed of their keys. This does not explain the broken bars, nor indeed the necessity for breaking them, nor the opening of outer doors: it is

45

unlikely that any one warder had a complete set of keys. In any case whence came the drugs? None of the doctor's patients suggested that he had any mesmeric gifts.

(2) The warders were bribed or connived at the escape. This is the view of several criminologists, notably Dr Frink of Illinois. It may be discounted since there is every evidence that both men had an old soldier's loyalty to their commanding officer. Each died in respectably modest circumstances and there is no suggestion of any outside source of income. Dr Gabbitas was a total stranger to all three.

(3) Watchit's account is in some measure true. This is the least likely. Some instrument must surely have been used to break those bars. Dr Gabbitas was a small man of sociable disposition, never at any time an athlete. After the verdict of guilty he received no visitors. There is no one who could conceivably have passed him a crowbar, drugs or a sum of money.

Until very recently no explanation covered all the facts and the mystery would remain for ever unsolved were it not for a document which was recently discovered among the effects of the late Dean of Gurney Magnus in Suffolk. It was the property of his father, Canon Woods. The item concerned, modestly titled *The Olympian*, is one of those amateur literary journals, fashionable in the '90s and even later. This particular issue is for March, 1908. It was never printed, but either typed or handwritten and circulated in folio form among members of a local literary society, each of whom contributed from his own personal stock of talent a drawing, a verse, or as in this case, a short story. It is clearly one of a series.

"The Professor's Escape" is No. 4 in "Tales of a Prison Chaplain"

"One Sunday evening late in the last century a man awoke from a light slumber in one of the big London prisons. Ah, now he remembered it all, the whole terrible story! He was John Robinson, a professor of science who had fallen low. He was a murderer, justly condemned by the world for his wickedness, a wretch with but two days to live before the dread penalty would be exacted.

"Rising from his truckle bed he glanced idly at the two warders who were with him both day and night. They were sitting by the table in the cell and one of them was apparently asleep.

"'By Jove!' exclaimed the professor, 'I believe your friend is ill! It is bitterly cold. Perhaps he has been overcome by the chill?'"

"'More likely he has had a fit,' rejoined the other in some

46

surprise. 'For he is an old soldier and has had these seizures before. It is due to long campaigns in Africa and the fevers he contracted there. Here, give me a hand with him.'

"The professor was about to spring to his aid, but a sudden wild thought had forced itself upon him and instead of rendering assistance he leapt upon his second guardian from behind.

"Within the flash of an eye the warder had been rendered unconscious, for the professor had learned secret tricks of self defence and attack whilst studying in distant corners of the world. Soon the poor man lay senseless, almost at death's door.

"It was a cold and foggy night. The strains of evensong from the prison chapel drowned say sound that might have come from the two helpless men, now at the mercy of a desperate criminal.

"It was the work of but a few moments for the professor to change clothes with one of the warders. He selected Sgt. Smith, the one he had personally attacked, and dragged him roughly upon the bed, covering his face with blankets.

"Once attired as Smith, he cut off his moustache with scissors from his victim's pocket, and donned the heavy uniform topcoat and peaked cap of the warder. His face was muffled in a woollen scarf, called in the Army a Balaclava. Then he rang the warning bell which sounded in the corridor beyond the cell.

"'Help! Help!' he called. 'Warder Brown has had a severe attack and needs immediate aid.'

"Two other warders now rushed in and perceived the plight of their comrade. Of this there could be no doubt for the unhappy man was perspiring freely, trembling and groaning piteously.

"'Merciful powers!' exclaimed one of the newcomers. 'He is utterly distraught. But surely our prisoner is a man of science and will come to the aid of a fellow man?'

"'Alas, no.' replied the disguised felon, adding a foul oath. 'He cares nothing for his captors. Quickly, now, give me a hand and we will take poor Brown to some place where he may receive aid.'

"Between them they carried him in a half dead condition to an adjoining room.

"In the confusion of the moment the Professor managed to obtain access to the outer yard, for he now had keys, and slipped away on the pretext of fetching the Doctor and the Governor, both of whom were at Divine Service.

"Fortune and the density of the fog, together with the confusion of the moment favoured the miserable fugitive. At the outer postern the guards mistook him for an officer going off duty and he vanished unnoticed into the dark streets of London.

"Inside the gaol the Governor and Doctor were soon upon the scene, shortly to be joined by the Chaplain (for Warder Brown was thought to be dying) and it was then that the discovery was made. A great search was ordered, but it was to no avail......

"The Governor, Colonel Johnson, then performed an action which many readers will find curious. He summoned the Chaplain and the Doctor to the condemned cell, which was now deserted, and spoke to them in quiet soldierly tones.

"'My poor warders have been duped by a treacherous foe,' he said. 'It would go ill with them if those in high authority learned of this trickery. For myself I care naught since my accommodation here does not befit an officer and gentleman and I am retiring to private life very shortly.

"'But these men are of my own regiment and as brave as lions, even if they have been outwitted by a cunning devil. Their livelihood, their pensions and their wives and children may suffer from this miscreant's scheming act.

"'I have therefore decided that their behaviour and their courage must not be called into question. We three are all old soldiers (though of different regiments) so you will both know that there are times when true loyalty must go the men under your command rather than to Headquarters.

"'If you will be good enough to leave me here in this dreadful place I shall make it clear to all investigators that this man did not escape by a mere trick, but by exercising superhuman force and overcoming my men, who were faithful to the best traditions of the British Army.'

"So saying, the Governor bade his colleagues a courteous farewell, and they retired for the night.

"Thus began a great mystery, the true solution of which has never been made public. Now that the good men concerned have entered into rest the truth may be revealed.

"But, the reader will ask, what befell the chief figure in this strange tale?

"As far as the present writer can tell (though it is by no means certain) he took refuge abroad, where, having undergone a change of heart and perhaps mindful of his deliverance, he devoted himself to good works and the healing of the sick.

"The purposes of Almighty God are inscrutable and it may well be that this man's later life atoned in some measure for a sinful past. Judge not, it is written, that ye be not judged."

Part of the interest in this illuminating little tale lies in the fact that it is written on headed notepaper. The address is: "The Excelsior Clinic, Davos. Switzerland. Under the personal supervision of Dr F. W. Amber and Dr Robert Gray".

Canon Woods, it should be noted, died at Davos on March 12th, 1909.

The Trouble with Locksmiths

"An unidentified object," said the first voice on the phone, "is moving upstream to your area, George. Now reported at about two thousand feet, roughly over Purfleet. Know anything about it?"

"Not on my books that I know of," said the second voice. "What sort of object? A club Proctor off course? Oh, I see, a helicopter. Registration? No? Well, can you type it?"

"We think it's one of those little Skyhook runabouts, but the old visibility is not too good and there's a bit of river mist. She's wearing no lights. Over to you, in fact, George."

* * * * * * *

Message from George to all concerned: "Unknown helicopter moving up Thames River, Tower Bridge area. Report movement and identification forthwith."

* * * * * * *

George, at his official H.Q. commands the Thames basin from an eagle's perch. He is youngish, an ex R.A.F. type and very important as far as air traffic over the metropolitan area is concerned. The lift carries him within twenty steps of his Observation Post penthouse, past the maps, the met. office and the installations offices, but the last flight has to be climbed. He was slightly puffed on arrival, but in full control.

"Got her taped?" he asked the duty officer.

"Yessir," said the man in charge of the glass box on the roof. "A little Skyhook. Wandering about all over the place. Been down as low as 300 feet. Might almost be a drunk on a joyride, but she's being handled beautifully. You can just catch her now in the glasses. Mucking about over the Houses of Parliament. Having a lovely time, I'd say."

"Blimey," said George. "This means trouble."

* * * * * * *

49

Message from the faithful commons, by telephone to George. "What the devil is a helicopter doing buzzing the House when in session? Identify, remove and report back."

* * * * * * *

From George to the faithful commons. "Helicopter shows no identification. R.A.F. engaged in Northern Exercise and not available for escort duties. Tracking aircraft from all observation posts. Helicopter now over St. Paul's and City area. Interference regretted."

* * * * * * *

"This is damnable," said George to his junior. "Trouble with a capital 'T'. He must be drunk. Right now it looks to me as if the silly ass was wandering up and down Fleet Street."

"I make him to be over Bloomsbury, sir, between us and London University - you see their tower. At about 250 feet. They move damn fast, these little Skyhooks. He must be mad as well as drunk."

"I have him precisely," said George and groaned, "and may the Almighty stone the crows. The insolent stinker! The illegitimate son of the Nine Blind Ones! He's circling Security House. Now indeed we are for it in a big way. Hold the fort whilst I pull out every stop known to mankind."

* * * * * * *

Security House, officially referred to as Gabrial's Court WC1 is the largest of the many modern triumphs (architecturally speaking) in the Bloomsbury area. It has much of the charm of a glass sided bootbox upended; containing four floors of income tax clerks, two of telephone accounts, six departments of the Agriculture (By-products) Marketing Board, a cultural lecture centre and, on the very roof, the Security Penthouse, the secret heart of all that is Hush Hush in Government research. This has its own direct lift from the ground floor, with two personal guardians, both ex-Sergeant Majors of the Brigade of Guards. The single approach, a door resembling a safe, gives on to a series of inner doors, covered by electric rays, bells, TV eyes and the whole paraphernalia of absolute security.

It also possesses a magnificent roof garden, rustic seats, a box hedge (in boxes), the best view in London and a sheer drop to the pavement.

On this particular Tuesday evening, it being long after civil service hours, there was nobody there, except for the outer guard, Sgt. Major Dunsford who possesses a minute bed-sitter beside the top of the lift shaft, and Sgt. Major Grigg, D.C.M. who has an exact replica on the ground floor.

Both these worthies were officially allerted within minutes, but they were already aware of the impending menace, and were indeed discussing the matter on the intercom.

Dunsford, from his window just below and outside the great steel curtain, had a fair view.

"He's all round us, Mr Grigg - like a ruddy wasp. Better get the police. If he lands on that roof......"

"Can't you get to that roof no-how?"

"Not a hope in hell. Locks went on at six thirty sharp. Control's at the Ministry and there's no one there, you can bet your sweet life."

*   *   *   *   *   *   *

The Minister however, if not in his office, was at least in the picture. Armed with his finest and heaviest racing glasses, for he was a sportsman at heart, he was watching the proceedings from his own roof top. Furthermore he was in direct communication by telephone with the Chief of the Metropolitan Police and the Home Secretary who happened to be taking wine with him.

"Looks as if he's coming in to land, Bertie," he said. "I say, what happens on that security roof - I mean, will it take the strain and all that?"

"Oh yes," said the Home Secretary. "It was built for the job if you must know, five years ago. Never thought anyone would use it unofficially. The trouble is....."

"Yes?"

"The trouble is that the infernal fortress is so damned secure from below that I bet every window in the place is open and probably the doors too - french windows, they are, onto the garden - remarkably pretty, I'm told."

To the telephone he said: "Running a cordon round it? Good. Can't we get a chaser plane on to him? No? Well, if there's nothing nearer than Gatwick you'd better get cracking. If he came up river he may go back that way. Get the River police - if we can't send a cruiser to the colonies let us at least send a launch to Wapping. Lay on everything - the coastguards, the C.D., the A.A., every one - the whole damned bag of tricks. But get him."

*   *   *   *   *   *   *

Said Sgt. Major Dunsford to Sgt. Major Grigg: "He's landed."

Said Grigg to Dunsford: "Can't you lean out of the window and take a pot at him?"

Said Dunsford to Grigg: "Not a hope in hell. He's right above my head - I'm unsighted for one thing. No gun, for another. And for a third.......he's off again."

* * * * * * *

Said the news editors of five London papers: "Make this a head across six, three col intro and play it big. Security House raided. Spy menace? Aircraft sub in Thames mouth? Bring in outer space if you can. Go to it, boys."

* * * * * * *

From a memo from the Chief Commissioner of the Metropolitan Police to the Minister. "Private and confidential. The aircraft which landed on the roof of Gabriel's Court at 8.17 p.m. on the 14th instant has now been identified as a Skyhook Mark 9 Helicopter and is certainly of British origin. No example of this type have been marketed abroad.

"It seems probable that it is a machine which took off from Marling in Essex where two recently reconditioned aircraft, the property of Hedgehops Ltd., have been on test. Pending re-granting of licence and repainting, one of them wore no identification marks. It is established that the premises were entered on the night in question by a person unknown and an unthorised flight was made. The machine was returned to a nearby field, undamaged. Visibility was poor and this would suggest an experienced pilot with considerable local knowledge. Evidence points to an ex Air Force officer, Anthony Frobisher-Hawkins, 31, of Neatsfoot near Marling, but he has an alibi which seems unlikely to be broken. Investigation is proceeding.

"With regard to Gabriel's Court and the security premises. It appears that only one room was entered by an open window and there is no trace of interference or damage. Any vital documents were under adequate cover. It is suggested that all Public Relations Officers be instructed to play down the incident."

* * * * * * *

From Miss Anne Louise Worthington, 26, personal secretary to the Director of the Security Department, Gabriel's Court, to Anthony Frobisher-Hawkins:

Pig and Monster,

When I got to the office this morning I found forty policemen in my room asking damn silly questions and one even had the impertinence to ask how come a red rose was lying on my blotter. I said I always left one there to remind me of civilization. He said he believed me, so I am a better liar than I thought. Pig, monster and darling I forgive you everything if you will promise never to do it again.

Anne

P.S: Now it will be months before I dare to resign.

The Proper Charley

If you turn left out of the prison gates the road runs fairly steeply uphill into a grim hinterland of Victorian suburbs where the bomb damage still reminds one of rotting teeth - an illusion aided by the untamed weeds. To the right the slope is gentle and from the far end the rumble of buses, a new petrol station and a straggle of side street shops give a suggestion of life. Half way down, where the pavement widens a trifle, stands Bert's Coffee Bar, a stall on jacked-up wheels, open day and night, under the personal supervision of Bert Maxton Jnr himself.

Those who leave gaol early on rainy mornings, suddenly finding themselves strangers in these parts, turn right without exception. Mr Maxton's establishment has therefore become, through the years, a certain rendezvous for those making their discreet exit and for any friends who are forming a welcome committee. A couple of taxis usually make their headquarters here and do a modest trade, especially on visiting days.

Bert's weatherbeaten awning with its thin flapping sides also makes an excellent hide for journalists covering executions and the release of prisoners who are still newsworthy. In its off-beat way this squalid little shelter is quite famous and many a good story has been picked up there in the small hours by perceptive newspapermen.

Business of this sort took me there that Wednesday morning. Prisoners are usually released at seven sharp and today's example was quite a celebrity in his particular world. At any rate my editor thought so and sent me off at the inglorious hour of six thirty to cover the dubious event.

The half hearted dawn was scarcely clear of the sky at that hour and it was of course raining. Even to think of this area without drizzle is an impossibility; it must have the highest rainfall in all suburban London.

I was not quite the first on the scene, for a little runt of a man was standing in the best corner, nearest the urn and out of the wind, reading a dog-eared paper and eating a cocoanut bun which looked as if it had started life as a bedroom slipper for an out of

54

work strip teaser. I greeted Bert respectfully as a valued friend and had some coffee. He is a large tub of a man who looks like Mr Noah in a grey apron. He must be very tall, for with the added height of his stall he towers above his customers, a fact which is useful to him on occasions. It may be that he has legs and feet, but they have never been seen.

"Morning, Mr C.," said. "Keeping busy?"

I explained diffidently that I was still alive, sufficiently at least to complain about my job and the kind of weather he always provided. I hoped to drink my coffee in silence and to keep a cautious eye on the little door in the grim castle wall just up the road, but my fellow customer had other views.

"Journalist, ain't yer?" he said and peered up at me from above thick steel rimmed spectacles. He had a straggling walnus moustache, damp at the edges, and a disgustingly rheumy sniff.

I grunted some sort of agreement and he continued half at me and half to himself, with Bert above us as the arbiter.

"I've seen 'em all," he said. "Ole Bill Forsdyke, who used to come up 'ere for the 'angings. Dead now, ole Bill is, on account of 'is chest I shouldn't wonder. And Mr Simmonds, a right gent 'e was, gimme 'alf a dollar many a time for a tip-off. 'E's dead now, come to think of it, ain't 'e Bert?"

"That's right," said the proprietor. "Pneumonia took 'im off, two years gone. You knew him of course, Mr C.?"

"Course 'e did," said the little man. "'E's like me, knows everything, I shouldn't wonder. Now," he hunched himself still further into the upturned collar of his mackintosh, "I can tell you why you're 'ere, I can. You're 'ere to see Mr Anthony Augustus Fitzroy Stevenson come out, ain't yer? You'll try and talk to 'im and you'll sign 'im up for a life story in ruddy great 'eadlines, I shouldn't wonder."

I was glad that there were only the three of us present for the little man was uncomfortably near the mark.

"I seen 'im done at the Bailey," said my companion, suddenly putting on a remarkable simulation of judicial tones. "You are a proper two-timer what 'as betrayed 'is birthright. You 'ave deliberately associated yourself with a gang of right wrong 'uns, a collection of Charleys of inferior intelligence what 'ave escaped detection thanks to your not 'aving split on 'em. So, chum, you will now take the 'ole bucketful. Five years, you."

He regarded me artfully over his glasses and sniffed.

"So down goes Mr Lah-di-dah Stevenson, and no appeal neither. Thank you, my Lord. I 'ave no comment to make what would get through your thick skull' he says, very sarcastic, and off down the steps 'e goes, lost to the world as you might say, until out 'e comes, seven sharp this morning, which is in five minutes time."

"Exactly," responded Mr Maxton and spat lightly on the chained tea spoon he was polishing. "Give us five minutes more, Mrs. Moore, that's what I say."

"And not such a fool, neither," continued the oracle, sucking a distant tooth with thoughtful efficiency. "Most of 'is lot - 'mere pawns in the underworld's battle for honest blokes' lolly'" (he was quoting again) "- they come unstuck they did. A year here, six months there. A proper set of Charleys. Not but what one or two of 'em might turn up to say welcome 'ome, eh, Bert?"

"Shouldn't wonder," said the proprietor. "What do you think, Mr C.?"

I did not answer because that was precisely what I thought, and so did my editor or he would not have sent me on this mission. Mr Anthony Augustus Fitzroy Stevenson had brought off a remarkable Hatton Garden burglary, capturing a hoard of uncut diamonds which had never been recovered. Mr Stevenson had certainly protected his associates and underlings, but it was he who held the booty, or so the prosecution maintained. My editor, who has a very fair nose for the coming event, took the view that there might be immediate repercussions once Mr Stevenson was a free man. My job was to get his story and watch for developments. My hope was to whirl my man away with the minimum of fuss once I had made contact.

"Oi! Oi!" said the little man suddenly. "What did I tell yer? Look who's 'ere. Give us another coffee, Bert, will yer, before the 'ouse blows up."

He had been peering through a tear in the flapping side canvas of the stall and he now shrank with his fresh cup in to the one warm corner. Here he sucked audibly at the strange beverage which Mr Maxton calls tea or coffee according to demand.

A couple of bulky young thugs, looking rather like Tweedeldum and Tweedledee appeared round the awning simultaneously. They might well have been wearing a uniform, for each had a black imitation leather jacket, tight trousers and all the regalia of insolence and menace. After them came a man with his hat pulled well down over his face so that below his dark glasses nothing appeared except a white rodent nose which looked as if it were prehensile.

They occupied the coffee stall, using it as a cover without acknowledgment to the proprietor and without making a purchase. For a minute the silence was only broken by a slowly rippling sniff from the little man. A clock struck, and a second echoed it and a couple of far off works' hooters sounded a drone's toxin. Then the little door up the road opened and a shabby man came out, looked up and down the road, and settled for the easier slope towards us.

"That's him," said the first blackjacket. "Must be."

"T'ain't," said the second, "I'd know him a mile off."

"Hold him," said Dark Glasses. "He'll know if there's anymore coming."

The two young men sidled into the drizzle almost as if they were performing a dance. The shabby man found one on each side of him before he knew what was happening. He was still protesting querulously as they reached the shelter.

"Now what's all this? Just you let me go. I've seen enough trouble already. I know my rights...I..."

"Shut up," said Dark Glasses. "Just answer our questions, friendly like....see. Where's this guy Stevenson who's coming out this morning? Just behind you, eh? Still saying ta-ta to the Screws?"

"I really don't know," said the shabby man. "I saw him this morning at breakfast. He wasn't in my block but I saw him, I think." He was free of their grip now and rubbing his left arm resentfully. "They don't let us out all in a batch, just one at a time. I don't know if he's out yet - and I don't care, neither. I'm on my way."

But the trio had lost interest. A new figure had emerged from the wall, a short fat man with greasy clothes who carried a shoddy card-board suitcase.

"That's Harry Sims - Harry the Dip," said Dark Glasses. "He'll know. Ask him in boys. Here..." he addressed himself to the proprietor, "Give us four coffees and a packet of twenty."

The fat man joined them without persuasion, grinning all over his face. "Well! Well! Well!" he said. "Just look who's here! Welcome home on behalf of the Mayor and Corporation. Give us the illuminated address and the solid silver mug. Thanking you one and all for your kind attention. Now I was just wondering if I should see you lot." He drank noisily at his coffee and drew hard on a cigarette.

"I said to myself I said," he continued, "Harry boy, they'll be waiting for a pal, a special pal of theirs, as like as not. They'll be waiting just down the road...."

"Cut it," said Dark Glasses. "Where is he?"

"Gone," said the fat man. "Early, he went, I expect, and just on account of you lot, I'd say. I'm the last - I know that. Half an hour extra and nothing for overtime, that's the way they treat you today. I'm writing to the *Times* about it, I......"

There was a moment of delayed reaction when each man seemed to be looking for something to hit or to kick.

Then the two young men began to swear repetitiously and in unison as if they were repeating some serious but obscene litany.

"He can't have," said Dark Glasses finally. "He bloody can't have. We've been here since a quarter past and only that snivelling little bastard and Harry here have come out. He's still inside."

"'Ave it your own way," said Harry. "I see Milord Lah-di-dah at breakfast and that was the last I seen of him. He had the full treatment according to regulations, same like we all do. He must have been in front of me because I know I was the last. A full bleeding half hour I was, standing in a corridor like a public lavatory waiting for the last blessing, and me a free man, according to law....."

No one in particular was listening to him. The old man in the corner gave a long corruscating sniff, a brief summing up of the weather, the company and the situation. He wiped his nose and his moustache reflectively with his fingers.

"I'm off, Bert," he said. "See you Thursday....'Ere, gimme my sandwiches."

Mr Maxton Jnr. sighed and rummaged beneath his counter.

"See you Thursday," he said. "Two 'am, one corner, with mustard. So long."

The old man collected his greasy little parcel and moved off. I waited a couple of minutes, but something told me, even better than the muffled conference which was going on in the far corner, that the morning was over. Mr Fitzroy Stevenson had evaded me and his erstwhile associates, and my best plan was to return to the office and explore other lines of communication.

I walked fairly briskly down the road, for the weather did not incite delay and the taxis had not come on duty. Ahead of me the old man shuffled at an even pace and it crossed my mind to catch up with him. It was possible, I thought, that he knew more than I: perhaps he had seen an early departure.

At the second corner he turned right and I quickened my pace to catch him, but as I rounded the bend by the newsagent it seemed that he had disappeared. A hundred yards ahead of me the only occupant of the street was striding along almost out of sight. Yet he had the same trench coat, the same cap....but now he appeared a foot taller, with a confident stride and a tough military look about his shoulders.

I had to run to catch him, to grab him by the arm and to make him pause. The man who faced me had a fierce almost bogus army moustache jutting sharply upwards and a bright informed suspicious eye. The steel rimmed glasses had disappeared.

"Mr Fitzroy Stevenson," I said. "I'm from the *Daily Record*. Could you spare me a moment? We have a proposition to make you."

He looked me up and down, a friendly man-to-man glance which was at once amiable and understanding but unyielding.

"Good for you," he said. "You rumbled me. Do you mind if we walk along?"

I had no choice, for he took my arm and we marched together in step whether I liked it or not.

"I'd only got five minutes, you know, before my ex-colleagues arrived. They can be very tricky boys to deal with and I had to use all the charm in the world to get the governor to open up before time. But I had to hang around to see what the form was. I hope you follow me, my dear chap?"

"I'm from the *Record*," I repeated, breathlessly. "We want to make you an offer for your memoirs. Now there's no difficulty about this. We have a re-write man, and we could probably pay you....."

I went into my routine story, but my companion was not really listening. We strode along into the main street like an avalanche, sweeping early workers and late cleaners out of our path like wind blown rubbish.

"Sorry, old boy," he said. "Nothing doing - nothing at all. Repentant fellow, going straight, catching a train to Scotland or Amsterdam or Cardiff or Pernambuco....make it wherever you like. Now this, I think, is where I pick up transport. If you're going back to Bert's, give the boys my very best wishes, won't you?"

He was one of those masterful types who can conjure a taxi out of the air. He was gone before I could even mumble a civil goodbye.

I stood there in the drizzle faced by dozens of buses going in the wrong direction, and obstructing honest pedestrians proceeding uncomfortably on their lawful occasions.

It was only when I pulled myself together, compounded a plausible story for my editor and at long last found an unwilling taxi, that it occurred to me to speculate idly on the contents of that packet of sandwiches which Bert had ready under the counter. Now I come to think of it, they seemed as if they had been in captivity for a long long time.

Uneasy Lies

Collecting villains has always been one of my major interests. Unless one is very rich it is a difficult hobby, for it can prove extremely, indeed disastrously, expensive. The best of my specimens, as it happened, cost me nothing except the loss of a first class newspaper sensation which might have made me a reputation. This, you see, was one that got away. On the other hand, I am intact, so honours are even.

His name is Baron Guilderstodt and he really is deliciously wicked.

I met him only once and that was due to the intervention of a waiter who made my acquaintance at an all-night coffee stall. It was one of those warm electric blue nights which London can produce once or twice in a good summer. The waiter and I, standing beside each other under the hospitable awning by Hyde Park Corner had something in common - a uniform, for we were both in evening clothes.

He said, with an endearing mixture of civility and irony, "Good evening, sir. Enjoy yourself tonight? I hope you did, for I was looking after your table, which probably you didn't notice."

I looked at him very carefully and for the life of me I couldn't recall him. He had the most ordinary of faces - round, smooth, inoffensive, mouse coloured trimmings, an easy manner and a reasonable accent - nothing to register at any point. He was neither effeminate nor gauche, a strict non-entity.

"Of course I remember you perfectly," I said, "and if you must know it was a horrible meal. Lukewarm soup, stale fish, strong sauce, chicken cooked far too long ago and re-heated. What else do you expect from a Charity Ball at sixty shillings a ticket?"

His amiable smile, the only memorable thing about him, flickered again.

"Well, that's true enough," he said, "But it didn't cost you anything, did it? I mean, sir, that you gentlemen of the press are invited just to write about who's there and you're not one of the ordinary suckers. You *are* a journalist, aren't you, sir?"

I admitted it.

"I thought so," he said. "I've seen you around and generally alone. Very few press people bring anyone with them to that sort of show - the food isn't good enough."

I agreed and added that there were always knobs and knutty persons and debs and dowagers to be observed and admired and written about and that anyway it was a means of earning a living, just like waiting at table, for example, and wearing precisely the same clothes.

This, he thought, was perfectly fair.

"I'm a casual," he said. "Not staff, I mean. If I was on the staff I'd change my kit on the premises and walk home in civvies, but we extras don't get the same accommodation below stairs."

He eyed me, very carefully with that same half mocking but wholly friendly smile about his eyes.

"You wouldn't be interested in a story, would you? I mean a real story - a headline job, not just gossip, but an honest-to-goodness riproarer?"

If you ask any journalist that sort of silly question you get the expected silly answer. We went back to my flat and I gave him a drink. The only odd thing about him was that his 'uniform' was remarkably well cut - rather better than my own.

"First of all," I said, "If we're going to talk seriously, what's your name and address?"

He paused for quite a long time, a calculated delay in which he took a deep emptying drink at the tumbler which he put down very precisely on the tray beside him. Then he straightened himself almost to the point of standing to attention.

"You could describe me," he said, "as an ex-member of the Court of His Most Exalted Majesty King Heinrich the Ninth of Plesse Weinstein and of the Province of Unter Weinstein, and in one way you'd be damn well right."

It was now my turn to produce the mocking but civil smile.

"Grand Duke becomes waiter?" I said. "That sort of story is fifty francs a time in Paris and even cheaper in New York or along Sunset Boulevard. You'll have to do better than that. Anyhow, I've never heard of Plesse Weinstein or King Heinrich the Ninth."

"Journalists are always abysmally ignorant," he said, and was not in the least abashed. "Look us up in the *Imperial Lexicon* or Duffy's *Royal Households* if you've got a copy - or better still-" he looked around him, "What liqueurs do you have?"

I indicated my modest collection of drinks and his eyes lit up.

"Ah," he said, "The very thing. Du Bellay Cognac, V.S.O.P. and very nice too." He picked up the bottle and read from the label. "'As supplied to His Exalted Highness' and here, by gum, is our coat of arms. Now do you believe in Plesse Weinstein? Not that

I'm blaming you for ignorance, my dear chap, because we haven't existed as a Kingdom since 1921."

He was perfectly right. Monsieur Du Bellay, I saw from his label, also supplied his liqueur to three other defunct but illustrious sounding realms.

I still did not see why I should be especially impressed or where the story could be of any great value to either of us.

"Your accent," I said, "suggests that you went to an English public school and though I'm not a Professor Higgins I'd be prepared to bet on which one - that's a guess helped on by a certain sort of arrogance in your manner when you stop remembering to be a waiter. I don't think you've got a drop of middle European blood in your veins. Suppose you come off it. If you've got a story, we'll go into it carefully and see if there's anything in it for either of us."

He helped himself to some more of my whisky, having asked for it perfunctorily by raising his eyebrows.

"As you say," he said, clearly considering his opening, "you may as well have it directly from the beginning. My name is - or to be accurate, was - Galbraith, Anthony Michael St. John Galbraith. Orthodox family, you see. I was an only son, very comfortably orphaned in India when I was twelve. I say comfortably, because of Rich Uncle James who spent quite a bit on my upbringing and who left me a pittance when he died. The old boy wasn't as rich as he'd thought, having bought a few gold bricks in his time. Still, he'd pulled what strings he could and got me into the lower reaches of the C.D. - the Diplomatic as you could call it."

He took a long sip and considered.

"The fact must be faced," he said, "That I was a ghastly flop. I liked the wrong sort of girl and I was generally pretty idle. All my own work with no sort of blame attaching to any other party. There was no future in it for my type, the best I could hope for being press secretary to H.E. for Mbongo-Mbongoland, if you follow me.

"Then there was a spot of real trouble. In fact it took all that was left of Uncle's well-known pittance to get me out from under without a blazing scandal. But out is what I did get and that without any sort of official row, which was pretty good going, all things being weighed fairly."

Another sip, another smile.

"Well there I was," he said, "on my uppers and behind with the installments. No talents, no real education to speak of. Expensive tastes, good wardrobe, French, German and Italian spoken fairly well - a natural job for the colonies if I'd been born fifty years earlier and had someone to send me pin-money. Old-fashioned and damned ordinary, the whole story. But wait for it, boys, wait for it. At this point I met the Baron Guilderstodt. Have you ever had that pleasure?"

I said I'd never even heard of him.

"A pity," he said. "Your loss. He's quite a personage, the Baron. Curly grey hair, handsome as the fiend, black eyes, deep voice, slight accent. Too bad to be true in fact. The old devil knows he looks like a stage character, feels he can't help it, and so keeps very much in the background.

"He sent a uniformed chauffeur and a footman to my rooms with a letter on royally crested paper - Plesse Weinstein, the court now in residence at Ganymede Hall in the County of Surrey, England. The Baron's compliments and would I do him the honour of lunching with him. If I happened by good fortune to be free, the carriage awaited me.

"Now it won't astonish you to know that I looked up the history of Plesse Weinstein pretty smartly. His Exalted Majest Heinrich the Eighth had removed his court abruptly from Europe to Surrey in 1921. He never abdicated and took a good deal of the top brass with him along with quite a large piece of cash money. He was no trouble to anyone, shunned publicity, very occasionally went shooting with Royalty here, although oddly enough he wasn't a relation, and generally behaved pretty well. In 1931 he astonished everyone including, I gather, Her Majesty the late Queen Ellen, by raising an heir. This chap was discreetly crowned in 1941 on the death of his father by the Bishop in Exile in the private chapel at Ganymede. End of information."

We both had a drink at this point and I felt that the bait was tasty enough for a nibble.

"The gallant Baron," said Mr Galbraith (though I still thought of him as a waiter), "lunched me extremely well in what he termed his private apartments. He also pumped me very thoroughly about my background and seemed pleased in a secretive sort of style about what I told him. I was reasonably honest about it because I had the feeling he knew it all anyhow.

"Then he came down to business. There was, he explained, a very nice little post awaiting me. A sort of Public Relations job to His Majesty but requiring very great discretion and considerable ingenuity. Life at Ganymede Hall wasn't too easy these days it seemed, and the Court had to be made to pay for itself.

"The job was in two parts. First, I must busy myself very cautiously making sure that the reference book people kept on including the Royal household in their lists although the Kingdom itself didn't exist any longer, and I gathered that this called for quite a bit of tactful pressure.

"Second, I had to find the right contacts."

"Contacts?" I enquired. "Meaning......?"

"Meaning," he explained, "tradespeople who want royal patronage and are prepared to pay annually for the privilege of a fine looking warrant and the use of the royal arms. Du Bellay, for example. They're a newish firm in the cognac world, but they like to look as old as they claim their product is.

"And then of course there are the real suckers to be catered for. You wouldn't care to be made a perfectly genuine Count by any chance? No? Well, if you did fancy that sort of thing the Baron could probably fix you up for a modest fee - say, five thousand pounds. He's reasonably selective, by the way and only advises His Majesty to make about three a year, including only one American. Quite a few Frenchmen go in for this sort of thing and we've even had an Arab who had decided to live over here for reasons best undisclosed. You'd be surprised.

"Honours, of course, for a much more reasonable fee. The best is the Order of St. Simeon which looks remarkably like the Legion d'honneur, strangely enough, and can be very useful in the buttonhole emblem form if travelling abroad. Yours for a thousand smackers, cash folding money. No cheques accepted but perfectly genuine gongs which you can sport at quite a lot of functions, and the sash gives you that air of distinction which women so admire. You can have an Order of Chastity for slightly less, but it's not so popular because it often raises a horse laugh, though that's a detail we never point out until it's too late.

"Well, that was the general outline of the business and the conditions were that I was to move to Court, bag and baggage, tell nobody what I was up to and to keep absolutely out of sight until I was completely briefed.

"It took me about a fortnight to get right into the run of things. Ganymede Hall is a vast rambling sort of pile, built about sixty years ago for a millionaire who went bust. I got to know the staff and what was left of the original household - a butler, a so-called wine steward who was obviously a thug, the Bishop who is over ninety, a male nurse described as an equerry and a physician in residence. There were others but they don't matter.

"The only chap I never met was the King himself. The Baron conveyed to me in a sophisticated roundabout way, that he was a pretty weak-headed specimen and the only time I ever saw him was at a distance, sitting all rugged up in a little summer house on the private lawn. Even that glimpse gave me some queer ideas about him. It rather frightened me."

"Why? Why *frightened*?"

"Oh, I don't know. It gave me a cold shiver. Pity, I suppose, for

64

instability, terrible weakness, - there was a kind of frail withering uselessness about the poor blighter.

"Somehow I wasn't altogether surprised when the Baron came into my office one morning - I was supposed to be swotting royal history - with a face like doomsday. He stood half in and half out of the room for a bit looking down the corridor and then he closed the door and locked it before he spoke.

"'My dear Mr Galbraith,' he said. 'A situation has arisen which I have envisaged for some time. Fortunately I have had the good intelligence to make your acquaintance and to assure myself of your friendship, your discretion and your integrity. I must now bring you some news which is so secret that you must really pledge yourself by whatever you hold sacred - money perhaps - never to reveal it.'

"I pledged myself.

"'His Majesty', he said, resuming his normal poker face, 'passed away at half past three this morning. It is of course very distressing but it raises rather vital problems if our association is to be continued, indeed if the Court is not to cease for ever. I have a certain suggestion to make which should prove extremely beneficial to your fortunes and to all of us here.'

"Suddenly I had a glimpse of what was coming, but I let him speak it all out in words - thousands of very long words in fact - just to enjoy listening to the smooth old villain. What it boiled down to was this. As long as there was a King there was a fat livelihood for one and all. But no King, then no honours, no royal appointments, no Court, no lolly. Not even a good book of juicy memoirs, there being no history for the last forty years.

"Why not, therefore, replace one nondescript and vague looking young man by another? Why shouldn't A. M. St. J. Galbraith disappear unloved and unlamented and His Majesty Heinrich the Ninth go on living happily ever after, dishing out royal favours to his heart's content?

"It took a bit of nerve, I can tell you, and quite a lot of criminal intelligence, but the Baron has bags of both. I grew a little straggly moustache and learned to see through very thick glasses which made me look suitably pop-eyed.

"I acquired a slow stiff hesitating walk and a gutteral accent. Heinrich had never written anything except his own name by hand and I learned the trick of his signature.

"After a month we had ourselves photographed, by royal appointment, by one of those Mayfair firms which do the thing in a light fog and print through veils with re-touching galore. It was officially issued and one or two society papers printed it. Six months later we pumped out a rather clearer one, sharp enough for people to get an impression of what His Majesty really looked like in this year of grace. I was even painted rather smoothly by a Royal Academician.

"Occasionally I was allowed out, heavily escorted. Ascot and shows like that. I even inspected the troops at a minor public school in the neighbourhood and gave the chaps an extra week's holiday. Later on when we got a bit more confident we used to go to some of the very best night spots just to show the flag and keep the good old name of Plesse Weinstein alive."

"You didn't swim into my pool," I said, "or I'd have spotted you."

"I doubt it," he said coolly. "We didn't go in for minor gossip. Royalty incognito - the sort of stuff good head waiters love and bad dowagers dote on. Twice we went to our villa at Cap Ferrat, but Estoril was considered dangerous and rather suburban - too many rival firms in the neighbourhood. In the meantime the cash rolled in very nicely, thank you."

"You did well for yourself?" I asked.

"Oh, beautifully," he admitted. "That is, in theory of course. I had all the usual trimmings; mostly on tick or on hire. Rolls Royce, swimming pool and so on. You never know, being a monarch, whether the bill is going to be twice what you commoners would pay or whether our splendid patronage is payment enough. The restaurant trade is especially tricky, you know, but the old Baron was wise to most of the snags. No, the real catch was the boredom. My God, you can have no idea how dull it can be. The people you meet are ninety per cent toadies and social climbers and those who aren't snobbish about meeting royalty are mostly half witted anyhow. In close on five years I never met a single human being with half the intellect or character of the first man who sits next you in a bus. It drove me very nearly nuts."

I said I could see his point.

He continued slowly. "After a bit it got to be like claustrophobia. I tried dodging off into a pub or a cafe once or twice, but the old Baron was after me like a hawk. He put a second thug, a detective personal bodyguard, on to me, in a very polite way and then I knew I really was a prisoner.

"I think I would have stuck even that for a year or two more, for the sake of the money, but then the final snag appeared. That defeated me."

"Someone blew the gaff?" I suggested.

"Oh dear me no," he said. "People just love royalty - they want you to be true and to say something unlikely so that they can repeat it. Oh no, it wasn't nearly so simple. It was the threat of eternity - in fact the Princess Gerda. The prospect of her finished me.

"The Baron produced her once or twice at Cap Ferrat and about a month ago he announced casually that I had invited her and her entourage to visit us at Ganymede. When I objected he said in his silkiest way, 'A great pity, your majesty. She is of excellent middle European stock and has quite a fortune in her own right. A marriage - you need only have one child provided it is an heir - could be very advantageous to our interests.'

"I told him flatly that her face reminded me of a rancid suet pudding and that it was something of a miracle that she had ever learned to speak and that it was out of the question. He didn't protest over much but said that the visit was fixed and that I must try to be both brave and civil. I knew damn well that he was going to return to the attack.

"That settled it. I made my plans for escape".

"Couldn't you just walk out?"

"It wasn't as easy as that, you know. In fact it was infernally difficult. The estate was wired like a prison camp and my two bloodhounds practically never let me out of their sight. I had to be very crafty. My plan took a week to fix, but it was pure genius and in the end it worked like a dream."

"The secret tunnel in the east wing?" I enquired.

"Not exactly," he said. "On Gerda's first evening we had a dinner - a very full blown affair, tiaras, medals and three or four ambassadors. My idea was simplicity itself. Late in the evening I sneaked into a washroom, shaved off my moustache with an electric razor, parted my hair differently, took off my horrible glasses and my gongs and orders, put on a black waistcoat and came out carrying a tray of drinks."

"You became a waiter?"

"That's it, my dear man. You have it in one. I just added myself to the extra staff hired for the evening and sneaked out on some one else's bicycle wearing a nasty inbound muffler, with clips, a soft hat and a mackintosh.

"I pedalled as if the fiends were after me all the way to the outer suburbs and slept in a bus shelter. My trouble was cash, strange as it seems. We kings live without the ready, you see. Still, I hocked my watch and a hereditary signet ring and bought myself a suit, a short back and sides and went to see my bank manager. I thought, you see, that I was sitting pretty, having been well paid, in theory at any rate. Then I found out that I was dead."

"Eh?"

"Well, somebody died down at Ganymede when I took over, and somebody had to be buried, it seems. It turned out to be me, the late Galbraith. The Baron said he'd take care of all that and he

67

certainly had. He'd also taken care to see that my salary cheques never reached the pillar box and had arranged a fine series of phoney bank statements to lull me into happiness. I was even flatter broke than the ghastly day I first entered Ganymede. The manager - a new boy - took a very poor view of my story and nearly had me arrested as a lunatic. I got out by the skin of knuckles, chased incidentally by one of my own bodyguard who was lurking around, and half the staff. I've been virtually in hiding ever since in darkest Pimlico and the service exits of the best hotels.

"Do you think you can use the story?"

* * * * * * *

I took the tale to old Copthall my news editor and he listened, holding his head on one side like an interested terrier, so I knew he was going to bite on it.

"Not bad," he said. "Not bad at all. The only worth while thing you've ever unearthed, *if* it holds water. The first step is for you to go down to Ganymede, see this Baron Guilderstodt and insist on a personal story from the King. It's all yours - take the day, take two, and handle it how you please."

The preliminaries were suspiciously easy. I used an office car and arrived at Ganymede in reasonable style. His Majesty, I had explained, was to figure in our new 'Royalty in Retirement' series.

Once inside I was given the full treatment, an impressive cloakroom complete with valet, a glass of good sherry in an ante-room and a long pause to cool my heels and make me feel like an insignificant outsider.

Finally I was escorted to the salon, a long beautiful room and to the presence of the Baron himself. He really is a remarkable man, olive skinned, suave, handsome, grey, distinguished and crammed with sixty odd years of condescending courtesy. I knew that every cliché in the book applied to him, that at best he was a bogus old hanger-on, but he handled me with a skill quite out of my class.

"My dear Mr Carter," he said, "this is extraordinarily kind of you and very thoughtful of your editor. What an excellent and enterprising paper you have. Quite fascinating - His Majesty tells me he prefers it infinitely to the more sedate - shall we say? - or pompous journals. Now what can we do for you?"

I said rather lamely that I had hoped to see the King personally, to get some of his views at first hand.

"It could be arranged of course," he said, "provided we saw your article before printing. Unfortunately His Majesty has one of his attacks today - nothing serious, you know, just a migraine - and we may have to delay matters for a day or so. In the meantime I have some of his latest photographs and one can be made exclusive to you, if you wish it. If I may, I myself will give you all the background you could need."

He was making me feel clumsy and ill-at-ease. His effortless polish, the beautiful white-walled room with its mirrors and portraits and long windows to the lawn, the whole atmosphere of ease and good manners made me aware that my shoes could do with a shine and that one of my cuffs was frayed. I stuck to my guns grimly.

"I'd hoped to see him," I said.

The Baron gave me a pleasant patronising smile, like an uncle offering a tip to a small boy.

"As it happens," he said, "You can *see* him almost from where you are sitting, for he is catching a little sun in his private pavilion on the lawn, but his doctor - he is with him now, standing next him, by the way - absolutely forbids visitors. Such a good man, Van Dongen by name. No relation of the painter, he tells me."

I got up and turned to the lawns outside knowing I was defeated. A hundred yards away in an elegant little temple, windowed on two sides, there reclined a young man wearing sunglasses and draped with rugs. At his side stood the doctor and behind him a manservant was mixing a drink. The sunlight made it look very luxurious and civilized and not in the least sinister.

I went back to my chair and began to shuffle through the portfolio of photographs which the Baron had offered me. He had returned to his chair behind a huge Louis XIV table which he was using as a desk. Gradually I became aware that his eyes had shifted from me to something behind and above my head. In one of the mirrors I could see quite clearly what it was, the great academic oil painting of King Heinrich the Ninth. Apart from the uniform it was quite without character or interest.

Presently his scrutiny, which was hard and speculative, moved back to my own insignificant features. It was a full minute before he spoke.

"Tell me, Mr Carter," he said. "Have you ever thought of growing a moustache? It occurs to me that it might suit you."

The thought behind his words was visible for no longer than it takes a moth to brush one's face on a summer evening.

"No," I said firmly. "It never occurred to me."

His Majesty, I learn, is to inspect the cadets at Oakridge College in about a fortnight's time and even though the Baron has invited me I do not think it will be worth my while to attend. I know from experience when a story is finished.

Collector's Item

Yesterday I sold my car for about four times as much as it cost brand new. This may sound like very good business, for I bought it second-hand at three years old - indeed, four, if you look in the road book carefully.

Yet, I'm afraid - no, I'm sure - that I'm a mug and that this is no sort of a bargain. The car is, or was, a Randolph sports two seater, 8 h.p., a reliable little job, and yesterday morning I was driving her around Regents Park in London heading north to Swiss Cottage. No traffic about at that hour, eleven thirtyish - only a few nurses and dogs and children playing around in the greenery. It was just the occasion to go slow and reflect how pleasant and rural London can be if you're in the mood.

It was all very lazy and civilized.

Quite suddenly I had one of those twinges which make people say someone is walking over your grave. In fact it was more like being near an ultra-rapid flash bulb, the type which is so fast that you cannot actually see the light.

Then the car went dead on me completely. Dead as a doornail. I let her wander to the curb and tried everything, but nothing responded. A broken connection somewhere vital, I supposed, not being an engineer by nature.

I got out with the forlorn intention of looking under the bonnet - a brave gesture in the face of fate so far as I'm concerned, for all the good I really expected to do.

Dear Providence, I thought, send me a friendly mechanic, and save me a half mile walk to a garage.

The answer to prayer was swift but rather odd. A young man, about twenty-two if that, walked from the bushes and stood beside me. He was wearing bright blue denims and at first I decided he must be a film actor, he looked so clean and unreal. He had tight curly yellow hair and a suntan which even close-to might have been make up - more of a south of France type than something you expect in London N.W.1. Then a couple of girls in white riding breeches cantered past on chestnut horses among the trees looking so glamorous that I felt sure there must be a camera team somewhere around.

"Well, by Zing, and by Zing!" said the young man, addressing me. "That's a Randolph, isn't it? A 1954 Randolph, by Zing!"

He had a rather high pitched voice, with a "refined" accent like a salesman in an expensive man's shop, but not altogether unpleasant. The only thing which was not slightly bogus about him was his obvious adoring admiration for my car.

"A Sports Randolph 1954," I admitted and thought to myself "and as it has conked out there's nothing so particularly wonderful about that."

Aloud, I added - since I hoped he knew something about these things - "The ignition seems to have gone west."

He was still enthralled. It was as if someone had walked up to him with a picture under his arm muttering "Psst! chum, what price the Mona Lisa?" and produced the genuine article. After a moment he said, in a casual after-thought tone, "Well, of course she won't run here - you're in a zone. But, by Zing, what a beauty she is."

He touched a wing almost reverently and then leaned across the driving seat to look at the panel. "Gears!" He said. "Speeds marked up to eighty! Incredible." Turning directly to me he began to eye me with rather the same admiration. "And you're pretty good yourself - very well done. Going to a rally?"

At this point it dawned on me that I was not exactly on his wavelength, even if I felt vaguely flattered by his unconcealed and wide-eyed admiration. Privately I was rather glad that I'd polished the old brute that morning, that I had my new suit on and that my camel hair coat lay in the back of the car, looking pretty sporting.

Then he put his hand into a pocket, pulled out a small transparent box and said, "Here, have some joy." He flicked it open, took out a pill, like an acid drop or sweet capsule, swallowed it, and offered one to me.

Now this, I think, was my undoing. He was so friendly, so easy to look at in his young film-star way, so openly delighted and anxious to be friends, that I took one and put it in my mouth.

It was delicious. All at once I felt as if I'd had a haircut, a massage, a turkish bath and half a bottle of champagne. I was on top of the world. The sun came out and the birds began to sing.

Another young man appeared behind him, equally smartly dressed. There must be a brand new garage somewhere round about, I thought, or perhaps they are making a commercial movie about garages?

"Look, Leo," said my friend. "A Randolph - a 1954 Randolph. Isn't she beautiful?"

The new boy was taller, with the same suntan but he clearly was a wider guy altogether, more sophisticated, more intelligent, but equally charming. He fingered my car as if it had been a piece of rare porcelain and he an expert in such things. Here, I saw, was another enthusiast. "It's atomic," he said at last, "simply atomic. The most astounding little kettle I've seen in years. You collect them I suppose? But this is a real prize. Finest complete outfit this side of Pernambuco."

By now I was so pleased with myself for my personal brilliance in owning this masterpiece and so delighted with my companions that I began to feel really magnaminous and expensive.

"If we can get her to go," I said, "I'll give you a run in her."

"Go? Of course she'll go," said my blonde friend. "She bowled in here alright. I watched you arrive. Just push her out of the zone and you'll see. I can't think why you came this way and hoped to get through."

As I was clearly puzzled he went on. "Look, you're in a zone, see? Stranger round these parts? Hunting, riding, recreation, sports and so on - you know. The ray has cut you out, see? Just push her down the alley and she'll go."

He put his hands on the wing and Leo, the tall one, was obviously going to give a hand too when he paused and eyed me squarely.

"I suppose," he said, "since you're certainly in the ring on these things, that you wouldn't like to sell her? I collect a little myself."

Joy was still with me: I felt like a Rothschild or Mr Rolls Royce in person.

"It depends," I said with a magnificently casual shrug, "what you're prepared to pay." After all, I'm in business myself and not doing too well. Two fifty would settle a lot of problems for me here and now.

"Have some joy," said Leo, and passed a box around. We all had some joy. Four hundred quid, I said to myself, not a penny less, and it'll be a bargain at that.

The two young men eyed each other, squaring up for some special bidding. Four fifty, if they're really keen, I calculated, and the birds were singing fit to burst my eardrums.

Leo, still giving his boy friend a rather old fashioned look, took out a notecase and said very deliberately. "I'll give you here and now, two thousand five hundred. Old Lucas the glory man –" he indicated his rival "- might offer more. But I said it first and I promise she'll go to a good home. I'd love her like my first born and look after her as if she was a Queen Commisar. What do you say?"

He thrust some notes at me and they stuck in my hand. I find it difficult to tell you how glorious it all was. The two sporting rivals, my new dear lifelong friends, the heavenly day, the warm sun, the laughing girls on their horses and my super glamour car, the Randolph Sports 8 - everything combined to make life as gay and colourful as the last act of a good musical.

There I stood, probably openmouthed, but with the notes clutched in my hand, uncounted. The deal was far too good to miss and this was a once-in-a-lifetime chance.

I temporised, just a little, with my conscience. I'd give them half chance at second thoughts, since I knew now what a superman I was at that moment.

"Just try her out," I began, "and the Road Fund - the licence book - the policy thing....."

By now they had their hands on the car, moving her quickly round so that she pointed downhill, but they paused in sudden and delighted astonishment. "By Zing!" said Leo. "All that too? Zip them on to me - my number is the easiest thing you ever recorded. Zero zero, one seven four on the Great Belt - you can't forget it."

They pushed her down the slope and I stood there with the things in my hand until I heard the engine start. Nothing wrong with the old Randolph, that glorious streamlined masterpiece of 1954 craftsmanship.

Then they rounded the corner and I was quite alone. Twenty yards away there was a public seat by the verge and I turned towards it with the ease of a man in seven league boots. If I wanted to, I thought, I could jump there.

But I didn't. I took one step, then another, and suddenly I had that someone-on-my-grave feeling again.

My teeth chattered and a nasty whipping little gust nearly took the notes out of my hand. It was a treacherous day and might be going to rain.

And here was I in Regents Park, without a car, without a coat, and late for an appointment. Somehow I knew in my bones that this vanishing trick was permanent.

But I have the notes. They are remarkable works of art in themselves, printed on a sort of transparent paper and engraved as brilliantly as a peacock's tail.

Two thousand five hundred pounds, they say. *We, the Governors of the United World Banks of America and Great Britain will pay the Bearer on Demand. Signed: W. Frost and E. Patmos. July 2059.*

I am leaving them to my grandchildren. What else can I do?

Peter the Blind

The house of Peter the Blind is closed. No trace of the foundations remains in Postillion Street and its only memorial is to be found in paragraphs under the heading "Exhibitions" in obsolete guide books to London.

Like its half brother, the Black Museum at Scotland Yard, it was devoted to crime, but it enjoyed one paramount advantage over that interesting establishment by the Thames: it was open to the public daily (Sundays excepted) upon the payment of one shilling and sixpence, children half price.

Before the war most uncles planning educational tours for their provincial nephews and all Londoners who played host to the English speaking peoples, included the tall Georgian dwelling in a bracket on their list with the British Museum. The two exhibits were within a stone's throw, ideally suited for the second morning of sightseeing, and leading naturally to Madame Tussaud's or the Zoo for the afternoon.

I remember my first visit, under the benevolent wing of my Uncle Harry Forsdyke, most eccentric of Edwardian philosophers. Even at the age of ten the gloomy depths of the house were impressive and the voice of Max Beit was capable of lowering the temperature of the room like a dead man's hand plucking at your heartstrings. It was as deep and as cold as a dungeon well; even to recall it today is to feel the sun go unexpectedly behind a thundercloud.

Max was more than a guide: he was the very essence of the place. He was an elocutionist and an actor of the first order. Without him the museum would have been just another collection of relics of dubious value, made significant only by their macabre associations. Before he took his sheepish parties round he would stand, as you may recall, where a single shaft of light, arranged through blue glass, would filter as if by accident to light the dome of his skull and to emphasise the dark caverns about his eyes. He could silence the most brazen tourist by this icy mesmerism even before he spoke.

"Here in this room you are in the presence of murder."

74

The words, so familiar still to innumerable middle aged cockneys, never failed to produce on me the dramatic effect of the opening of the Fifth Symphony. To conjure them back is to invite that involuntary spasm of the spine which makes people say that someone has walked over their grave.

"Here were planned the deaths of Doctor Carmichael, of Lottie Soames, of the younger Bertini, and of many others. It seems certain that Trefusis, once Lord Mayor of London, drank his poison and died in terror within these four walls."

Max must have conducted hundreds of thousands of sightseers over the old house, but his grip on his audience never failed and his performance was as ominous and icy the last time I heard it as it was in the golden era of Uncle Harry Forsdyke.

Very few people, I suppose, realised that Max Beit was the owner of the place. He called himself the Curator, but the house, the freehold and the exhibits were all his personal property. He bought them in 1904 from Van Tromp the showman who went bankrupt very sensationally that year and involved Royalty in the crash.

At first the profits from this investment cannot have been very large. Success must have come like the slowest of avalanches, but its culmination is not to be doubted.

Peter the Blind himself, it appears, lived in that grimy house in Postillion Street from 1874 until his death in 1888. It was a magnificent romantic period, the heyday of fogs, hansom cabs, gas lamps, untold wealth and, of course, crime.

In the public mind Peter is associated with Jack the Ripper, Professor Moriarty, Charles Peace and Sherlock Holmes.

He was not, in fact, blind, but his white stick (exhibit 13) with which he was heard on more than one terrifying occasion tapping along a foggy street, earned him the nickname in Bloomsbury long before his name became synonymous with blackhearted Victorian infamy.

For his career Max Beit is the supreme authority. His book *Napoleon of Night* is the standard work on the life of the mysterious Peter Chatsworth Yates, called Peter the Blind, and it seems impossible now that it can ever be improved upon. No man, certainly no eminent criminal, ever had a keener biographer. His researches on the subject never ceased and each time I heard Max's blood-chilling lecture he seemed to have added a new item of shocking or fascinating information.

In the 80's and 90's disappearances and mysterious deaths were commoner than they are now. How far Max embellished his subject's record we may never rightly discover, but he lists no more than twenty four victims in considerable detail and infers at least as many again.

At one time he claimed, though the reason for this is hard to find, the wretched Marie Gomez as Peter's handiwork, though the authorities now place her death with the Ripper.

Peter was certainly far more Catholic in his tastes than his distinguished contemporary. He murdered for pleasure, for gain, and sometimes for self preservation. His house contained almost every means of slaughter known to the Victorians and his medicine cabinet alone held more poisons than ever a Borgia wielded.

As a child I coupled him in my imagination and my nightmares with Old Pew of Treasure Island, and even now the sight of an ill-lit London street gives me a shiver, for I half expect to hear the tap-tap of that white stick along the gutter and to see that monstrous vulpine shadow flapping inexorably towards me.

The stick itself enjoyed a prominent place in the museum. A late acquisition probably, for only on my recent visits do I recall seeing it although it always featured in Max's discourse. It was, you remember, a swordstick.

To such a figure and in such a period, legend attaches itself easily. In the 1900's a series of penny dreadfuls added their quota of obviously apochryphal adventures. Among collectors such as Ernest Turner these highly coloured, though fading, little paper volumes have had a fair vogue, but they contain only a few authentic grains. In them Peter is shown as a Machiavelli of modern crime, the most sinister murderer of all time, a fiend whose powers were both scientific and magical. The blood writers of fifty years ago were not particular.

With Max Beit's *Napoleon of Night* came the first and indeed the only semblance of a balanced and authenticated story. It was quite brilliantly done. The work has something of the quality of Strachey's "Eminent Victorians" and it is, as the catalogues say, 'copiously illustrated'.

Barnabas, who first published it in 1930, did extremely well. There was one vogue for biographies at the time and another for crime. *Napoleon of Night* rode to best-sellerdom on the crest of both waves.

The dates and details of the 'authentic' crimes were set out and analysed with clarity and no little sardonic wit; the 'doubtful' cases were judged impartially on the available evidence. The index is commendable as such and is as well an incomparable guide to the period. Beit must have made a good deal of money out of it, for it not only cemented Peter into the Victorian scene, but established the author as an unquestionable figure of literary importance in London life.

It was at this time that I began to know Max really well. He was a member of the Corduroy and, of all curious things, a keen card player. In those days I spent too many of my evenings in that most respectable of Bohemian clubs and was modestly expert myself. He played with a sort of vicious accuracy which could be, and generally was, devastating. My own play, though vastly inferior, is after this style, which is probably why he came to be civil to me.

His first nod to acknowledge my existence - I mean as a player - came after several years of acquaintance. It was as unnerving as a sudden bow from a Sphinx, but it said quite clearly that I was accepted. I became, as nearly as one might, a crony.

There was something about the lighting of the card room which suited Max. He would sit back in the shadows watching the other players, very much as he stood in his own museum lecturing his audience in that inhumanly deep voice of his. He was in every way a terrifying opponent. His tongue was bitter enough, but with the depth of his intonation he could give a sinister twist to the most casual of observations. I think most of us could feel our spines quiver a trifle when he said, "Singularly ill-advised. I fear I shall inevitably profit from your lack of judgment."

There is a portrait of Max in the dining room (just above the cold table) painted by James Pryde. It is a fine piece of subdued bravura, very nearly one of the great portraits of our time. Certainly the whole spirit of the subject is there - neither Rembrandt nor Reynolds would have disowned the composition nor the handling of the paint, but it has just that extra touch of the theatre which stops it in some curious way from being completely dramatic at the second glance.

It was Simmonds who damned it for most of us. "It looks," he said, "like Irving trying to play Hannen Swaffer," a criticism which was so devastingly true that it was repeated to every member of the Club and certainly a dozen times to Max himself.

Simmonds described himself as a jobbing journalist: he looked like a caricature of all one's less beloved schoolmasters, and his pockets one suspected were full of string, toffee and catapults confiscated from small boys. He wore his dirty white hair too long over his collar and affected (there is no other word for it, since it was out of character) a large black sombrero. He took snuff from a tortoiseshell box and seemed always too consciously Bohemian in appearance to be quite genuine. The inner Simmonds was schoolmaster.

Erudition was his stock-in-trade: he could and did knock out remarkably informed articles about politics in the Antipodes, aluminium clay deposits in Nova Scotia, or the incidence of Siamese twins in the Irrawaddy basin, at very short notice. He was fluent, speedy, reliable and possessed of an excellent news sense. If Theodore Simmonds began to discuss the Priesthood of Lhassa or the White Slave Trade of Madagascar you could be sure that both were due for headlines in the near future.

Whether the dislike he had for Max, and Max for him, dated from his remark about the picture is hard to say. Simmonds had a trick of debunking most things with a hard fact and a sniff.

The first open quarrel between the two men was not without a touch of drama, which is not remarkable for they both had a high sense of theatre. Max was standing, as was his habit, beside the table at which a game had just finished. It was towards the middle of the war, late at night. We were all in a state of tension with one ear half cocked for the grimmer sounds of the outer world.

The green shade cast its usual horrid pallor over his face and the whiter light streamed directly upon his hands, particularly upon signet ring with a large black stone in it which he wore upon his left forefinger.

Somebody said: "Is that a new acquisition, Max?" He drew it off and let it lie upon his palm. "A poison ring," he said, "of ingenious and devilish construction. The work of a master, but later than Cellini. A new item for my collection. The last of the Blind Man's instruments."

Several people handled it, myself included. Indeed it was I who passed it to Simmonds. He took it up as if it were a little dirty and peeked at it through a jeweller's glass.

At this there was a pause. Most of us felt something pungent might be on the way.

Simmonds turned the ring over and over. Then he let his glass fall into his left hand and tossed the ring on to the table.

"Made, I should say - hmm - about three years ago. Viennese in design, but probably the work of the Jewish evacuees now carrying on their trade in Jerusalem." He paused and sniffed. "A silly trinket, Max; you ... hmm ... should be more careful with your little ... hmm ... embroideries. You had better consult me in future."

The silence which followed grew more intense with each of its twenty seconds. Finally Max picked up the ring. "I shall consult you," he said, "when I am next in need of a farrago of vulgarity, inaccuracy and pompous stupidity."

Fortunately little Louis Bidon, who was with the group and a touch tipsy, gave one of his delicious child-like chuckles which would have warmed the heart of the oldest carp in Versailles, and after that no one could maintain anger publicly. Max made a casual departure instead of a dramatic exit and I walked home with him. His living quarters were above the Museum, now closed for the duration, and my own were in Great Russell Street. But he was fuming with a cold venom which stopped him on the corner of Bloomsbury Street as if his heart would fail from the acid which was eating into it. He leaned against some railings and suddenly the moonlight made him look very old.

"That man's mind," he said, "is like petrol spilt upon a wet road. A sloppy assortment of tasteless colours with no depth. He has every sort of accomplishment - I don't suppose you know the half of his interests and his interferences. He's a dabbler, a half-cock dilettante. You may think of him as a journalist. It may amuse you to know he pretends to the restoring of antique clocks. He never mends them. He makes dry-fly fishing rods and never completes them. He backs horses, but in halfpenny packets. His fingers itch for thrills he hasn't the guts to taste. He plays the Bohemian because it's easy. But he achieves nothing. Nothing. Nothing."

He straightened himself. "Forgive me. I expect some company before the night is out. Let us see if there is any civilisation or any whiskey up above the Museum."

The 'company', late at night, which Max entertained was various and fascinating, and particularly, I think, during wartime. Somehow the streets themselves seemed to have returned with the blackout to their Victorian mystery and the whole scene made the ghost of Peter the Blind a malignant possibility, to be glimpsed in the first shrouded doorway across the street.

Max's guests were infinitely varied, but apart from occasional actors, who came, I suspect, solely in order to study his voice, they had one interest in common: crime.

That particular night's flotsam was typical. At one o'clock a young airman who had been charged with a *crime passionel* and acquitted through the ineptitude of the public prosecutor, arrived not drunk but loquacious. He was a rarity: an aristocrat and a murderer. The Battle of Britain had turned him from an Oxford poet to a fallen Lucifer. His conversation was obscene, Olympian and wickedly funny. With him was George Braham of Fleet Street who had covered his case for the *Post*, gasping as usual with asthma and memories of even better murders, and a girl with a dead white face and the figure and tongue of a Jonsonian drab, who turned out to be a Junior Commander in the A.T.S. At two the local Divisional Detective Inspector arrived. He was a short pawky Scot, a sound member of the Elks and other men's societies, but he knew his London and was not without a relish for the humour, or the gossip, of his trade. The whiskey, a miracle in those difficult times, was abundant.

George Braham lamented the passing of the 32-page paper and

the days when he could turn a murder into an epic and began to cite instances. "Crippen today would be lucky if he got half a par," he said. "There is no good crime in war because there are no good newspapers to transform a corpse with a well slit throat into history. Now take Seddon, for instance."

"To hell with yesterday and Seddon," said the airman. "Seddon and Sodom, the Brides in the Bath and Gomorra. It's all very well for you, Max, to batten on the past, but what about today, Inspector? Tell us that. What will tonight's blackout bring drifting to your desk on the morning tide?"

"Nothing new," said the Inspector, "nothing new, for a level shilling. And if there's any to come on that one I'll bet that Mr Braham will get it wrong if he gets a line of it into his newspaper. Breaking and entering, up ninety per cent through the blackout, you know, but still they get it wrong when it comes to print."

"Never wrong on a fact in my life," said Braham, pouring three fingers without turning his head. "I remember out at Box Hill when the lot of us went down to see the homicidal gypsy..."

"Never a fact right," said the Inspector, "if it sounds better the other way round. And I'll prove it, even today. Now take the girl you boys in Fleet Street call the Painted Lady. She breaks and she enters and she leaves her handwriting all over the place. She uses scent and she smokes whilst she's on the job. Very good, and very likely we'll happen on her as soon as maybe. But it has to be glamorous for the lads of the Fourth Estate. 'A rich perfume from the salons of Paris' - 'Exclusive pink petalled oriental cigarettes' - 'A dark mink clad figure' - and so on. And what's the truth? The fact is we've never seen her, so we don't know how she dresses. But her scent is the cheapest you can buy - cheap stuff, even now. And her cigarettes come in the well known yellow packet. As for being pink tipped, all they've got on their butts is lipstick. Balderdash, George, and bunkum is what you dish out when the papers might tell us more of what's happening on the beach-heads."

There was much more fine talk in this vein, for the pigeon was amongst several cats, and the attic filled with smoke, whiskey fumes and the hangover of impassioned wordy digressions.

I remember the whole night with a particular vividness, for it was the last occasion on which I saw Max Beit alive.

It was the time of the Flying Bombs and the V2's, which Londoners called, with a spiritual snook cocked at Fate, the Doodlebugs and the Gas Mains, and I was by no means sorry to be called out of the city for a month or so. Rumours however did reach me, for Louis Bidon, who was a great gossip both in the flesh and on paper, kept me primed with all that he considered civilised.

"The Max-Theodore quarrel progresses with great bravura," he wrote. "They do not speak now and one regrets that one may no longer carry a sword along with a glove and an ivory card-case. At the Club, the porter receives messages and enquiries. They are like the figures in a Swiss weather toy. If Max is in, Theodore must needs be out. If one lunches, the other dines. But from both, what great rhetoric! It is worth the bombs to hear Max pronounce, during one of those exciting pauses, on 'a creature upon whom one's mental heel turns without even revulsion'. Or Theodore - 'Eccentrics of - sniff - an era which is too recent to be amusing. Balloons of conceit which a pea-shooter could destroy'. It is all splendid and the betting is slightly in Max's favour, for though the written word may be powerful, there is nothing to equal the great phrase in that deep voice which we all mimic and, I suppose, envy..."

In February of that year, 1945, I returned to the city and about a week later - it was a Wednesday evening with a cold whip of rain in the dark streets - the shocking thing occurred.

It was about half past six when I became aware of a timid knocking at my door, a sound which I knew subconsciously must have been going on for some time. The little old person who stood outside was so clearly a London charwoman that she had no need to explain the fact.

"You'll excuse the liberty, I know, sir," she said, "but my friend is Mrs. Cook, who does for you. She says you know Mr Beit over at the Peter Museum and often go to visit him. I look after the gentleman, you see, myself, and I'd be easier in my mind for your advice."

She was a pathetic little sketch for an outmoded joke: my heart warmed to her.

"It's like this," she said, "I let myself into the museum with the one key at six, but I only go up through it to the gentleman's rooms. He has his own front door, sir, and either leaves his keys so I can find it, or lets me in himself. This is the third evening, and I can't get no reply. What with the doodles and all, I'm worried. Mrs. Cook and I wondered if - you being a friend..."

We went across with upturned collars through the rain and through the shrouded museum, which seemed to hold an even more sinister menace behind those dusty coverings. Max's door was indeed locked.

The little old lady, so like a courageous mouse, stimulated me to take hold of the situation boldly. The door was half glass, leaded with Victorian panels, and I stove a couple of them in with my umbrella, opening the look from inside. The half minute which followed was and is my worst nightmare. I switched on the living room light, saw what there was to see, and realised that the curtains were undrawn.

It meant inevitably, for this was wartime and first things had to come first, switching into darkness and stepping across the floor to make the blackout complete.

Across the floor. Avoiding the dead man who lay sprawled upon it.

The charlady was gallant and gentle as only old ladies who know trouble and have the habit of courage can be. She bent down and touched what had once been Max Beit's skull. "The poor gentleman," she said, "the poor gentleman."

It was hard to say if the room had been ransacked or if it was in greater chaos than usual. It had always looked like a cross between a theatrical prop store, a taxidermist's lair and a lazy artist's studio. Both of us, I think, felt there was no longer any urgency. We looked around summing up what there was to see and to be done according to our own lights.

I am no detective, but presently the weapon became obvious. It was a large stone pestle with a wooden handle and my guess was that Max had been killed with a single blow. He lay face downwards in the midst of tumbled books, trinkets and papers and it did not seem to me that he had ever moved again.

Books ... trinkets. The books were legion, but there were oddments missing. The 'poison ring' had gone from his left hand. 'Peter's snuffbox', a fine inlaid tortoiseshell affair, had vanished from the mantelpiece, so had a jewelled paperknife, some ivory miniatures of 17th century villains, Colonel Blood's inkhorn and Charlotte Corday's little handmirror.

As the old lady and I stood side by side, neither moving nor speaking, the room, which had been very cold, became slowly foetid and close. There was the sickly stomach turning warning of decay, but there was an afterthought haunting the air - a perfume which was as out of place in that *nature mort* as a paper rose lying amongst a display of glass eyes.

Exactly as I put my hand on the old lady's shoulder and said "We'd best get out of here and let the police know," I noticed the last detail. In the big pewter ashtray on the drinks table there was a cigarette stub tipped with lipstick. Another lay in the empty fireplace and a third had been trodden into the carpet.

For me the picture was as complete and as ugly as a verdict in a headline.

We both, I suspect, saw the gleam of a policeman's cape in an opposite doorway as we quitted the museum and felt that it was unseemly to break the news to a constable in the rain. We went back to my own rooms and my companion, whose silent agreement had been very comforting, said, "You do the telephoning and tell them what's happened. I'll be making some tea if you'll show me the kitchen." She took off her old black straw hat, put the pin back through it, shook out her coat and hung it up on the peg by the door as if she were used to violent death, as perhaps she was, being a Londoner.

I rang Holborn Police Station and asked for the Divisional Detective Inspector who had known Max. There was a bit of a delay and it emerged that he was not there. Just as I was bracing myself to find cold blooded phrases to explain to a stranger the bomb fell. It was a V2.

The thunderclap of a building having its heart torn out came first, then the hysterical supersonic whine of the bomb's arrival. The windows on both sides of the flat were blown in but the curtains saved us from glass.

The whole house swayed from its foundations and shuddered. An angry wind smacked at our faces, foreign and insulting. In a few moments there was an irregular clatter of debris on the roof above our heads and the air became thick with brickdust. The phone, still in my hand, went dead. The bomb had been very close.

The blast made us both very slow and careful in our thought and movement: we were like automatons testing every step to see if the cords of life still worked.

I sat her down on a wooden chair in the kitchen and searched for brandy. This she refused and presently the forgotten kettle began to scream. We made tea before we set out to see the damage and were grateful for our own wisdom and restraint.

The crowd of sightseers, rescue workers and firemen stopped us almost at my door. The end of Postillion Street was barricaded off already but even from the corner the news was clear. The House of Peter the Blind and everything in it had been blown into infinity. Only a hole like the socket of a giant's tooth remained. Max, his treasures and his vanities, his body with its final secret and above all his voice, which still seemed to echo in my throbbing eardrums, were only a memory, a fragment of the odd backstreet antiquarian history of the town.

I did indeed report the night's adventure to the Inspector, but on the next morning. He made heavy weather of it, promising the impossible, for his phrase, I remember, was "Well, we'll look into it. Write me a statement of it in your own time." He showed me out of the station himself, walking to the corner with me as if I were fragile, and it dawned upon me that he only half believed my awkward story and put a mental note against my name with the word "Concussion".

83

Newspapers in those days did not report the incidence of bombs directly. Max's death appeared first as an obituary announcement in *The Times*, paid for by the Club, and his career rated half a column a day or two later in that distinguished journal. It was bye-lined (which meant it had been contributed by a friend and had not been part of the usual newspaper mortuary service) and the initials only were given - T.S.

Theodore Simmonds - his writing style was not to be mistaken - was guarded in his appreciation but he was, as ever, knowledgeable and respectfully cordial. He spoke of *Napoleon of Night* as being "A scholarly example of research into trivia, executed with that touch of sardonic wit which will make it memorable amongst his large and eclectic circle of friends ... still a piece of desiderata for all students of the late nineteenth century".

There was no other public reference to Max: the popular dailies had better stories on hand and the Sundays were hampered by the censor's ban on the location of bomb craters. Without the annihilation of the museum only half the story remained.

At the Club Simmonds suffered slightly from one of those declines in popularity which move like a wave of schoolboy emotion over any male community, however sophisticated. Here too only half the story remained. Simmonds merely reminded us of Max who had been, we felt, the real force in the team.

This trend was not improved by the contents of Max Beit's will. His capital, which was small, went with the freehold of the vanished house and contents to cousins in Bath, whose existence he had never mentioned. But Simmonds became his literary heir and executor: it was the last ironical gesture from the old master.

The legatee was shaken by this news: he aged ten years in a few weeks, and his hair lost its last touch of grey. However, being a practical if sporadic worker, he did not neglect the bequest but arranged in 1947 for a cheap edition of "Napoleon" by the largest and best of the reprint publishers. It caused a small literary vogue for Max, a little Indian Summer of posthumous glory, and must have made several hundred pounds for Theodore.

But he still wilted. Shifting his interests like a dilettante schoolmaster on holiday, he took up archery, was bitten briefly by the Vintage Car bug (buying a fine Model T Ford which he paraded outside the Club) and invented a not very successful pipelighter.

By 1950 the last ripples of Max's personality had reached the final backwaters and were still. There were so many other absorbing topics for club conversation - the Haig Murders, the Russian Menace, Don Bradman's Retirement, the Painted Lady

Still Uncaught, the Linsky Tribunal, Baby Brumas and Existentialism.

What did emerge through the parti-coloured passing of the months was that Theodore was slowly losing his grip. He established one corner of the bar as his own, an ominous and not altogether original gesture, and kept longer hours than most in that stronghold of weakness.

He still exercised his extraordinary talent for assembling out-of-the-way facts. I remember the flutter in the Air Ministry dovecote when he published information about the Russian MIG six months before it was official. He had not done more than assemble known details with skill and make logical deductions, but after a lot of hurried denials in Parliament he was proved perfectly accurate.

He did not get actively, demonstrably drunk, but late in the evening he became maudlin and garrulous with casual victims whether they were willing or no.

And there were occasions which gradually increased in regularity when he talked alone, or to an unseen listener.

On such an evening when the bar had long been closed officially, though Bates the barman was always around, he caught my eye and insisted that we drank brandy together.

"I see you too seldom," he said and sniffed. "Cold blooded impartial characters are rare nowadays. Partizanship is the way of it in this year of inelegance. Did you know, by the way, that there is trouble is Odessa? They have produced a new sort of wheat in large quantities in that area. It seems that it has a tendency to promote cancer and it is very easy to grow even on the poorest soil. But I digress - I ramble - I spread out my husks before a pearl fancier."

Suddenly he straightened himself and emptied his glass. "You were a friend of Max's," he said. "Now I will tell you something which you will not find dull. Here is a joke, the last and greatest joke of the lot. You know I was - I am - his literary heir?"

I nodded and he commenced another drink. "The joke is upon me for ever," he said. "A long nose pulled from the pit of Acheron by a tuppenny charlatan. And there is no escape."

I waited and warmed my brandy.

"Hoist on my own petard," he said. "I am, or I was, among other things, a ghost - that is, a literary ghost, a writer of other men's works. I wrote *Napoleon of Night*."

He clearly expected me to be astonished, although in fact I was only half surprised. Apart from the one sound work Max had never as far as I knew written a single word. A 'ghost' had always been a possibility, but the quality of the text had suggested that perhaps he was after all a man of one book and that *Napoleon*.

Theodore was not altogether gratified by my silence: he had expected some tangible sign of incredulity and there was an Ancient Mariner look in his eye which made it clear he had determined to achieve an effect.

"You may, or ... hmm ... you may not believe me," he said, "I am as neuter. But this joke was doubly redundant upon me. If I was a fake, imitating on paper Max's verbal mannerisms - not an easy matter - I had to infer his voice, as it were, in every sentence. Max was the greatest fake of all time.

"Listen, Peter the Blind was a myth. He never had any real existence as such at all."

This did rouse me. I protested that the book had been indexed and documented at every turn.

"A fake," said Theodore, and repeated, "an ingenious, erudite, brilliant literary fake. I will now tell you the truth about Peter Chatsworth Yates, the involuntary charlatan of the century. He was not blind, you know, but very shortsighted. He walked with the aid of a stick and wore a large old-fashioned eye shade. The place in Postillion Street was a second rate lodging house and the tenants were mostly recruited from the Seven Dials area, bad characters even at that. Peter was a picturesque figure, much chased by children, like the prophet, and gifted with a fine turn of invective. He was a character all right. Daubeny's "Memoirs of Soho" describe him very accurately. "Half man, half raven..." - you remember the passage no doubt. It is one of the few genuine quotations in the book.

"Peter never murdered anybody as far as I could trace. All he did was to conceal a body or so rather inefficiently in quicklime and mortar in his cellars. These people were either killed in brawls or died of drunkenness. He concealed their bodies to avoid trouble with the police. He was not a greedy antiquarian with a fine residence grown rich on the spoils from his victims, but a man who was afraid of losing his livelihood by reason of the attentions of the police, of whom he was in terror. He probably fenced a little stolen property and he had a taste for cheap ornate jewellery and miniatures, which was all his eyesight permitted him. At his death the relics of two or three bodies were discovered by the new owner of the house and an open verdict was returned. A sensational pamphlet - again we quoted, although it was full of obvious inaccuracies - was published about him, and that began the legend. A dozen unsolved crimes were laid to his account, mostly deaths or disappearances of people who couldn't conceivably have moved in his dirty half-world."

Theodore had me now, firmly gripped by the lapels of my mind.

He paused only to order more drink and to drown my protestations.

"You have no idea how simple it was to improve on the crude publications of the time - to magnify their importance and to add here and there a touch of truth. Old police notices of missing persons, old photographs from forgotten family albums, penny bloods - they all added their quota of colour and authenticity.

"It was exciting, you know. One pitted oneself against the experts in the period - destroying evidence here, creating it there, and deciding where to chance the laziness of any researcher who might follow us. Quotations can tell lies by punctuation. Whole books can be invented if their publishers no longer exist.

"We were lucky at every turn. In 1890 the house was bought by a man called Corney Griffin, who owned a waxwork show. He built on the legend which was already growing and made the place a tuppenny Chamber of Horrors. No fool, our Mr Griffin. He helped us quite a lot, for he published his own booklet on Peter and made him the centre piece of the show - gave him all the ground floor and the cellars, in fact.

"He lasted ten years and did very well indeed by the careful encouragement of blood-writers. Then he sold out to Van Tromp, who used Barnum and Bailey methods. He helped us too - a lot of photographs in the book had been fixed by him. And all, in the end, to bolster up the most stupendously bogus figure of the lot - Max Beit."

Theodore was so excited now that he lost what was left of his control. He dribbled, let his voice wander from squeaky to husky, broke the stem of his glass and poured out an orgy of detail.

In the end the three of them, Max, Theodore and Peter, were stripped bare: the vain, cynical showman, the literary trickster who had gloried in his own small cunning and the wretched myopic keeper of a Victorian doss house.

Suddenly Theodore yawned, shuddered, nodded his head once or twice and fell asleep. The bar was cold and stuffy and it was nearly dawn. I let myself quietly out and left the author of *Napoleon of Night* to his dreams.

Now unless our invaluable Mr Bates was listening to part of the story, and he certainly was not there at its conclusion, no one besides myself shared the secret. Bates is a superb listener, but comment is beyond him and gossip beneath him and so I think there were only the two of us. Theodore was certainly never so garrulous again and possibly his doctor gave him reasons for modifying part of the cause. At all events he gradually gave up his throne in the corner of the bar and took to sipping, as often as not alone, in an armchair in the smoking room.

His walk was still sprightly enough, indeed I once saw him

vault like a cat on to a 15 bus, and he could not have been more than sixty. But at the Club he had decided to play the quaint old character in the window, courteous to the younger members and acknowledging the existence of only a few chosen contemporaries. As I say, perhaps his doctor had a hand in the change.

One afternoon last May, at a quarter to four in the afternoon, he died in that chair. He had greeted me fairly civilly and said, "I've just made a discovery about Aphra Behn. Just your line of country. I'll tell you about it sometime."

About twenty minutes later I happened to be looking in his direction, or rather beyond him at the clock. He coughed twice, quite gently, and tapped his chest with a closed fist. Then his face went a cold grey and he lay back.

It was half an hour before anyone noticed anything wrong. I had assumed him asleep and it was Bates, scurrying silent and purposeful through the room, who made the discovery. He stopped on one heel, turned and went over to the chair in a single flow of movement. After a little while he, Louis Bidon and I carried the body to the secretary's quarters where there was a small outer room furnished with a grimly appropriate horsehair couch. There was hardly any fuss at all and not more than six people ever guessed what happened.

Our secretary is an abominably efficient person. He took charge of the situation as if he had been an ambulance man dealing with a fainting case.

"Dead," he said. "Dead without the shadow of a doubt. And I should say the trouble was heart failure. Now, Mr Bidon, you take that cushion away so that he is down flat. It'll make things easier. You don't know his doctor? No? Then we must try to find him, and at once. That will avoid calling the police and we may be able to save an inquest or any of the wrong sort of publicity. In his notebook or diary perhaps we'll find a name. It's awkward, because we don't even know an address for him, so we must find it. He always gave me his bank to forward any letters. I'm afraid we must turn out his pockets."

It was a most repulsive task, but the results justified our clumsy search. We found all that we needed and more.

There were three items which I now confess that I stole from the dead body of Theodore Simmonds.

The first was what looked like a multi-bladed penknife, only it was a more ingenious tool than that. Instead of blades there were innumerable flexible pieces of fine steel, some of them very like keys. One, the largest, was not unlike a screwdriver or a chisel except that it had a forked tongue. There is no doubt about its purpose, or so I am told by experts.

The second was a tin box with very curious contents: six half smoked cigarettes of a well known brand. Their oddity lay in the fact that the tips were smothered in lipstick.

The third of my thefts was a small bottle which contained, as the analysts say, a quantity of colourless liquid. The Divisional Detective Inspector had been quite right in describing the fluid. There was nothing glamorous or exotic about it at all - it was a cheap scent, cheap even for these days.

Alias Mr Manchester

The only one of the gang who looked like a criminal was George Arthur Gabel and it was characteristic of him that he came into the room first, and by an unexpected doorway. A massive slovenly figure, he wore perpetually an old-fashioned grey Homburg hat with a bound brim - he was bald - and very dark glasses which also magnified - his eyes were weak. Beneath this a large nose, a grey slab of a face and a rather greasy blue suit made up the unsavoury picture. He had come into the darkening room by the garden door and had sat down in an armchair which only just fitted his huge bulk.

Charles Dixon, who owned the house, discovered him when he turned on the light. Dixon had the air of a commercial traveller, which was how he usually described himself.

"You give me a shock, Mr Gabel," Dixon said. "You're early. Half-past, I was told. Never mind, it gives us time for a word."

"It doesn't," said the fat man in a wheezy whisper. "I know who's done this and I'm going to settle it here and now. In front of us all."

"That's good, Mr Gabel. Very good indeed. A drink, then?"

"My usual."

The suburban room had been furnished by a woman with a talent for the worst and a pocket to make it a triumph of trumpery. Dixon produced whisky and water from an illuminated cabinet of chromium and glass which might well have contained a fruit-vending machine and a juke box as an optional extra. They drank in oppressive silence.

Tony and Ron Myers, who were twins, announced their arrival by the echo-chamber exhaust of their car. A pair of cheerful dirty young mechanics, they ran a garage and could not be mistaken for followers of any other trade. They came in, sheepish but truculent, like a couple of schoolboys hoping to brazen out some discovered insolence.

"What's all this lark?" said Ron.

"We don't like this caper." said Tony. "Not one bit."

"Best to wait for the others, we thought," said their host.

90

"George'll do the talking then. You two gentlemen take beer?"

"Our bet is that George is behind this whole ruddy business," said Ron. "And if he is, then we're going to do him up so rotten he'll never walk again."

The gathering, it was clear, was not destined for social success. To complete it came a scarecrow of a man named Foster-Brown who might have been a seedy schoolmaster, and 'Doc' Tidmarsh, who suggested gymnasiums or prize-fighting but followed neither employment. The twins continued to stand side by side before the multi-tiled fireplace, glowering like young bulls considering what to smash first. For a full minute no-one spoke.

At length the fat man called Gabel pushed his hat to the back of his head, tilted his dark glasses and heaved himself forward on his chair. His soft asthmatic voice necessitated attention if it was to be heard and he had about him the curious magnetism which goes with command.

"Sit down, boys. Sit down," he whispered, and when the silence became frozen he pulled some sheets of paper from his pocket, unfolded them and waved them gently before his audience. "Now, if you've all brought yours, get 'em out. I want to compare them. Then we'll each have our say. In turn. *Then* we'll decide."

Papers were unfolded by each of the older men.

"We burned ours," said Ron. "No sense in keeping them. But we remember them okay."

"Very well then," said Gabel. "I hope you do. But just in case, Charlie-boy here is going to read his out to us. If there's any difference, even a comma, just say so. Otherwise belt up, see?"

"Why me?" said Dixon. "Why pick on me? You don't think that-"

"Nobody's going to think yet," said the fat man. "You'll read it because it's your house we're in and you've got a lovely voice. Get on with it." He nudged his hat forward again and slid back in the chair.

Their host glanced round the company and cleared his throat.

"Dear Mr Dixon," he began. "It's on a sheet of ordinary typing paper, typed, top copy with no address; plain envelope, also typed.

"Dear Mr Dixon.

"About the Saunders Electronics payroll job which we carried off with such remarkable success that a total of £35,317 was netted without any special complications, I wish to draw your attention to a new development.

"The fact is that I am not satisfied with the share-out and propose for it to be adjusted in my favour. I know I did not say this at the time but I have been reconsidering my position, which I think is remarkably strong.

"You will all, therefore, make me a contribution according to

91

what I feel to be right and fair. I have included myself as one of the contributors, and will put in my proportion because I do not wish to court trouble by revealing my identity.

"Here is the list and the sums you will all pay me.

"*George Arthur Gabel.*

"You are the so-called brains of the act but you are also the meanest of us and have always pocketed the last halfpenny of the small change. This time you'll return it. To straighten the record you will hand over £1,317.

"*Charlie Dixon.*

"You have the guts of a field mouse but a neat way of arranging things. To compensate me for putting up with you and your horrible house you will pay me £1,000.

"*Hamish Foster-Brown.*

"You did a neat job with the alarms but let's face it, they were dead simple, which makes you overpaid. From you, £750.

"*'Doc' Tidmarsh.*

You may be clever with gelignite but you took a risk with those of us who were inside by failing to blanket properly. To teach you to be more careful next time you'll pay £750.

"*Tony and Ron Myers.*

"Your sort are two a penny and you are inclined to talk too much. To encourage you, for all our sakes, to keep your mouths shut, you'll pay £750, each of you.

"I make this a total of £4,317. This is not much considering the take as advertised in the Press. You will put the cash in a box neatly wrapped and labelled Mr Manchester and place it in a locker at Waterloo Station, and for all our sakes this will be done at 8.45 a.m. on a weekday. The key to the locker will be posted to Mr Manchester, care of Clarke's Stores, 17 Postillion Street, London WC2, which is a tobacconists-news shop where they take letters.

"If by agreement you keep observation on Waterloo or Postillion Street I shall know all about it, of course, and if any of you decide to operate on your own account you will still be rumbled. That, too, is obvious. Nor do I advise any of you getting in some pals to help, since we know just who they'd be and they'd want a bigger cut than I'm asking.

"If I suspect any funny business I shall blow the whole story, go Queen's Evidence and collect the reward, which is 10% - so I won't do badly if you don't come across.

"I am allowing two days from receipt of this to make up our minds. We will meet at Charlie's on Monday at 7.30 p.m. sharp, which gives us until Wednesday. If any of us don't turn up there will be trouble.

92

"If any of us decide to play silly beggars about this I will lay a little information on one of us on Thursday morning with Detective-Inspector Hungerford who is in charge of inquiries according to the Press. He is a lazy buzzard and has better things on his mind by now, probably. This will be just enough to remind him and to tip him off on one of us, and I hope the man I pick on has an alibi which stands up. He'll need it.

"This will just be a gentle warning to show I mean business.

"Best to agree, don't you think?

"Yours sincerely,

"*Mr Manchester.*"

As Dixon paused, the fat man struck the leather arm of his chair with the flat of his hand.

"Right," he said. "Everyone get the same note?"

"Seems right," said Ron. "Same sort of line anyhow. As far as we're concerned you can all go to hell."

"That's right," added Tony, "just as soon as we've fixed whoever's done this."

The fat man struck the chair again.

"One at a time. But since you two have piped up we'll start with you."

"Flaming silly," said Ron. "Stands to reason it's not us. A letter like that - all fancy talk-" - he imitated Dixon's clerical accents with skill - "'I wish to draw your attention to a new development.' Can you see Tony or me coming up with that kind of lingo? We can't type, anyway."

"About all Ron can do is to write his name and he don't do that so good. We keep a skirt in the office for that lark," said his brother.

"Exactly," said the fat man. "A bit of skirt. Mavis Wilson, a right little doll by all accounts. No, it's not her. She's not got the brains any more than you two. But -" he slapped the chair again. "She has a sister. Young Stella. Now there's a clever lass. Went to a good school, ought to have done even better than she did if she hadn't got herself a bit of bad luck. Only sixteen then, but she knew quite a bit about blackmailing filthy old men. A pity one of them had a tape recorder and a couple of narks in the next room when she came to the final push. But it was blackmail."

He paused. "And this is blackmail."

There was a murmur of agreement.

"What about it, Ron?" said Doc Tidmarsh. "Stella's a clever kid and her sister is your typist. You two always did talk too much. Mavis might have known about the Saunders job all along and put her sister up to it."

The twins rounded on them, Ron in the lead. "Nuts," he said.

"You're raving bonkers, the lot of you. We haven't seen Stella in months. Anyhow, she's in -" he stopped in full flight. "She's in Manchester," he finished.

The obvious shock that his admission produced brought with it more sincerity than the outburst itself. He went on with the protest but the truculence was gone; he had become a puzzled man.

"No, No, it couldn't be Stella. She's living with a bloke in the rag trade who's loaded. Even sends her blasted old mother clothes. You can write her off. Not that she knew a thing about it - couldn't have."

Instinctively the group appeared to recognise sincerity when that rare commodity appeared among them. The Myers brothers were for the moment clear.

"Very well, then," continued the fat man, calling the meeting back to order with his hand. "Now we come to you, Mr Foster-Brown. 'Overpaid because the job was dead easy' - that's what the man said. Could it be that you meant underpaid? You write a good hand, read books and all that. Good education. Good job with Standard Alarms until you got too good for it. How about it?"

Hamish Foster-Brown had a certain dignity about him, something clinging to him from a different epoch in his career. Alone among the gang, he stood up to answer the charge and spoke in a gentle Scots burr, as if he were lecturing students.

"All that you say, Mr Gabel, is true. It was an easy one, as it turned out. I said I was satisfied with my cut - it was agreed beforehand in any case. I might not have been and for that you have only my word. But I am not your Mr Manchester.

"You will want some proof of this, no doubt. Well, I'll give you what I can. Your letter was forwarded to me in the Waltham Hospital where I've been flat on my back for two weeks. Not a fatal complaint, you understand. I'd had a bad fall when I was doing a little research for another enterprise and had to walk quite a wee way before I dared collapse. It did me no good, that walk. I had to explain, you see, that it was my own stairs I'd fallen down. Then they took me off in an ambulance. I only came out yesterday morning. You can check all of this, you know, if you've a mind to."

He sat down gingerly. Each of the group recalled that he had limped into the room. Now they saw that his face betrayed him as a sick man.

Doc Tidmarsh muttered, "Okay, Guv'nor, okay," and Charlie Dixon expressed the general opinion. "Not you, Mr Brown, not you. I've got my own ideas, but you're not in my way of thinking."

Even the twins seemed disposed to accept the verdict.

Unexpectedly Doc Tidmarsh took the floor. "It's my turn," he said, "and you'd better listen good and proper. I can't write, I can't type, and I can't spell. I done a good job with that safe and you all know it even if the blowoff was more than we reckoned. My cut was fair and I got no complaints.

"But I tell you one thing, so catch on to it. When I get my hands on whatever sod among you is trying this little game, I'll fill his backside so full of jelly that there won't be no pieces. If it's you, Charlie boy, I'll see you take your flaming doll's house with you, and if it's you, Mr Fat Gabel, I'll cut you in slices first and I give you my oath on that."

The explosion was impressive. In his more social moments Doc Tidmarsh had a range of Army reminiscences concerning the amusement to be obtained from little packets of gelignite delicately arranged as booby traps, calculated to turn even a cast-iron stomach. He had learned his trade with a Commando unit, and the group recalled uneasily a recent incident at a betting shop where the proprietor had failed to win Doc's admiration. No one seemed disposed to carry this part of the discussion any further.

"Charlie-boy," whispered the fat man, his dark glasses glinting venomously. "You've got some explaining to do now. You can write, you can spell, you can type, and what's more you've the right sort of double-crossing mind for this lark. I wouldn't put it past you to squeal to the coppers.

"And another thing puts you right on the spot," Gabel produced an envelope from his pocket and flung it on to the table. "Postmark. This postmark says Wembley, right here where we're sitting. Posted just at the end of this road I shouldn't wonder."

An ominous rumble of approval greeted this charge. It was halted by Foster-Brown.

"That doesn't mean a thing." He spoke with authority. "Not a damn thing, D'you think I'd not notice something like that? Just look at this, Mr Gabel – my envelope."

He thrust it under the fat man's nose. "Posted from Walthamstow or thereabouts, E.17 anyway. It could be from just opposite your little hideout. When I saw it in the hospital I was sure it was from you before I opened it. Maybe there's nothing in that, but I've been looking at Mr Dixon's copy – just checking on it, you know – and his was posted *south* of the river in Blackheath, which might make us all think of the Myers' garage.

"No, definitely no. Whichever of us is responsible is too clever by half and in my opinion it's not the owner of this little birdcage of a villa we're in at this moment – he's too vain and too cautious. *But* – someone is just a mite too clever. You, Mr Gabel."

"That's right," chimed in the Myers brothers.

"It looks like it," said Doc Tidmarsh.

"I give you my solemn word and may I drop dead this moment – " Charlie Dixon began before he realized the heat was off him.

The storm centre veered to the man in the armchair. He shifted his enormous bulk and by turning his head conveyed that he was considering each of them in turn. He spoke only when he had achieved complete silence and he held the pause with calculated authority.

"You perishing gibbering nitwits," he whispered. "You're almost too stupid to be allowed out. If it weren't for me you'd all be inside by now. It was I who taught you to blow your noses on your handkerchiefs. I taught you how to take care of yourselves, I got you together, and you're a useless bunch without me."

He surveyed them again in turn and then a wheedling note came into his whisper.

"Now think, boys, think if you can. I don't know who did this, though I thought I did when I came here. I admit I've changed my mind. *But I do know one thing.* We're bust. We're clean bust, finite, kaput as a team, and we'd better face it. It there's no trust we're done for, and we were the best in the business. It'll take me years to find a bunch half as good. If you think I'd kick all this in for an extra cut – who arranged the perishing cuts anyhow? – then you're even bigger fools than I thought."

He stood up with some effort. "That's the lot, as far as I'm concerned. I'm off now and you'll give me ten minutes start because I move slowly. I'm not giving Mr Smart Guy Manchester a single solitary penny, and if you take my advice you'll do the same. Good night."

This was not the end of the meeting, which continued for over an hour, but as usual Gabel's word was final. The group decided unanimously to do nothing – which, after all, was the easiest – if not the safest – course.

It was not until the afternoon of the following Saturday that Charles Wilberforce Dixon, 43, described as a commercial traveler, residing at 17, Ponders Way, North Wembley, was taken into custody for questioning to assist the police in their enquiries into a patrol robbery at Saunders Electronics.

* * * * * * *

Inspector Hungerford eyed his victim with a friendly, almost intimate smile. The Inspector had a reputation for smoothness which some translated as a crafty use of the softly-softly-catchee-monkey technique.

"Charlie," he began, "a little bird has been whispering to me about you. Now don't get me wrong, this isn't something from an ordinary stoolie. This is rather special. My guess is that you've got a pal who isn't quite as fond of you as you've been supposing. Now we've time for a nice long chat and if you want some legal gentleman to hold your hand we can wait all night for him to arrive."

The discussions did indeed last all night and well into the next day. Mr Dixon was a cautious and painstaking man who knew just how sharp was the razor's edge on which he was teetering. But on Sunday evening he walked into the street a free man, having proved conclusively with the aid of his passport, two coloured postcards, four hotel bills, six impartial witnesses and a Continental telephone call, that at the relevant time he had been enjoying himself in Rome. Signer Emilio Valconi, manager of the Palazzo Valconi, personally recalled ejecting Mr Dixon from his premises for conduct unbecoming to a guest in that elegant establishment. Even Inspector Hungerford did not know that Mr Dixon had a brother who resembled him very closely whenever he bothered to grow a moustache.

Two days later, on a Tuesday morning at the uncomfortable hour of 8.45 a.m., Tony and Ronald Myers, Charles Dixon and William Tidmarsh were arrested in front of a locker at Waterloo Station, together with George Gabel, whom the four of them were escorting very closely. George Gabel had in his possession a parcel wrapped in brown paper addressed to Mr Manchester, and the parcel contained £4,317 in banknotes.

It was typical of them, as Inspector Hungerford pointed out, that each had paid his share of the demand in new banknotes which were part of the Saunders Electronics haul - the banknotes most dangerous to get rid of. It made the notes simple to identify and their possession was convincing evidence, especially when taken in conjunction with letters that all six of them were known to have received.

"You look remarkably pleased with yourself," said Inspector Hungerford's senior colleague as they took their mid-morning tea that day. "Can't say I blame you, but you took a damn long chance with those letters. Had your share of luck too."

The Inspector permitted himself the smile of a contented Cheshire cat.

"There was no luck about it, my boy, no luck at all," he said. "The whole thing had George Gabel written all over it, but he's far too fly to leave himself uncovered. Where George is, Charlie Dixon is close behind - that's been true for years now. Charlie Dixon always uses Foster-Brown for the alarms and Doc Tidmarsh for any jelly work and the Myers brothers do his get-away driving. There you have the entire gang, as I knew from the start. But Charlie's real specialty is the perfect alibi; he's a master at it and he probably fixes them for all concerned - as near as dammit watertight.

"No, they had to be tricked out into the open - it was the only way. So I wrote all six of them the same 'blackmail' letter.

"I wondered," he added, "if I might be overplaying my hand when I described myself as a lazy buzzard. But of course, in some ways I am."

The Last Hangman

Albert ("Sniffy") Bates was the last hangman in our part of the world, and it is not so long ago that he went out of business. He only served one gaol, Chalfonts, which has now been turned into an unbarred garden city for juvenile delinquents. This new effort by the Home Office may satisfy their statistical department, but it terrifies those of us who live roundabout. We never used to lock up at night but recent experience has taught us a caution which we used to think discourteous.

Sniffy Bates had a few months of glory when this epoch began. People used to say to him, "Ah, if you were still at work old Mrs Forsdyke wouldn't have been beaten up in her cottage with a lump of gravel in an old sock," and he would sniff mildly and say, "Ah well, I can only cure them once."

Unlike other members of his profession, he didn't run a public house, nor even a barber's shop, a sideline which has proved a considerable attraction to keen exponents of the art before now. He was, and indeed is, a partner in a small garage in my village.

I have had two secondhand cars from him myself and never felt the need to grumble. After all, it makes a very good conversational gambit to be able to say, "My little buzzbox? I bought her from the public hangman."

For more years than I can remember, being a stranger of only twenty five years standing in these parts, Sniffy has been a known and marked figure. On certain ominous days, he would stand at the bus stop in his flat cloth cap and belted mackintosh, carrying a sinister black bag - a scruffy affair with a handle mended with twine, fixed at the top by two brass clamps. The girls at the fruit packers who use this early transport were always twittering at his appearance and he got the best seat, a solo affair in front just behind the driver, without competition.

When he came back, a couple of days later, no one spoke to him for a week or more, out of a decent sort of reticence. He has a particular corner in the Bull where he is available, at hours and dates decided by Mrs Bates, for a pint or a game of shove h'appeny, but he always did ten days or so of solitary before he became accepted as a member of the community once again.

His wife, a grim woman who had purchased her wardrobe many years before in evident anticipation of widowhood, never accompanied him. He is not a great conversationalist, but when he wishes, he can join this discussion with the aid of two words: "Ah!" and "Exactly" which can mean anything he chooses. The 'Ah' when it descends in tone to a bass 'Ahhhh' possesses a profundity of agreement beyond question, whilst his 'Ex-zakkerly' conveys, if required, 'That's what you say but I don't believe a word of it.'

With tourists, rare birds in our part of the world, he was a little more forthcoming, and once or twice on a late summer evening I have seen him pass a six inch piece of soft white rope into an eager hand, rather as if he were doing a black market deal.

Locals, like myself, 'fancied' him and cultivated him like an *object d'art*. We bought our petrol from him rather than at the big garage at the crossroads.

After each departure he would return silent and red-eyed, sitting huddled in his personal corner. It used to occur to me that he was not the ideal man for the job, and perhaps that perceptive officials might be well advised to pension him off, if indeed there is a pension scheme for government servants in this branch.

But he kept at it right to the end, and indeed followed the debates in parliament about the abolition of his profession with a very keen eye. He had curious steel rimmed glasses, working on a principle I have never seen before which he used for reading. He reversed both lenses which worked on a swivel, and hooked them on his beaky little snout upside down, as it were, for the study of small print. We sometimes wondered grimly which aspect he used for his work, but lacked the courage to enquire.

But at least the debates made him loquacious. "They can't do it," he would say. "Hanging's the only cure."

His opinion was absolute. Unfortunately the Royal Commission did not think fit to consult him, but we regulars at the Bull were in no doubt as to his views.

The changes in the law reduced trade for Sniffy very considerably. Old Dixon the postman delivered far fewer of those sinister buff envelopes summoning him to toil, but he and his little black bag did leave the village from time to time by the early bus, for nationalised transport, it seemed, was required for government matters.

Then the death blow, so to speak, was dealt to his business. Prison arrangements were changed by the Home Office and executions ceased permanently at the gaol. Sniffy was condemned to the ignominious nonentity of garage service.

For some months he bore up pretty well, even riposting sharply from his corner to the occasional tasteful allusions to his past career which the members of the Bull thought fit to offer.

"Missing that little old rope o' your'n, Sniffy?"

"Some on you 'ud be the better for a taste of it, I doubt not."

It was good, witty, thrust-and-parry stuff, but I could see that he felt bitterly. At the end of a year he had lost a stone - too much for a thin man - and the itch to travel afield was upon him. He hugged his corner silently, white of face and red of eye.

Then came the news of the accident. Bill Emms, his partner at the garage told me of it briefly one morning when I stopped to fill my tank. He was markedly non-committal about the affair.

"Fell down here in the corner by the Inspection pit, so he did," he said briefly. "Broke an ankle and bashed his head right hard. Little boy Clive what washes the cars found him. Policeman come - fetched him to hospital. They say he's took no real harm."

But that evening in the Bull, little boy Clive was in his full glory as an authoritative witness of vital events.

"Hanged himself, so he did," he explained, and was completely fluent in the story by the time I arrived. "Hanged himself just like a real execution, rope and noose and all. It couldn't have worked proper, though - he must have jumped off the bumper of that old chara we've got jacked up above the pit. Rope broke - that's what it did - and he hit himself two ways falling down. Proper knocked out he was when I found him."

It was not a nine days wonder, but it did rivet local attention for the forty-eight hours during which poor old Sniffy was held incommunicado at Chalfonts hospital. Mrs Bates in her rusty prophetic weeds visited him on the second day and returned sour and tight-lipped as ever.

Soon after, I received a very surprising telephone call. It was from the hospital and the voice said that their patient Albert Bates who was suffering from concussion and a broken ankle was asking very urgently to see me. I would be admitted for a few minutes if I presented myself at four o'clock.

I found him as pathetic a picture of misery as anything I have ever clapped eyes on. His head was heavily bandaged and his left foot was encased in a gouty caricature of Stonehenge. He was immobile and despairing, even his sniff was no longer a comment on life.

"I'm done for," he said. "Done for. Finished. Be the laugh of the village for the rest of my days, that's what I'll be. Never hold my head up again."

"Don't take it too badly," I said. "Remember you asked to see me? Is there anything I can do?"

101

"Well, you might," he said, and there was a long pause, "You might. You being a real journalist and knowing about these things. You was always a gentleman to me, sir. I hardly like to ask."

I promised to do my best. After a while he poured out the whole story.

"It was a sort of an accident," he said. "You see I've been properly down ever since I was abolished, as you might say. It's Mrs Bates as is the trouble. A right turmagent as maybe you know. Silent as the grave outside, but to live with she's like an old gramophone record with a crack in it, going on for ever. Not a moment's peace do I get and sometimes it drives me near mad. I've often wished I could cut off my ears to save myself. A day or two off over at Chalfonts was like water in the desert.

"Now it's finished and last week I was feeling so low I started messing around with a rope in the garage, just for old times' sake."

He paused and eyed me over his sinister steel rims.

"It wasn't suicide I was thinking of, you know, sir," he said. "I was just reminding myself of happier days. I just slipped off me perch and banged myself up very nasty. But you see the trouble I'm in."

"Not quite," I said.

"Well," he explained, "Whatever I was up to, I made a mess of it. 'Hangman makes proper old fool of self', that's what the papers will say and no mistake. Charged with attempted suicide as like as not, after all the talk there's been, and proved to be no good at it into the bargain. Just what do you reckon I ought to do?"

As it happened, I was able to give him the answer. Sniffy's misadventure had drawn attention to him once again. A wave of sympathy for him was sweeping the village and in an underground way was probably reaching even Mrs Bates herself. In my capacity as a 'fancier' I had taken the precaution of sounding out our policeman. No charge was in prospect, for it was very doubtful how far his experiments had gone; it was only the dark inference of Sniffy messing about with a rope which had started the story.

"So don't do anything, don't say anything," I advised. "I know what the stars foretell for you. Everything's going to be all right."

A week later, when he did get back, he got the nearest thing to a hero's welcome that we run to at the Bull: that is to say there was a low amiable groan from the company which could almost be interpreted as a cheer, when he hobbled in. Several of us bought him drinks and everyone wished him well. The truth is we love our celebrity and would feel very bitter if we were to be deprived of reflected glory.

Now for a great deal of this I take the major credit, particularly for talking very privately to the proprietor of the local newspaper. If that suicide story had ever come out the London press would inevitably have discovered it sooner or later, and then there might have been investigations into Sniffy's career as an executioner.

For the sad truth is that our hero never hanged a man in his life.

The story was the Great Excuse, the escape route to a couple of days' peace of mind and freedom from the inexorable tongue of Mrs Bates. His expeditions to Chalfonts were made to see his cousin, a Mr Charles Peek, who works at the local Labour Exchange, and it was he who had invented the idea.

Mrs Bates, though strictly forbidding him the house, even for a Christmas visit, never opened letters in official envelopes in case they came from tax collectors and Charles had an unlimited supply at his fingertips. What began as a single ingenious spree developed over the years into a legend. A little investigation of my own had unearthed the secret long ago. But even if I am a journalist I also have a heart. I never breathed a word nor winked an eyelid.

That is, until last week, when Sniffy's sudden popularity had relaxed into normal tolerant amiability. Everything was precisely as usual when the customary wisecrack was made.

"Missing that old rope of your'n?"

Mr Bates reversed his glasses to survey the company. Then he gave me, I thought, an extra special stare that could almost have been interpreted as a wink. He sniffed very happily.

"Ex-actly," he said, "but I've retired. Only go to Chalfonts now for the electric treatment after my accident. Doctor says it'll be years before I'm cured."

The Second Saint

There was a man on all fours in the middle of the road close to the corner at which Carraway Street joins Hampden Lane in the suburb of Carfax Green, where I used to live.

Though it was long past twelve on a bright moonlit night it seemed a dangerous position to adopt, even if he was drunk and therefore entitled to some protection by the gods. But he did not look as if he was drunk; his head was on one side, very close to the ground and he appeared to be watching something carefully. Perhaps he had dropped some valuable and was looking for it.

I crossed the road and stood beside him.

"Are you all right?" I asked.

Presently he looked up. A shrewd, wizened face peered from steel-rimmed glasses. He rose to his knees, brushed his hands together and retrieved a black homburg hat which had been on the road beside him.

"Thank you, indeed. Yes. I am quite all right. Kneeling like this is inclined to make one giddy, but I am quite all right."

He had a precise legal voice and his mouth split into a smile of synthetic teeth. He was certainly sober.

"Lost something?"

He stood up, brushed his knees and straightened his back, hands on hips.

"You are very kind. No. I have not lost anything—or, rather, I have found what I was looking for."

He had certainly picked nothing up: in fact he had been looking towards the wall at the corner of Hampden Lane, twenty yards distant. For a moment he surveyed me quizzically, making up his mind about me. The books I was carrying under my arm evidently suggested that I was a helpful stranger rather than a menace.

"I have found something, my friend," he said, "and very interesting too. Now, perceive this very slight dip in the road surface. You don't, of course, and pray don't trouble yourself to imitate my undignified posture—take my word for it—and follow the line of my finger across to the garden wall. Now, what do you see?"

He took my arm and pointed directly.

"Nothing," I said. "That is, nothing unusual. A garden wall made of brick with laurels and rhodedendrons beyond."

"Precisely. Precisely, my young friend. A brick wall. But the bricks are fifteenth century and the wall is clearly Victorian. Does that suggest nothing, and you a man of letters?"

"That the bricks have been used again or that the wall is older than it looks?"

He chuckled like a schoolmaster with a promising pupil.

"Aha! Now we begin to advance. But we must start with first principles. *Festina lente*, remember. This little dip in the road surface is our first clue, and a very important one. It shows quite clearly that the present street line is comparatively new. An old road, my friend, is often an extremely obstinate thing, difficult to erase, especially by slipshod modern methods. No, no; a good road leaves its imprint, regardless of concrete and steamrollers. Now, come with me."

He still had my arm and he trotted me to the pavement and along the wall.

"Let us observe. Even the paving-stones tell their tale, and—just here—is where we must lose it again unless we are to trespass."

He halted me some yards from the corner itself, and looked up at me, hoping for some sign of intelligence. I saw nothing remarkable and said so.

"Oh, but you must use your eyes," he reproached. "An informed and observant eye is essential to this little exercise. Now the road surface dips, does it not? Just here, you see, and this dip, which if you consider it from the other side is, in fact, a rise, continues through the pavement, where these four stones are slightly uneven, and so to the wall. You follow me?"

"And the wall has a slight crack in it which has been repointed at some time or other," I suggested. "An old road once ran through the garden?"

He was delighted. "Capital! Capital! You have the makings of a worker in this field. Now, let me see, where do you live?"

I was in no mood for a lecture on cartography, for it was a night with a touch of frost, but he still held me by the arm.

"Martin's Close," I said ungraciously. "I must be on my way."

"A terrible monstrosity," he said. "There is Roman tessera beneath it but no amount of protest would make the authorities relent when it was built. But it is on my way and we shall cross the ancient track at two points."

As we set off, for there was no gainsaying him, I had a very strong feeling that the direction relieved him and that he was leading me away from whatever goal he himself had been pursuing.

"My name is Widgeon," he said. "A mere clerk in the Chaucerian sense of the word. This is my hobby and I generally follow it at night. Moonlight is especially favourable. Less traffic, few spectators, and the light gives far more informative shadows than the sun. Now just here..." We paused perforce. "Just here is our road again, which, of course, is the old Hampden Highway, Norman and Roman before that, running beside a pool. It is shown on some old maps but their topography is inexact and one must do the research personally. I think the gateway to Carfax's lodge stood hereabout, in fact I know it. There are corner-stones in the Carfax Arms which undoubtedly come from it, even if the hostelry was built in eighteen eighty. Builders, especially local builders, are like magpies, you know. They thrive from the ruins and the rubble they hoard. A Roman consul's villa dissolves into a confetti of stones still used by later generations. Thirty years ago one could have rebuilt the *Royal Ensign,* one of Elizabeth's first great ships, from timbers in this street, for they were all used in houses hereabouts. Now nothing remains except a couple of beams in the cellar of the Carfax Arms. Tragic, you know, tragic."

There was no escaping this ancient mariner; he accompanied me right to the door of my block of flats.

"A terrible place," he said looking up at it and shivering with either cold or revulsion. "To think that the Consul Cinna once had his villa here and looked towards the river—the course has changed as you must know—but here, where the pond once was, the Romans watered their horses and their lines ran just behind the Carfax Arms. And what of the Consul's fine marble around his private bath? For marble, you know, never decays—it is for ever. I'll tell you: it was looted long centuries ago, just like the seats in the amphitheatre at Vienne, to make tables, wash-stand tops, even tiles, heaven knows what. Scattered, dispersed, but never really lost if one knows where to look. Yes indeed, stone is for ever—a great virtue. But I mustn't keep you, my young friend. I bid you good night."

He released my arm and set off into the moonlight at a gentle pigeon-toed trot. I was heartily relieved to see him go, for his lecture showed every sign of continuing indefinitely. Next time, I thought, I will be careful about asking old gentlemen crawling over the highway if they need help.

* * * * * * *

It was a couple of months, high summer in fact, before I saw Mr Widgeon again. Again it was at full moon and this time I was more wary. But his antics were so odd as he paused, peered and trotted alternately, that I could not leave well alone. I stalked him as he darted from point to point like a black beetle.

This time he was skirting an open car-park which had been fashioned out of an area laid waste by bomb damage. There are several of such gaps in Carfax Green, where the authorities are dilatory.

He was following the same technique, squatting, peering, scampering and darting his head from side to side as if it were independent of his body.

And then without warning he vanished. It had all the surprise of a conjuring trick and it was several seconds before I realised that he must have nipped over a little wall and landed on the far side, where the irregular ground lay lower than the pavement. He had been absorbed into the jagged, bleak shadows of a bombed-out ruin.

I gave up the chase, turned homewards and had gone a good hundred yards, rounding the corner of the derelict wreck, when his head suddenly appeared at ground level from a hole in the wall a couple of paces in front of me. He must have scampered diagonally through the ruins, for he was now standing, I guessed, in what had been a Victorian semi-basement.

"Aha, my young friend!" he squeaked. "Still pursuing your studies? I am. Indeed I am, and not without success. Tonight I have made discoveries of great importance. Come now, nip down beside me and I'll show you history."

It was a squalid and dirty setting for research but I managed to scramble into what had once been a kitchen. Only half of it remained, open to the sky.

Again he seized my arm and jabbed towards the rubble wall with an incisive finger.

"Our lost road again, you perceive? How rich these layers are! How informative! Saxon flints, Roman stone and some of their great flat bricks now sadly decaying, the Tudor cobbles above— once a fine thoroughfare ran here. But the world moves on. People steal roads; you know when they die. A great lord enlarges his garden and who is to forbid him? Some Victorian magnate builds a row of slums and bribes an official to close an eye. A planner decides to wipe it all out and start afresh, and where is your great open way? It has become a twisted alley at best, or it lies as it does here, just beneath the surface, lost for ever."

"Do you record all this?" I asked. "Are you writing a book?"

He tapped his forehead. "It is recorded here," he said. "Every foot of the way towards my goal. You felt instinctively I had a purpose? Of course I have. I am unravelling one of the great mysteries. Indeed, you could say I was seeking the fountain of life, the lost elixir."

I was too surprised to say anything but "Eh?" To have been cornered by an eccentric with an oddly fascinating hobby was one thing, but to find that he was chasing the fountain of life was quite another.

He evidently felt my lack of enthusiasm for after a moment he continued.

"Perhaps I disappoint you. Perhaps you are forming an opinion based on ignorance. Let me enlighten you. Consider the Legend, my boy, consider the Legend. St Alban's Spring, the Elixir of St Alban, first of English martyrs, even if he was a Roman. It had miraculous powers; it was nearby, you know—there is no peradventure or doubt about it—and it was reputed to flow with the water of life. Think of it. Supposing it could be discovered once more—analysed—given again to mankind. What a triumph!"

He paused. "You don't think so?"

"No," I said. "My experience of springs and spas is that they're salt and dirty. If you find one hereabouts the likely gift it will bring will be a nice dose of typhoid."

For a full minute he seemed downcast, but suddenly he looked up at me with his quick quizzical smile.

"You don't share my enthusiasm?" he said. "A pity. A very great pity, young man. I shall bid you good-night."

We parted on that but I had an odd feeling that things had gone his way, not mine. He was not at all perturbed but had merely tried out an idea, failed in his objective and was now glad to be rid of me.

* * * * * * *

Though I glimpsed him once or twice on his midnight prowls during the next nine months I avoided discovery and had almost forgotten his existence when one evening towards closing time he appeared at my elbow in the bar-parlour of the Carfax Arms. He was unchanged—the same black dusty clothes, the same look of an enquiring beetle, or perhaps a speculative tortoise.

"We meet again, my young friend," he said, "and not entirely by chance as the song says. No, indeed, I have been seeking you out. I shall buy you a drink—I insist upon it—for I am in dire need of your youthful services. Come, now."

He bustled me to a small marble-topped table and I could not help speculating where the stone had originated, when he returned with, of all unlikely drinks, a couple of glasses of port.

"It is to your taste, I trust? I don't know what young people prefer today, but this is sound enough and it is a young person I am in need of today. Your strong right arm, my boy, that is my *desideratum.* I cannot command your aid, I can only ask it."

I was mollified by the port: it had been a curiously naïve and endearing gesture.

"What can I do for you?"

He jerked his head forward, nearer my face.

"Splendid! Splendid! I felt I could count upon you; you have an open, friendly countenance, and I feel sure that is an earnest of a keen intelligence. Now, when I said I could not command your aid—though you have freely offered it—I was perhaps not making myself clear. I am prepared to pay for it. The labourer is worthy of his hire, and I am offering you ten pounds for your services for one evening."

He pulled out a dog-eared black pocket-case and thrust a wad of notes into my hand. I did not close my fist but let the money stay where he had left it. Nor did I answer.

"You hesitate?" he enquired. "I can assure you that you need have no qualms. There is nothing unsavoury about my project, indeed you could say with justice that you are humouring me in a fancy in which you have no faith."

"The St Alban's Elixir?" I exclaimed. "You're still chasing that fantasy?"

"You could put it that way," he said. "You very well might, and with complete accuracy. Then it is agreed? Splendid!"

He raised his glass to me.

"A bargain! You cannot be a loser in the matter. Now listen very carefully. Tomorrow evening you must meet me at the scene of our first encounter, the corner of Carraway Street. Midnight is a good hour and let us pray for a clear night, for the moon will be at its zenith. You must come equipped."

"With what?"

"With a small crowbar, dear boy, nothing more uncouth than you could borrow from, say, the porter of your horrible block of flats. Oh, yes, a beetle and a wedge might be handy with, perhaps, a gardener's trowel. And of course, a sack. You can carry your impedimenta in it."

"It sounds like breaking and entering," I said.

He gave me his gleaming porcelain smile.

"Oh, dear me, no!" he chuckled. "Nothing of the sort. Indeed where we are going—and this has been the goal of my investigations for some time—is a spot which has no known owner today, not even the District Council. I have been most meticulous in my researches on the question. St Alban, remember, is dead and the secret was his, and his alone. You have my word upon it."

"Very well, then," I said. "It's a bargain."

"A small point before we part," he said. "The token which you

109

have accepted is a fee. You have been too nice—in the Elizabethan sense—to count it but when you do you will find that it consists of ten guineas, which makes it a professional matter. In return I am counting upon your discretion. It is a sum paid *in toto*. You understand?"

I didn't but I was too perverse to say so. I was committed to his adventure and I had ten guineas in my pocket which was a rare experience for me.

I was as prompt upon the hour as he on the following evening. A flawless night with a bright moon sailing magnificently through light cumulus cloud.

He seized my arm and scuttled me along in the opposite direction to the one we had taken at our first meeting. True to form he discoursed continually as he piloted me.

"Those Tudor bricks, you appreciate, came from the orchard wall of Sir Montague Hampton's mansion. Peaches he grew, too, nectarines and strawberries. Lost forever. I suppose I am the last man in the world to know where it stood. Here were his stables, running diagonally through those two little suburban homesteads. And just beyond us—aha—just beyond us, stood yet another house, destroyed much later."

We were now beside a patch of wasteland at the approach to Carfax Common, a place of surrealist horror. An abandoned car lay rotting amongst a welter of broken prams, tin baths, old mattresses, and the thrown out junk of a quarter of a century. I tagged along with my burden as he skipped delicately through the mess. The ground was uneven with the partially obliterated foundations of walls showing here and there. A narrow flight of steps led to a small open area about eight feet below ground level, where children had evidently made a den, for there were broken toys, pieces of a bicycle and an old gramophone lying about.

Here we halted.

"This is it, my friend," he said. "Here your task begins. It should not prove difficult."

"What am I to do?"

"Just apply your mind and your strength. You mind first. You will not fail to have remarked that we are standing in the remnants of what was once a cellar? No? Then consider, pray, the conformation of this wall. Despite the layers of rotting whitewash you should notice something."

I examined it carefully. "Two different types of brick?" I suggested.

"Precisely. I knew you were very acute. There was once a door here, but it has been bricked up. Now for your strong right arm. Unpack your equipment and let us discover what lies beyond that door. We must hope to reach out to St Alban."

It was really remarkably easy. The wall was only the thickness of a single brick and it had been laid without proper foundation. Three or four jabs with my crowbar smashed out half a dozen bricks and when I put my shoulder against the rest, I very nearly fell into the recess beyond as the bricks tumbled into a dusty heap.

Mr Widgeon brushed me aside and stepped nimbly through the gap. Almost before I crept through after him he was flashing a pocket torch, for the interior was a narrow room about four feet by twelve. It smelt abominably and except for the remains of something that might have been a hassock or a footstool, it was quite empty.

Built into the opposite wall was a wrought iron object which I thought at first must be an old oven but as he played his torch full on it I realised that it was probably the door to a small Victorian furnace for some early form of central heating. A moulded inscription with a trademark proclaimed: *Edwardes Patent Combustion Company*. It had a heavy latch rusted hard to its socket and this took me a couple of minutes to raise. The door creaked open.

"Stand back, pray," he said, his voice squeaking with tension. "Stand back. Hold the torch. This is the supreme moment. Aha! I thought so." Squatting on his haunches he inserted an arm and withdrew it slowly, dragging into the light what had once been a leather Gladstone bag. As he gripped the handle to lift it to the ground the upper part ripped away and the bag itself thudded to the ground.

It was full of golden sovereigns.

It would be natural to say that there was a moment of stupefied silence, but it would not be true as far as Mr Widgeon was concerned. He chuckled with delight, ran a handful of the coins through his fingers and finally held one steady in the beam of the torch.

"St Alban's secret, my boy," he whispered, "and here it is at last. You observe the date?"

"Eighteen hundred and seventy-eight!"

"Precisely," he said. "A very good year for secrets." He tossed the gold piece back into the broken bag.

"Now if I had any sense I should say to you 'Be off, my boy, be off. Never let me see you again.' And so I will in a minute, make no mistake about that. But though I owe you nothing in cash, for a bargain is a bargain, you are entitled to an explanation."

"All that bunk about the mystic spring, the legend and the elixir," I said. "A proper old fairy tale. Ancient Roman roads, my foot."

"Oh, dear me!" He protested. "You do me a great injustice. Without my little hobby, history, cartography, call it what you will, this discovery could never have been made. My only deception, a very mild one you will agree, I feel sure, was about St Alban. You see there were two St Albans and one of them is totally forgotten in this day and age. Fortunately, I must admit."

"This certainly wasn't the Saint," I said.

"As you remark so aptly, certainly not our English Martyr; just a forgotten man, a namesake, Alistair St Alban, a Victorian romantic novelist, of whom no doubt, you have never heard. But he once had a great reputation. Another Sir Walter Scott they thought him, but he really wrote the most dreadful balderdash. No one has read him since, which is not surprising, but in his time he sold in his tens of thousands. He made, I am happy to state, a fortune."

"So I see," I remarked.

"Just so. But he had, as I discovered some time since—my researches are always useful and sometimes rewarding—two especial qualities. He was a miser and a humbug. When he died people wondered how it was he came to be almost penniless but he was buried in the odour of great sanctity. There is the most repulsive memorial to him at St Margaret's in Sydenham, all pious platitudes and weeping angels. Quite nauseating, I assure you."

"And this was once his house?" I suggested.

He eyed me with pained surprise.

"Certainly not. His own residence in Sydenham, of course, was searched from attic to cellar but not a halfpenny was found. No, no. But there was a modest little house just here, burned to the ground, alas, within a few years of his death. It was the property of a Miss Amelia Mulberry who was, as they say, just a friend. He was very discreet about the whole business. It took a great deal of research and deduction to discover that she ever existed and the labour of locating the site of her establishment has been extremely tiring. The lady died in very reduced circumstances in eighteen eighty-nine, which left me assured of two things: that his fortune rested here, concealed, and that she guessed nothing of its existence.

"Now run along, my boy. If you will be so good as to leave me your sack—I'll return it to you if you wish. I feel I can look after myself for the rest of the night. Goodbye, my boy, and a thousand thanks for all your help."

I only saw Mr Widgeon once after our adventure. He was driving in a small open car with a comfortable and jolly blonde companion of about his own age. I can say this because he himself was certainly looking ten years younger, so there was something in that business of the elixir of life after all.

A for Assassins

The oddest things always happen at the oddest times. In 1939 during the "phoney war" days I had an experience which was so peculiar that for several years it was pigeonholed into that department of the mind which says 'It's so damn silly that it couldn't have happened. You dreamed it.'

But it wasn't a dream. It happened at 9.05 a.m. on a pavement in London W1, on a cold damp November monday morning. I was a Second-Lieutenant in those days and had just begun to realise that this was indeed the lowest form of animal life. I had very little to do with war and was in fact a plain unglorified clerk in a department of the War Office known as "The Dustbin". Officially it was called A.G.19 (Surplus and Redundant Personnel) and quite what it was all about I shall never know.

But next door to us at No. 21 Rowena Street, was a mystery bag. We called them Department Z (just in fun) and they were certainly cloak-and-dagger boys, popping up in uniform one day and the next day in bowlers, umbrellas and brief cases, exactly like City types. Strange characters wandered about too, tramps and organ-grinders with monkeys, and ladies who might, at a pinch, be considered to come into the glamorous spy category. Most of these looked either like modern beatniks or overworked Rep actresses, but we poor slaves wove highly coloured tales about them. There was very little else to do.

However on this particular morning there was literally movement afoot. The road was blocked by a couple of W.D. lorries, there were packing cases everywhere and occasionally a squad of stalwarts appeared and lifted a heavy armchair into the pantechnicons.

Department Z was transferring elsewhere.

I watched this for some time, having nothing more urgent on hand, leaning, I remember, against a large green filing cabinet which stood on the pavement, sloping awkwardly towards the gutter.

Now whether I touched the top drawer or whether it moved on its own account I do not remember, but with very little encouragement it slid slowly open on its rollers until the entire contents were displayed for inspection.

Idly I pulled up the leading docket and had a look.

A - Assassins it said.

A little waft of fog had begun to eddy around the pavement and the air was cold and moist. There was not a soul around. The atmosphere was at once unpleasant and theatrical. We had been three months at war and hardly a shot had been fired in anger. I took out two or three of the files near the front.

Aumonier, Jean-Paul ran the first of them, *b.1904 Lyons, French (atheist); Method: Garotte* and the second: *Abrahams, Anatole, b.1909 Prague? Holds passports for Brazil, Holland, Austria; Method: Razor.*

I suppose I ran through half a dozen of these files goggle-eyed. Each one of them made remarkable reading but common caution warned me against enjoying too much of a good thing. I closed the drawer, jammed it tight with a match stick (for security) and walked stolidly into my office to deal with the day's supplies of redundancies and surplus.

All that morning I was saying to myself, "This is ridiculous: this is cloak-and-dagger and spies with false beards and beautiful women with the plans secreted in their cleavage. This is a third rate film which sent me to sleep and I am now wide awake."

Despite the unreality of the whole episode one of the entries remained with me, etched permanently on my memory like the surprise element in a routine nightmare.

Duvivier, Gabriel b.1901 - French subject - access to all passports. Sp. French, German, English (cockney). Caution: height 4'10" (recognisable). Methods: Various - Knife, poisons (practising chemist holding certificates and qualifications Warsaw, Memphis, Quebec, etc.) Rifle shot, knowledge of high explosive. Location: Les Moinneaux, Touraine, France, Café des Moinneaux. Approach: Carry mackintosh and local newspaper "Matin du Vent des Moinneaux" under left arm. Drink: Pernod (2). Whistle "Au près de ma blonde".Fees: moderate, according to currency supplied."

Underneath in the notes section were various remarks by different hands. "Reliable - too noticeable for important work owing to height - J." "Not explosives – W." "Employed 17/1/32 (ref: A/123707/B) - 25/4/35 (ref: B/5574/J)"

Now it would not be true to way that I remembered all of this as accurately as I have now written it down. But parts of it stuck: all through the war years I found my imagination wandering off to Touraine and to a mysterious little figure hunched in a corner minding his own business. Was he a Resistance man now? How was trade? Had he gone over to the Germans?

He began to edge his way into my dreams, for by this time I had a clear mind's eye picture of him, almost a dwarf, a sort of dirty Quilp from the Old Curiosity Shop, with darting eyes and a sharp unshaven chin - a mercurial mystery figure played by a ham actor. Always as I crept along a rocky precipice ledge in my dreams I found that the path petered out and Duvivier was behind me, waiting unhurriedly, but with a knife in his hand. Sometimes I was in a bistro, in pyjamas and of course penniless but when the barman turned to face me - it was Duvivier again.

I suppose it was because I could not share the story that the little man became such as obsession. I had a roving war, largely in forgotten corners of creation and the more I thought about it the more fugitive became my first picture of that drab November morning and the more unlikely the tale. I told no one and Duvivier came nearer and nearer to me once my eyes closed at night.

Even with the war over I did not quite forget him, but he did at least have the grace not to call so often. I went into business as a dealer in paintings, most of them contemporary, but occasionally touching the established French masters if we could find them at the right price. It was not altogether a happy venture because from the start I began to quarrel with my partner. He is, I consider, dishonest in his way of thinking, and indeed I know I am (to some extent) in mine. But we know too much of our mutual failings to be able separate: it is an uneasy brotherhood.

Last summer a picture scout brought us news of a Van Gogh privately owned by an elderly widow living in a dilapidated château outside Tours: it was reputed to have been a gift from the painter himself and although she was said to be a difficult old lady the chance of a cheap purchase was too good to miss.

I set off for Tours with reasonably high hopes and a rare old wild goose chase it turned out to be. The picture was not a Van Gogh, the old lady was foul tempered garrulous and senile and she had no intention of selling in any case. I got back to my hotel on a wet Sunday evening, tired, irritated and extremely bored, although such adventures are common enough in my profession.

A series of slow lonely drinks in assorted cafés finally brought me to one of the larger joints, with brighter lights and a small orchestra. Opposite me on the wall was a touring map of the area, a nice bright modern affair with all the great Chateaux of the district clearly shown, and the major motor trips vividly marked. But a name in smaller print caught my eye, and this I felt was the irresistible finger of Destiny pointing. "Les Moinneaux" it said, "Ancient ruins of Monastery, 14th cent., local pottery, view over 100 km. Musee. Hotel de la Poste".

By Monday evening of course I was there, my bag in a room at the hotel, and myself discreetly sitting in a corner of the café des

Moinneaux, for this was my heaven sent opportunity to break my dream. I brought my mackintosh, carefully tucked over my left arm, but the local newspaper no longer existed. I made do with the *Echo de Tours*.

It was not at all what I had expected, this café, and this I felt was all to the good if I was to effect a cure. It was large, barely populated and patronised chiefly by regulars playing billiards in a far corner. The little town is comparatively high and sunny, a few streets round a large market place. Life is leisurely and the French language is beautiful on the tongue, as it always is in that region. Here I would stay, I decided, and live elegantly until the nightmare was broken for good and all.

I had chosen a particular seat for myself in the corner of a banquette where I could see the street and, through the wall mirrors, most of the clients. After three days I became almost a regular inasmuch as the patron recognised me and brought my Pernod without asking.

On the Thursday he wiped the marble top of my table with more care than usual. "It seams to me," he said, "that perhaps Monsieur is looking for somebody?"

"Such things are entirely possible," I said cautiously. "Do you think you can assist me in the matter?"

He gave me a long straight look. "At nine o'clock," he said, "I will place a little glass of cognac here - so...." he indicated the far end of the table "...for the entertainment of a friend, a very good friend."

It was neither a promise nor a threat, but there was a sort of warning to me, as evasive as a wisp of cigarette smoke, that said, "You are here on suffrance. It would be just as well not to try any tricks."

It was half an hour by the clock but a tingling, chilling century if one reckons time as it really matters. And quite suddenly he was there in front of me as unexpectedly as if he had materialised out of the air.

He was very small, with a round face and round pale eyes, blank as empty saucers. His hair was cropped close, but he was grey and balding. His lips were puffy and pale and had the curious appearance of being made-up in the modern female ultra-pallid style. He had dark respectable flappy clothes and very small hands which were so clean and precise that they might have been professionally manicured.

He sat delicately in front of me, having removed a black homburg hat. After a moment he picked up the cognac and sipped at it with the faintest suggestion of a salute.

I let my eyes travel from my Pernod to my mackintosh and to the newspaper.

"I cannot whistle," I said, "but I am thinking of an old song called *Au près de ma blonde*. Perhaps you recall it?"

He had a very soft voice, neither a whisper nor a whine, but it had all the charm of a caress from a slug.

"My friend," he said. "You are many years out of date with your little song. I am a chemist here in Moinneaux. I mix medicines and sell pills. I do no other business."

And yet he sighed. A little sibilant, tired rasp escaped his lips. Not a sigh of regret nor even of relish in retrospect, but a sigh that left the conversational door only half closed, because it was deliberate.

"The war," I said, "changed many things. But I remember your name from the past, though we never met. That is why, though I am no longer in any service, finding myself in your city, I felt I must give myself the privilege of meeting you."

Then I noticed that he had a little ribbon in his buttonhole, one of those odd insignia which only the French understand, for they represent anything from the Legion d'Honneur to the presidency of the rifle club.

I remembered too the oddly protective attitude of the patron.

"The Resistance, perhaps?" I suggested.

He made a gesture and the patron produced Pernod and cognac without asking for instructions.

"Yes," he said and gave his little rasping sigh again. "I had a share of all that. Too much for my liking. But it makes for loneliness. Not everyone wants to remember patriotism in this country. A hero of one moment is often recalled only as a man of mystery, a suspect, a year later. Only a little year and one's friends are gone. They remember too much and too little."

"Yet you still live here?" I enquired.

He shrugged his shoulders. "Where else? In another town I would be pointed out for what I was and old scores might be paid off. Here I am respected, but at a distance. I am even regarded with pride, like a monument. But wives do not like to see their husbands talking to me in the café and husbands suspect wives who patronise my shop too frequently. But I live, my friend, I live. Doctors must have their prescriptions made up and corns must be cured. It is necessary and it is respectable - or very nearly so."

We had another drink. There was something pathetic about him, a whine in his voice that said more clearly than words that he was a victim of social injustice, that he should be regarded and treated with affection. Yet he was cold: his blood one felt was of the temperature of a toad and his mind did not work along quite the lines of yours and mine.

I told him of my troubles on the trail of the false Van Gogh and of the occasional triumphs I had enjoyed in my hunt for undiscovered masters. All this he understood perfectly and his interest was curiously flattering, particularly because he was so anxious to talk as one human being to another.

He had several drinks, yet he remained a reptile.

"I could have had some rare pictures, once," he said, "but I should have had to have hidden them, and what is the use of a masterpiece without an audience? Even if you are a miser you should be seen counting your gold - that is half the pleasure.

"It was a very simple affair, this - just the matter of an officer, a Colonel-General, who very foolishly set up his mistress in the little house - the dower house you would say - of a château near here. A sort of hunting box, it could be called. He thought, you see, that only he, and his servant and the young woman knew about this arrangement, but of course he was terribly wrong."

He sighed again: really a most unpleasant sound.

"You dealt with him?" I enquired.

"I dealt with them all," he explained and gestured with his small white hands. "All three. It had to be that way, to avoid witnesses. A mildly interesting little problem, not in a class with my international commissions but it required thought."

"And your method?" I asked. "Your dossier with us described you as having many resources."

"Drugs," he said. "Drugs in the first instance. It was the batman's task to cook the evening meal and he drank Pilsner whilst he was at work. I put enough in each of the dozen he brought with him to put him out at the first sip. He did not drink until the meal was half cooked and the wine for his master was warming by the stove. By eight that evening he was in a stupor, so that I could get into the cottage and deal with the wine. When they found him they thought he was drunk and so they fixed the meal for themselves. By nine they were all in deep sleep and snoring like pigs. I was able to finish my business without interruption.

"Very rarely can one conclude such a task at one's leisure, so as to make it a masterpiece, but this was one of those fortunate occasions. The general, it was thought, was stabbed to death by his mistress, who poisoned herself whilst the servant was drugged or drunk.

"But we were talking of pictures...yes, there were several fine things on the walls, looted from various of our Chateaux. A set of miniatures, a couple of Ingres sketches and a Watteau, too famous to be valuable. It was sad, but to complete my own masterpiece I had to abandon the best work of other artists. It is also very funny, if you look at it in that light."

It was getting late and the billiard players had gone home. But in this leisurely town the Cafe des Moinneaux never seemed to close. In the mirror I could see the patron half asleep behind his zinc counter. He was an elderly man, a widower, whose life was without complications.

"Do you ever," I said, "make plans, even now, in your mind's eye? I mean, do you plan in imagination a *coup* that could make you rich, or satisfy your interest in craftsmanship?"

Duvivier's pale eyes were looking directly through me to the wall and the red plush fittings at my back.

"But certainly," he said. "One sees problems and devises solutions - sometimes the only possible solution. But this is no longer for me. I have retired. I can be respectable and hope to die in my bed, even if I am not acceptable to my neighbours in the next coffins. Yet one studies cases....Mme. Ledoux, the Mayor's wife for example...what happiness for all the family if that virago were to collapse of apoplexy."

He sighed again. "I should be a Professor of the Academy of Death...and advisor..."

"I have my own problem," I said, for an idea had suddenly intruded into the forepart of my mind.

"But of course," he answered, and now he was looking at me directly. "I knew that when I first heard you were sitting in this café, with your mackintosh and paper. That was why you came here, you know. Tell me about it. Not about the friend of a friend whom you happen to know, but about the man himself, for I think it is a man."

I found this abominable, for it was less than a quarter accurate, but there was just a grain of truth, and, now that I was more than a little drunk, an enormous curiosity seized me. Was I really sitting there in Les Moinneaux talking to a man who less than two hours before had been a total stranger and asking him to advise me about a murder? Perhaps, I thought, this is my dream of Duvivier taking a new turn.

"We will call him," I said, speaking with slow and precise enunciation now I knew I was drunk, "the friend of a friend. He is one of a partnership – two men who are linked in business and who do not get on together but who cannot break their chains. He has few friends, virtually none. He is over sixty, I think. He is mean and petty and very greedy. He travels by bus to and from his place of business though he could afford a chauffeur. His hobbies are mending rare porcelain and the careful restoring and altering of pictures..."

I wandered on and on. In the end I had given a pretty fair picture of my partner Robin.

"Very interesting," said Duvivier at last, "very interesting indeed, as a problem."

He paused and was clearly delving into his own mental filing system.

"A recluse, you say, and a mean man who drinks very little. Without studying the subject directly one cannot really devise an accurate, foolproof method. The solution would lie, I suppose, in his weakness - one should always capitalise on secretiveness - it can be a great help. A little gift of cognac, perhaps - say some samples sent out as advertising, which he would keep but not acknowledge. Three miniature bottles in a box, not to be shared with anyone....three in a row, the middle one only to be doctored. People always pull out an end bottle first - did you know that? It is very important, for it provides time, weeks maybe, after the wrappings have been destroyed. Any link is broken, so.

"You should give the matter some thought yourself. Think along these lines - probe these weaknesses. Very possibly something simpler will occur to you. A half smoked packet of cigarettes left on a bus seat next to your friend? Or a new pair of expensive gloves dropped on his doorstep - risky, but sometimes effective if the hidden needle cuts deep enough. A specimen electric light bulb left in his hall...but toys like these are expensive and messy and they involve enquiries. Bombs can be traced far too easily once the remains get into the hands of experts.

"Above everything remember that simplicity is a saving grace. Be simple, be above suspicion and be out of the country when any accident occurs."

He stood up, not altogether steadily despite his teetotum figure.

"I shall wish you goodnight," he said. "Perhaps I shall see you again, but in view of all we have said to each other I doubt it - I very much doubt it. The people who ask my advice never come back to say thank you. That is one of the many reasons why I am a lonely man. I should cure myself of the wish for conversation. Goodnight."

He tottered out. I took one for the road with the tireless patron, a calvados drinker, whose single observation remained with me despite the difficulties I found in reaching my own bed.

"And odd fellow, that Duvivier," he said. "He has no friends, but those whom one might think should be his enemies have a sort of affection for him. Perhaps respect is a better word."

*   *   *   *   *   *   *

In the morning, to improve my hangover, there was a sheaf of telegrams and a letter awaiting me. They had been forwarded,

120

with unexpected efficiency from Tours and I had the devil's own job sorting out their various dispatch dates. Their style needed no signature for they were all from my partner.

"*Return at once, by fastest aeroplane.*" - "*Stay and await letter, new instructions.*" - "*Shall come myself and deal personally. Meet me best hotel Tours.*" - "*Impossible to leave owing to pressure here but await letter.*"

Finally there was a letter.

"*Dear boy,*" it ran, "*I was going to say that it is not for me to teach you your business, but clearly such is the case. Now do please pay attention. The painting in question may or may not be all we could wish but there is enough background to suggest that it might be - our man Gregory had certainly heard that it was, for example. Now the painting is contemporary with Van Gogh, it is reputed by the ignorant to be by him and it has had only one owner, who seems to have had associations of some sort with the master.*

"*There could be no better set-up, particularly if she is really old and as senile as you suggest. All we are buying is a pedigree and a canvas of exactly the right date. If the painting itself is unsatisfactory (and I have no doubt it is) this is a matter which can be adjusted over here. Forsdyke or Dakers could cover that side of it.*

"*Now do as I say. Swallow your pride and your ill temper and get hold of it at the lowest figure which will force it out of the old beldame. Be back by the 14th when the Cox Martin show opens, for I am too exhausted to cope alone.*

"*Robin.*"

The cumulative effect of all this was to put me into a black fury, for he was clearly in one of his ghastly moods when he changed his mind and his plans every half hour. Even the patron of the café noticed my mood sympathetically. As I tore the messages into little pieces I explained to him that I was giving up work, probably for good, that my partner was a knave and an impossible imbecile into the bargain and that I proposed to stay and sun myself on the square at Les Moinneaux which in my considered opinion was the last centre of civilization left in the world. I would also visit their historic ruin.

"Nothing could be simpler," he said. "My brother-in-law, a fine chauffeur, who drives only very old ladies in his barouche will be free tomorrow. He will drive you around it in great comfort and he knows every one of the forty seven places on the route where it is fitting for a gentleman of your station to refresh himself."

The whole affair arranged itself to perfection. After the expedition I returned to my café tired and controlled, arm in arm with my new friend and mentor. He was, I decided, the best and wisest of men, a natural philosopher and a gargantuan wit. We sat together on the first banquette and communed in a silence which was magnificent in its profundity.

Then I heard the voice. It was low and sibilant and unmistakable. It was Duvivier's and he was sitting just around the corner.

"This man, you say, is impetuous, he drinks too much and he is given to bouts of very bad temper?"

I gestured to my new friend and we listened together in an omnipotent conspiracy.

"It is no great problem," Duvivier continued, "One should always capitalise on weaknesses of this sort. A hundred ideas suggest themselves at once, but one cannot be certain without studying the subject in person. In such a mood a man would be induced to threaten suicide, in front of witnesses? Then, a gas jet left on can work very well. Or perhaps he takes a foolish risk at such a time - then a traffic accident can surely be manipulated, though this is often chancy and the subject might merely be injured and survive. Has he a private supply of liquor - some little secret *cache* of brandy he keeps for himself and believes is unknown to you? Remember that the simplest means are always the best, and capitalise on weakness. Many a satisfactory exit has been arranged by damp sheets, slept in whilst drunk and helped by an icy draft, but unfortunately pneumonia is too easily cured in these days. A little trip wire at the head of a stone staircase is often helpful. Be simple, my friend, be simple, and, if you can, be a long way away should any accident occur."

I could not see Duvivier's companion without exposing myself in one of the wall mirrors, but long before he spoke I knew whose voice it would be. I could even forecast the phrase.

"How madly droll," said my partner, the execrable man Robin. "What a macabre fellow you are. You give me a whole series of quite delicious ideas. I see hours of pleasure ahead of me in the long winter evenings. Not that I'd harm a fly, you know, even if it were an insect privately owned by the friend of a friend, but what stimulating reveries you are providing. I shall apply my imagination - nothing more of course..."

My new found brother and fellow philosopher had not, fortunately, understood a single word of the conversation, for it had been conducted in English, but he responded to my earnest signals and together we sneaked out. The situation did not admit of explanation and we finished the evening in a minor bistro that seemed to be his personal property.

In the morning I delayed my meeting with Robin until I had a couple of cognacs under my belt. The problem had taken me all night and I felt that the solution must be tackled at precisely the right moment.

It arrived at the blissful pause after a good lunch when our business strategy had been finally agreed and the sun drowsed over the empty cobbled square and all the world was at peace.

"About your friend of yesterday evening," I ventured. "Do you know him well?"

Robin had the grace to go a trifle pale and to spill his coffee. I pursued the advantage.

"He is a very odd fellow," I said. "His reputation is pretty formidable. Some say that he is a little mad, others that he is a blackmailer or at least a dealer in black magic. They still believe in witches and wizards in these parts, you know. As it happens I know the truth about him."

"Yes?" said my partner without looking at me.

"He is an informer," I explained blandly. "Some sort of international policeman, I understand. I met him during the war - he's often in London, he tells me, working with Scotland Yard."

Well, at least my dream is broken and this is important to me because I tend to sleep fitfully.

ARMY STORIES

Kane's Doll

At the back of the lorry on the hard sand the puppet danced. She moved slowly with luxurious lazy gestures: the dance of a woman pleasing herself.

The moonlight was as bitter as a blue arc-lamp, making black pools of shadow on the desert where the column of waggons lay dispersed. It was a very still night.

I did not see the man who was watching until I was within a hand's touch: he stood so rigid that he might have been a sack or a piece of canvas hanging from the waggon, nor did he turn his head at my approach.

The puppet danced and the man who was manipulating her strings as he leaned over the tailboard crooned very quietly to her as she twisted and swayed over the caked dust. It was hard to believe she was not human, so lithe and easy were her gestures.

I knew, although I had never seen it before, that this was "Kane's Doll," Everybody in the company knew Kane's Doll or at least had heard of it. But it was not, as you might have expected, a joke. People said "I saw Kane's Doll last night. He's a queer blighter," and left it at that.

It was not often he made her dance. He was not a professional manipulator of marionettes, and the puppet danced only by night. He made no effort to entertain with his toy, and the spectators, if they happened to collect, watched in silence. He was not a man who encouraged conversation and his tongue could whip any would-be wit into discretion. He was tall, thin, gangling and so darkly sallow that even the desert sun could not remove the suggestion that he had been grown underground. He crooned to the dancer in a soft, whining cockney tenor.

If Kane had no friends in the company he had at least a faithful companion, almost, you might say, a slave: the bulky Hicks whose immobile figure seemed petrified as he leaned in the shadows, watching. I recognised him by his strong, thick neck and the vague look he always had of being a stocky edition of Rodin's Thinker.

125

He continued to stand and watch the puppet without moving, although he must have known someone was very close behind him.

Kane was humming, I think, a bolero, though I was never very hot at identifying people like Da Falla or Ravel, and it was the dance rather than the background which cast the spell.

The puppet wheeled and twisted over the dust as lightly as a cat, a living feline creature which was completely sensual. Her face was pale and her mouth wide and carmine, a purple smear in the moonlight. The figure was arrogant, voluptuous, with high breasts clearly indicated in a clinging black corsage. When she turned, the fluted folds of her skirt flared out to reveal long white limbs.

I do not think I have ever seen anything so wholly female in my life. The thing was the quintessence of sex: desire radiated from her as surely and purposefully as an electric current.

The tilt of the waggon cast a black curtain of shade over Kane himself so that only his thin vibrant hands showed as he manipulated the two wooden bars from which dangled the puppet's strings.

She whirled suddenly across the ground, flung out a graceful arm to Hicks, turned, seeming to invite him with every curve of her body and flaunted away. Her gestures were so fluid, so utterly and deliberately abandoned that in the cold deceptive light it was almost impossible to think that we were watching the antics of a doll made of wood, joints, wires, paint and rags.

For a moment or two the creature coquetted at Hicks as she pirouetted and then, with an impudent flouting twist of her body she suddenly drifted open armed into the air and the dark cavern of the lorry. The dance was over.

I heard Kane moving about and then his sharp thin voice.

"I'm packing in now. Get me another blanket."

He vaulted out of the vehicle and disappeared in the direction of his bivvy. Hicks came out of his coma with a jerk of the head, fumbled clumsily in the cab and then followed the other across the stony waste, carrying a blanket with him. They were an odd couple: master and man.

The power lay in the magnetism of the toy. Hicks was obviously fascinated by it, but as he passed me I had one of those sudden clear emotional waves of insight which are as vivid and undeniable as a plain fact stated by a loudspeaker. There was no look of hatred or venom or murder in his hooded eyes as he lumbered by me but I drew in my breath and thanked God that I was not Kane.

At that moment I realised why the men referred to "The Doll" in that curious guarded way of theirs: she danced for two men only, two men who had nothing but an obscene puppet to bind the one to the other.

I did not see the thing any more, although I knew from odd remarks in the canteen that she had danced again. One of these irritating instincts about which one can do nothing was gnawing at me, whispering that something violent would happen to the puppet and its creator. You cannot take action on an uneasy presentiment of this sort. At the same time when it did happen I was cursed with the unhappy feeling that I ought to have done something to try to avert what really looked like pure chance.

You know, if you have been in the desert at all, the horrid black plume of smoke which suddenly curls up from the horizon to mark a crashed plane or a burning vehicle. I was on my way to a detachment when this ominous sight began to creep up into the sky beyond the escarpment ahead of me. The mirage distorted it into fantastic shapes, but I was going on a bearing and the nearer I got the more certain it became that it was one of ours.

As I came over the top I saw the black skeleton of a three-tonner settling for her last collapse onto the sands. She was almost burnt out. A solitary tyre still flickered and stank in the breeze. But the circle of men which I had expected to see around the disaster waiting for me with a cheerful shamefacedness was concentrated about a figure lying on the ground. It was Kane and he was dead.

The story was simple and unlucky enough. His truck had gone up apparently entirely of its own accord, in the way trucks do, when he had been at the cook-house. There had been a dash to save what could be saved, though the flames had caught hold by then. But Kane was not to be stopped. He had made a wild dash towards the back of the waggon, and had been killed, not by burning, but by one of those freakish chances which do sometimes send men to their graves. Some odd ammunition lying in the lorry exploded just as he was climbing in. The first cracker to be touched off had killed him before he had even got his balance above the tailboard, so that he fell back clear of the wreck. Hicks had gone up, regardless of the rest of the fireworks and dragged him clear.

It was just one of those things. To my lot fell the cleaning-up, the Court of Enquiry, the forms, and worst of all, the collection and parcelling of the dead man's personal stuff. I was surprised how little there was. A wrist watch, an A.B.64, some money in a leather case and a very expensive knife. By this time there was a tendency to speak of Kane as if he had been a bit of a hero who had gone back to try to save his truck or what he could of it.

Hicks had helped me to go through the dead man's kit. They had shared one of the bags in common and it had to be sorted. He was quite unemotional.

"His," he said, tossing the knife over; "Mine," as he pushed aside a vest or an old letter.

"Why did he go back?" I asked. "The truck must have been well ablaze by then."

"It was the doll," said Hicks. "He kept her there."

That was the end. The wretched rigmarole of enquiry dragged on and was finally pigeon-holed and dropped out of sight. I think it is true to say that I had very nearly forgotten the doll herself until I was reminded of her rather violently several weeks later.

I was taking a pay parade and not giving overmuch attention to names when a man who had been rather careless in getting his pay book ready let a photograph fall onto the pay table directly under my nose. There was no mistaking the woman in the picture. She was the original of the doll.

"Driver Hicks, sir," said the Sergeant. "One pound."

I picked up the photograph. Hicks stood rigid and wooden before me.

"Yours?"

"She was, sir....once," he said, and stuffed it clumsily into his wallet.

Mr Healy's Day

From his box in the hall old Chatters surveyed the fine marble sweep of the club staircase. For forty years, except when the Harcourt was closed, he had sat there booking the members in and out, controlling the page-boys and turning them into decorous and imperturbable lackeys.

On his right, through a shimmer of swinging glass, he could look down into St. James's; facing him was the bland formality of the memorial panel, on his left the staircase.

The old man was looking over the top of his thick steel-rimmed spectacles, but he knew by the voices who was descending. His eyes were getting very bad those days but his memory was infallible. He knew every member, often their fathers, sometimes even their grandfathers, though it was a bit of a strain getting clear about some of the club's newer acquisitions. He sighed when he thought what the Harcourt might be landed with after the war.

It was Bernaise, one of the older members, who had been on the committee for years and his nephew who were approaching. He recognised the senior member's solemn cough - as if he were perpetually clearing his throat to address a Board of Directors - and the creak of young Mr Bryan's new shoes.

So the boy was going East at last; they all seemed to go that way. The camp kit and the bed-roll and the bright green canvas equipment with its bold printing and fluttering labels lay stacked in the vestibule in front of the leather sarcophagus chair in which Chatters kept doubtful visitors waiting.

There were no page-boys left; the old man unhinged himself slowly and made a gesture towards assisting with the bundles.

"I'll get you a taxi, Mr Bernaise. I expect I can find one." As he had hoped, the young officer stopped him.

"That's all right, Chatters. Everything's laid on. Look, this is good-bye, for the time being. Mind you're still here when I get back......the place wouldn't look right without you, you know."

Suddenly, almost for the first time in a quarter of a century, Bernaise saw the old man clearly. No, the place wouldn't be the same without him. The war had postponed pensioning him off, but he was more like a bit of furniture than a human being. Bernaise looked at him objectively, being aware that there was a moment of emotion impending, and closing his mind to it. A wrinkled, bald old figure with a fuzz of white behind the ears in a seedy tail-coat on which only the bright buttons were respectable. Even the old man's glasses had been repaired with tape, he observed.

Chatters unhooked them with a gnarled hand which was not quite steady.

"I'd like to wish you good luck, Mr Bryan, if I may," he said, "and a safe return. This club needs young gentlemen like you, sir...that is if we're going to carry on."

Bernaise coughed; he had been afraid of something like this. The old man was still talking.

"You know, Mr Bryan, you put me in mind of another young gentleman who used to be a member here years ago. A Mr Healy. You wouldn't remember him, but a very nice young gentleman he was. The club was a very nice place in those days." He straightened his back and turned to Bernaise.

"You'll recall Mr Healy, sir? It was very pleasant in his day."

"Young Healy? Oh, yes. I remember him. A very pleasant feller. Ahem! Yes, those were the days, indeed they were. Well, we must get along. Come on, Bryan, my boy. And- er - Chatters: if there's a telephone call I'll be in to tea."

Within five minutes, only the diminishing swing of the big half-glass door remained to indicate their departure.

Bernaise was ill at ease with his nephew. He was acutely sensible of the discrepancy in their ages and felt old and awkward. On the platform at King's Cross he was gauche with the women porters and irritable when he found he was unable to buy an evening paper.

He stood at the door of the carriage and looked at his nephew. What the devil was he to say to the boy's mother when she rang him at his club? Come to that, what was he going to say to young Bryan himself for the next twenty minutes? Young people were difficult to talk to in the ordinary way; they knew too much and were too inclined to adopt a protective attitude to their elders.

A sudden thought occurred to him - an anecdote, a story he'd never been able to tell before. He cleared his throat.

"You know, Bryan," he said, "it was curious old Chatters should mention that name....Healy. Reminds me of something I thought I'd clean forgotten. Sensation with a few of us at the time, not that it ever came out, of course."

His nephew seemed genuinely amused. "Not a real scandal at the old Harcourt? I can't imagine it."

"Oh, dear me, no! Not a scandal by any manner of means. Just an - er - what shall I say? An embarrassment to the committee. It must have been round about nineteen eleven or twelve when we had a lot of new men in. Old Pennyfeather was one, I remember, and several of his friends. Well, amongst them was this fellow Healy, quite a nice boy, introduced by a group of young feller-me-lads who'd been up at the Varsity with him. Nothing wrong in that, of course, and he behaved himself very well when he used the place, which wasn't often.

"As a matter of fact I hardly noticed the fellow, and I don't suppose I should have done, but one day, during the summer it was....strikes and suffragettes and things going on, you know....Sims, who used to be the secretary came to me with a face as long as your father's tailor's bill and said did I know anything about young Healy?

"I said I knew nothing at all, and what was there to know about him? Well, Sims puffed and blew and made a damn long roundabout thing of it, but the upshot was that Healy was in point of fact the son - the legitimate son, mark you - of old Chatters. He seemed to think that if it came out we'd be made a laughing stock, and so in his long-winded way he wanted me to do something about it."

"What the deuce could you do?" said Bryan. "He was a perfectly good member, wasn't he?"

"Just so," said his uncle. "As you say, a perfectly good member. If it hadn't been for Sims we'd have let it drop, truth or no truth, but he got at the committee in his silly bickering way and I was forced to investigate things.

"It was quite true. Young Healy himself told me all about it. Much more embarrassed that I was, and offered to resign, though of course we wouldn't hear of it. Quite a simple affair, really. His father had a great friend, it seems, who was a commissionaire at the old Imperial, just round the corner - a very swell hotel in those days.

"Now these two cronies made up their minds to send their sons to a decent school, you see. Nothing wrong in that; very laudable, in fact. Johnny at the Imperial was making pots of money and could easily afford it. Chatters couldn't by rights, but scraped his little all together until he did. At all events, to a good school the boys went, and young Healy did very well out of it. He must have had good brains, for he got a scholarship to the Varsity, did very well there, and came up to town with a first-class job and a lot of friends, most of whom, as it happened, were members of the Harcourt. It appears they knew nothing about the boy's father and dragged him into the club practically without his consent."

Bryan was laughing. "A jolly good show. Why on earth shouldn't he be a member?"

"No reason at all," said Bernaise. "That's what most of us thought. We weren't so starchy as you seem to imagine; even in those days there was Bernard Shaw and Keir Hardie and Democracy and all that. No....."

He chuckled. "We were rather amused, as a matter of fact. It was one over on Sims, who was a dreadful old woman, you know. Well, the upshot was that we decided to shut the old bore up, say no more about it, and congratulate ourselves on getting hold of a very decent member. Chatters never guessed we even knew he had a son. I'd forgotten it myself until to-day, come to that."

"What happened to Healy?" said Bryan.

"I dunno," said his uncle. "I went abroad just after that, you know. Didn't see the club for ten years....Well, no last message for anyone? Love to your mother, I suppose? Usual sort of thing?"

Whistles were blowing, men leaning further out of carriages, women in uniform fumbling for handkerchiefs. The engine gave a long-drawn snort, as if feeling its pack loaded.

Bernaise was relieved; really the time was going far more quickly than he had expected. He cleared his throat and blew his nose with unnecessary vigour. Scenes of this sort were remarkably distasteful.

In the vestibule of the Harcourt, old Chatters rubbed his glasses, twitched them comfortably into the ploughed furrow half-way down his nose, and settled in his cane chair. On his left was the staircase, on his right St. James's Street, just as it had always been, always would be. Facing him on the wall was the tablet.

He leaned back to discern the blur through the lenses. "Proud and loving memory....members of this club....Arthur, Lord Amblehurst, Theobald Cranleigh, Hugh James Dale, Captain the Honourable Mostyn Gwynne....Thomas Chatterton Healy....*Dulce et Decorum*...."

He sighed.

Yes, things had been very pleasant in Mr Healy's day.

The Green Box

Graham knew that he was lost as soon as he got to the top of the ridge.

He pulled the jeep to a stop and looked round. There was no trig point, no distant escarpment as there should have been, no guiding hummock; nothing. Nothing at all but sand and rock and scrub.

He turned to his companion contemptuously. "I suppose you've no ideas?"

The man in the flying kit with a three-day beard grinned. "No," he said, "I was off my course before I baled out. Jerry to the north and west, minefields east, soft stuff south. Does that help any?"

Graham drew his breath through his teeth. If he hadn't been a sentimental ass and gone after the descending parachute his own calculations wouldn't be astray and he'd be back in his lines. He wondered now why the devil he'd done it. After all he'd had enough trouble for one trip; his driver killed and all his spare petrol riddled. Fifty miles left in the tank, with luck. The course must be roughly east.

He spun her round and headed away from the wadi: the plain was as flat as a table and quite featureless. It was infuriating and the more he thought about it the less he liked it.

The sergeant pilot began to whistle *We are Wanderers of the Wasteland*, a tune he had always disliked because of the memories it carried with it. He stopped the Jeep.

"Listen," he said, "What's your name?"

"Cook."

"Well, Cook, if you want to stay in this truck, don't make such an infernal noise. Do you know *anything* about this bit of country?"

The pilot rubbed his stubble, "Not really," he said. "No more than you. If we could find something definite to work on could you locate yourself?"

"I might," said Graham icily. "And what do you suggest we do about discovering some recognisable object?"

Cook stood up unsteadily in the confined space of the truck.

"Go to your left a bit. There's something. May be just a wreck, but it might give us a line. It looked to me like a pranged crate."

Graham winced. He was as meticulous with his mind as with his fingernails. He disliked slang, he disliked being lost and he disliked the man at his side. Nor did he approve of people with eyes sharper than his own.

He drove in silence. The wrecked plane lay in a small clay pan so that only the tail jutted above the horizon. A recent wreck he decided. It still smelt faintly of burnt rubber and nothing appeared to have been touched.

They got out and walked over to it together. It had Allied markings and was in two parts, the engine having been thrown some distance beyond. The clay was only half hard beneath its shiny surface and they reached the wing- tip gingerly.

"Does this mean anything to you?" said Graham.

Cook considered. "Not a lot," he admitted. "A pursuit ship of some sort. New on me - might be one of those American jobs. You can't keep up to date on everything."

"So it would appear," said Graham. "And I cannot see that its presence helps in the slightest degree. Have you anything to propose before we move on?"

Cook did not reply. He was casting a professional eye over the dashboard instruments; half in and half out of the cockpit. A queer job, a very queer job, he decided.

Presently he extracted himself with an object in his hand. It was a green oblong metal case, not unlike a cash box, with a metal handle on the top of it. "Let's take a shufti at this. I reckon the pilot baled out and left it behind. It's not first aid or his lunch basket."

He put it down on the wing and began to play with the catch which was of some patent design. Graham took it from him and prized it up with his two thumbs. The top flew up on a spring.

Inside were a number of packets each bound in a strip of white paper. He pulled one out and broke the band.

Cook whistled. "Blimey, we've found something all right."

Each packet contained notes, brand new bank notes, fresh from the press. A pound a time. A fortune.

The evening wind played with the broken band, lifted the upper sheet of precious paper into the air.

Graham grabbed at it. "We'll get on," he said and snapped the box shut. "Another hour's driving still left and if we strike no landmark we'll wait for first light. We will discuss this matter in the morning, if you please. There's nothing else in the cabin of the plane is there?"

"If you mean boodle," said Cook, "No." He was about to add

that there was a great deal to interest him there, but thought better of it. Queer instruments for an allied plane. It was all wrong. He continued to whistle as they drove off.

The brief desert twilight dramatised the sky until the clouds looked like an over-filtered photograph. They stopped. Graham shook the Jeep, examined the petrol guage and made a calculation: twenty-five miles.

To the north there was a faint rumbling of guns, remote as traffic heard from a high building. Then flashes began to flick the horizon like summer lightning.

The two men got out, stretched, rummaged for food. Graham arranged his own blankets and after some thought handed one to Cook.

"That's all there is," he said "You must do the best you can. I intend to sleep now. Have the goodness to rouse me if you wake first."

He did not sleep but lay considering the green box. It must be worth ten thousand pounds, he decided. A fortune if he could get away with it. Ten thousand would see him through, settled for years to come.

But there was Cook to think of. Suppose he wanted a share; suppose he wanted to explain the find to somebody? He reviewed the situation methodically. Cook did not know his name or his unit. The Jeep had no markings. To all intents the man was a total stranger, a stranger whose life he had probably saved out of the goodness of his heart.

With twenty-five miles still in his tank he could certainly strike something: one of our patrols would be sure to pick him up.

He sat up and looked at the stars. His prismatic compass would give him a bearing. He'd risk it. Cook grunted in his sleep and turned over on the sand.

The Jeep stood on a gentle slope. Graham folded his blankets silently, took off the brake and pushed. She moved easily down the incline. At a hundred yards from the sleeping figure he took a bearing on a star and started up. The night closed in upon him in indigo folds.

* * * * * * *

The dawn wind was blowing a thin mist of sand waist high when Cook awoke. The situation was clear, however. He decided he'd been a bit of an ass to expect anything else from his ex-rescuer. That box was too tempting to produce any other result. Well, he'd have to walk it.

He set off grimly, following the trail of the Jeep's tyres in the sand. It was quite easy even in the bad going the ground offered.

Ten miles saw him to the top of a ridge where the desert was hard and stony and the wheel tracks lost themselves in an outcrop of flat rocks and scrub. In the wadi beyond was a mass of trails, tanks, Brens, sand grips, every wheel mark in the world, spread out like a diagram of a railway junction.

That at least meant civilisation again. He plunged forward.

As the wadi turned, a shout brought him to a standstill. A man was waving to him frantically. Behind him were trucks, moving figures in the mist.

He stood still and waited whilst one of them came forward by a devious route.

"Hold everything, chum. You're on a field." As the man came up to him he saw a burly Royal Engineers sergeant with a broken nose and a grin.

"You're lucky, chum. We stopped you just on the edge of it. Jerry's very smart the way he slips the old mine in these days. Look what's happened to this chap."

They came up to the main group and it was clear enough. Graham's jeep lay upside down and what was left of Graham lay beneath, a grim twisted travesty of man and machine. Kit, blankets, and equipment were scattered over the ground. Of the green box there was no sign but as the wind suddenly eddied it carried with it to Cook's feet a single slip of stiff paper. A pound note.

He grabbed at it and his rescuers began to laugh.

"A nice little souvenir for you, chum," said the sergeant, "the whole area is covered with them. We can't quite make it out. They're queer sort of notes - wouldn't deceive a child really. We think perhaps they're what somebody's going to use for money when he gets to the Delta. Have a look at the watermark."

Cook examined his trophy. No, by broad daylight it wouldn't deceive a child. He held the note carefully to the light. The watermark was a swastika.

The Genuine Article

The technique of the pick-up in Petronis' (Old Swiss Firm) Cairo Garden Cafe is not difficult. You sit at your table under the trees until something catches your eye. When you get the high-sign from the girl you either move over, or if you're more discreet, go into the patisserie and wait for her to come along to join you. What happens then is up to you.

My attention was drawn to all this in rather a curious way, because the cafe is pleasant and comfortable and sunny, and really very respectable even if one does see every type and nationality in creation taking their morning coffee under the big coloured umbrellas. It was the sun in fact which gave me the tip-off. A sudden winking spark in my eye suggested that somebody was flashing a mirror in my face. I looked about but could see nothing very likely and had almost forgotten about it, because it was the last day of leave, when it happened again.

People were gossiping and laughing in French, Polish, Arabic, English and even Italian - it was like the BBC's old *Café Continental* come to life - but no one seemed very interested in me. Not enough to signal to me with a mirror.

Then I tumbled to it. In the opposite corner, which the sun blinds just missed so that a dusty golden shaft of yellow light picked out the colours, was a girl. She had diamond earrings.

Once spotted, you couldn't miss them. They winked and flashed as she turned her head and the little flicks of brilliance leapt about the garden like a gala night at the *Palais de Danse*. Real watery diamonds.

They didn't seem quite right on the girl who was wearing them. She was blonde, faded and painted in a sort of half-hearted way. Her clothes, too, were a muddle, almost as if she hadn't been able to make up her mind whether she wanted to be mistaken for the Vicar's wife or just a tottie looking for a man. She had a smart little hat worn at the wrong angle, a costume which ought to have been tailor-made, but wasn't, and a really appalling red patent leather handbag, much too big.

I must have stared pretty hard for she caught my eye and gave

137

me a half-hearted smile, a routine kind of thing, and then looked away. Presently she turned her head again, bared her teeth mechanically for a second or two and then picked up the dreadful bag and began messing about with her make-up. Her diamonds flashed.

There is no mistaking that kind of smile: it says "The goods are here if you want them. And for sale." Yet it was half-hearted. I think if it hadn't been for those incredibly live earrings I wouldn't have gone across.

Close to, she looked her age. She was very refined. She said. "Oew, hew naice to see you again. I wondered if you would remember me. Do sit down, won't you?"

I'd never set eyes on her in my life before, but this was plainly her standard conversational gambit. We went through a good deal of this patter until I felt I was almost part of stale old Music Hall act. We drank iced coffee and her thin hands against the tall white cup drew attention to the chipped varnish on her finger nails. The conversation was remarkably stereotyped. Whenever I strayed from what appeared to be my correct lines I came up against a brick wall. She knew just what I was expected to say, word for word. Progress was slow.

"Your earrings are attractive," I said at last. "Real diamonds?"

She unscrewed one and held it in the palm of her hand. "I don't often wear them," she said. "They're not very nice for the mornings and they never bring me any luck. They're not real, you know - just cheap fakes. I don't know why I keep them, really."

It didn't seem possible that she could be as dumb as all that. The thing in her hand flashed and glinted as if an electric bulb lay behind it.

"That's a real diamond," I said. "You can't mistake them. The little stones round it are sapphire chips. They must have cost a lot of money."

She sighed. "You're quite wrong. They're paste. Cheap rotten paste, you know. They were a present to me from a gentleman friend a long time ago."

"My dear good girl," I said, "don't talk rot. I'm not a jeweller but I give you my solemn word they're genuine."

"Oh, no." She shook her head and looked at me with great bovine pale blue eyes. "They couldn't be. Reelly they couldn't. My friend gave them to me and I didn't think it was very kind of him, being a gentleman. I hardly ever wear them, because they don't go with my costumes. They're not real, you see. Look."

She began to fumble in her tawdry bag, which seemed to contain half the rubbishy powder puffs in the world, and brought with it a whiff of cheap scent.

"Look, here's the box they came in. I've always kept it because it was the last present he gave me - my friend, I mean. It's Marks and Spencers, you see, so I know I'm right."

She put the shabby little thing down on the table.

"I don't know why I should tell you this," she said. "reelly I don't, but my friend, well, he was very kind to me generally, and then when he got into trouble he went and did that."

"Trouble?" I asked.

Her pale eyes widened. "Oh yes, terrible trouble. He used to laugh at me and make jokes I couldn't understand. But I told him he'd get into trouble in the end."

She unscrewed the other earring and put the two blazing stones back in their pitiful container.

"I was quite right," she said. "I'm not often right, but I was that time. It was the last time I saw him, too - that's why I keep them, reelly. He came to my flat. Such a nice place - I'm sure it must have cost him a lot of money. 'Jenny,' he said, 'I'm finished'. He used to call me Jenny, though I call myself Yola now, being more chic. 'What's the matter?' I said. 'Here's my last present for you,' he said, 'and that's a cheap one.' Then he laughed in his funny way, just as if he wasn't laughing at all, reelly, and went away. I never saw him again, of course."

Somehow she didn't seem quite that type. She ought to have been silly and loyal and not wholly mercenary. I said something of the sort.

"Oh I couldn't," she said. "You see, he was terribly famous and important and when he went to prison with his name in the papers and all that, I just couldn't see him. The rent on the flat ran out and so I had to find something else. That's how I wandered out here. One job after another, and nothing coming of it."

It was nearly a year to the day before I saw Cairo or Petronis' Garden Cafe (Old Swiss Firm) again. When I fetched up there my companion was a fellow called Sanders who was in one of those obscure Army departments which have just a touch of Scotland Yard about them.

We found a table under one of the same old umbrellas and after the normal exchange of gossip he began to show off.

"You see that old buffer over there - the one in the dirty white suit? He must be worth a million. Used to be the biggest black marketeer going. Got out of the business just in time. We're watching that fat woman in the red blouse, too. She's some sort of agent. The fellow in the tarbush with the big moustache is..."

Sitting in the same corner as when I had last seen her was the girl whose name was Jenny but thought it more chic to call herself

Yola. She had a companion at her table, a sergeant whose face I could not see.

"Know anything about that girl?" I enquired.

Sanders turned his head. "Not a lot," he said, "beyond what you can see for yourself of course. But - just a moment - the chap with her....that's funny."

He paused and watched until Jenny's friend looked up. "Yes, I thought so. Now that fellow's a character. His name is Calthorpe - remember? The financier who crashed, like Hatry and all the rest, just before the war."

"He doesn't look like a financier now," I said. "How's he doing in the Army?"

"Pretty well," said Sanders. "As you know, he took a bit of a rap and mostly for other people. Been in the Army three years now. Two gongs and he seems to be a hell of a fellow."

He went on talking, but I lost the thread of it all, for I could not take my eyes off the couple. Presently she opened her bag and took out the little box which contained the earrings. As I watched she put them on. Sergeant Calthorpe called the *safragi* and they got up to go.

They passed close to my table and they were laughing together, quite oblivious of everything else in the world. I don't think I've ever seen a woman look happier - certainly not in Petronis' Garden Cafe (Old Swiss Firm).

Old School Type

Mystery, if you like a dramatic word, was about the best to describe Ffolliatt. His A.B.64 gave his full name as Charles Hilary Windham Ffolliatt and added that he had once been 'Independent'. Even with a mouthful like that he didn't rate a lance stripe, which was one of the curious things about him. He was good looking, able and what is called 'nicely spoken'. By reason of these attributes he finally gravitated into the office of H.Q. Platoon.

Here he came directly under my own eagle eye, but try as I might I could discover very little about him. Obviously he had money, excellent taste and a natural easy manner. Whilst he was not bone lazy, he contrived to do a bare minimum very efficiently. But that was all. He did not want a stripe and was not prepared to exert himself in that direction.

The company office consisted of a canvas lean-to at the side of a three-tonner, since we were, for excellent reasons, fully mobile. Ffolliatt and I shared a table in this drafty dusty hovel for twelve long desert months. Yet at the end of them I knew almost as little about him as at the start.

In the comparative peace which followed the second Msus Stakes the company breathed a trifle more easily, and began to reorganize. We had among other surprises an intake of several warriors fresh from the Delta. The Sergeant-Major, that mighty administrator, distributed them through the platoons with an impartial pen.

To us in H.Q. fell Messrs Williams, Walker, Waites, White and Wendon, five tired, crumpled and un-exciting bodies who were thankful to be wheeled off to the cookhouse. I watched them go and ran through the list of their civil trades which lay before me.

"An undertaker, two clerks, a baker's roundsman and a chemist," I said. "What are we going to do with this lot, Ffolliatt?"

For the first time in our association he seemed put out. "I wonder, Sir," he said, "if I might ask you a favour."

"Anything you like."

He paused and offered me one of the very expensive cigarettes he used to have sent him regularly from Cairo.

"It's about Walker," he said at last, "one of those new men; the short gingery fellow with the freckles. Probably you had no occasion to remark him, Sir. Could he be transferred, say, to D Platoon?"

Now D Platoon was detached for reasons best known to the Powers and we saw very little of them. They were supposed to have special duties and were popularly reputed to do nothing at all.

"What's wrong with this chap Walker?" I enquired. "Do you know him?"

Again Ffolliatt hesitated. "I'd hardly admit to his acquaintance," he said. "But I recognise him. A curious type. He claims - or rather claimed - to have been to a good school."

"Yours, for example?"

He smiled in his slow, easy way and took a deep puff at his cigarette. "I see I shall have to tell you about Master Walker. In confidence of course, Sir?"

I agreed.

"It's some years since I had the distinction of meeting this gentleman," he began. "But I have excellent reason to remember him, though I only saw him once. We used to have a Founder's Day at school. Theoretically it was in honour of the sacred memory of Edward the Confessor, but it worked out as a party for Old Boys. You know the kind of thing - cricket match, re-union, speeches, lots and lots of beer, pleasant green lawns, white flannels and strawberries and cream."

He sighed.

"A glorious time. One of the dormitories was turned over to a few of us who wanted to stay on late and we used to motor back to town in the morning. Great days. That was when I met Walker. He was one of the few who stayed on one occasion. He just drifted in and seemed to get pleasantly pickled along with the rest. I even remember him asking me what house I'd been in and if I knew a bloke called Guffy Randall, which was a pretty safe bet because he was expected to captain the Gentlemen that year and was one of our best and brightest. We sang and laughed and drank and swapped all the classic stories and went to sleep very late. We were pretty late in the morning, too. All except Walker, that is.

"Mr Walker was up and away with the lark and he took with him the contents of all our pocket books. It must have been quite a tidy sum."

"Are you sure about this?" I said. "It's a bit stiff after ten years or so."

"It was Walker right enough," said Ffolliatt. "It seems the police knew quite a bit about him. He made a specialty of Old Boys' gatherings. Easy enough, I suppose. You just say you were in a different house or a different year if you're taxed. And you stay sober when others are less well advised. I don't know if he was ever caught. I think he'd do better in D Platoon."

I was inclined to agree, although I had some difficulty in persuading the C.S.M. to see my point of view without revealing my reasons for an exchange.

To D Platoon however, went Walker and they promptly fulfilled H.Q.'s most dismal prophesies by seeing we got the worst of the bargain. A lazy ungrateful independent hoity-toity lot were D Platoon, and they were asking to be straightened out.

Straightening out, in fact, was in the air. As a result of several changes I found myself bumping along a wretched track only a week later to perform this unenviable task. D was about as pleased to see me as I was to see them. A long period of independence had made strangers from H.Q. unwelcome.

I was made aware of unsurmountable reasons against any change and fobbed off with a multitude of minor problems. D had dug itself in and had no intention of altering its habits.

"I wonder, Sir," said the Sergeant, with a calculating eye on my notes, "If you could help one of new chaps; Walker, his name is."

I knew that this was just a delaying action, but my curiosity to see this ingenious person was strong. He was sent in to me.

Walker's problem was really very simple. His mother was ill and he wanted to send her some money. Being a new man, his credits were a bit uncertain. A dozen hands had been at work on his pay book and the result was chaotic.

He stood in front of me, hopeful, worried and puzzled. The sun had bleached his hair and intensified his freckles. A rather pathetic figure; not much like my idea of a crook.

His trouble took some time to adjust - longer, I think, than even the Sergeant had hoped. He had a wife and two children in London, but his mother lived in the country.

"At Crowshurst, Sir," he said. "Near the big school, you know."

The temptation was too much for me.

"Do you know the School?" I asked.

"Oh, yes, Sir," he said, "very well indeed. My mother used to work there, and so did I, come to that. I was born and bred there as you might say."

He hesitated and twisted his cap in his hands. "I don't wish to be rude Sir, but I think I recognise you. Weren't you in Mr King's house, there?"

I had to admit it. The mischief was out, so I plunged on.

"I suppose you don't remember a fellow called Ffolliatt, who's now in H.Q. Platoon?"

"Ffolliatt?" he said. "No Sir. There was no one of that name there in my time. I was call-boy for the Headmaster for years and I reckon to remember everyone's name - yours for example, Sir."

It was quite a relief. It meant that Ffolliatt and I shared a secret, though from rather different angles.

Thinking it over, I managed to recall him quite clearly at that old school party. We were, in fact, in the dormitory together on the fatal and scandalous occasion when the pocket books were stolen.

* * * * * * *

But it was Ffolliatt who had left us at the crack of dawn.

TALES OF UNEASE

The Evil Eye of Brother Polidor

EVERY secret admirer of rascals has a favourite character. Some settle for Casanova the great lover, or Cagliostro the sorcerer. For me it has always been Brother Polidor, a comparatively obscure monk reputed to have the true secret of the evil eye and to have received the formula from the Devil himself.

Brother Polidor was burnt at the stake in the year that also saw the death of Joan of Arc. This was in the great square at Cacharel, and his crimes included heresy, blasphemy, and of course communication with the Devil in person.

At that time both towers of the Abbey looked down on the scene, for this was before the *Tire-Bouchon*, the famous Twisted Tower of Cacharel, crashed to the ground to emphasise another death, that of the last of the real Kings of France. And if you ask local opinion, so ended the greatness of France, for both happenings were contrived by the Prince of Darkness.

There is of course some doubt about Brother Polidor. The Abbé of Cacharel, writing some twenty years later, says, "He gave up his spirit almost before the kindling wood had begun to crackle or the smoke enveloped him."

Writing from Mont St Michel in 1462, Brother Francis, his confessor, said, "Of the manner of Brother Polidor's death there is much discourse, some holding that the Devil himself carried him out of the smoke, meaning to burn him eternally as it should please him. Though earthly fire may not have consumed him, his spirit seemed to depart before the brands had flamed, perhaps by reason of a poison or the executioner's dagger used in mercy on a most unworthy sinner. The pile did burn a day and a night in despite of foul weather and no part of him, no, not so much as his heart, remained."

Later in the Chronicle, the old man says, "Of Brother Polidor's black chest, said to contain a treaty with the Devil and much else that did offend, no remnant was ever found and that in defiance of a great search by the Abbé of Cacharel himself.

"Polidor was said to open it only in the dark, for what it contained was writ in letters of fire from the pit. Yet though fire doubtless had him at the last, for his proven sins, many say he did not die at Cacharel but escaping by aid of the executioner or the Devil travelled to another kingdom. This I do doubt."

In the records of the municipality of Cacharel, the entry runs, "The ex-communicate Monk Polidor was this day burnt at the stake having been delivered into the hands of the civil authority by the powers spiritual as guilty of sorcery, blasphemy, heresy, and communication with the Devil. Wood supplied by foresters to the Abbey. Executioner: Master Gaston of Cacharel."

There is no more contemporary material about Brother Polidor in his death or his disappearance, but he established a small legend, nurtured by charlatans for a credulous public. Every confidence trickster and apothecary in that line of business since then, including Cagliostro himself, has claimed to know the secrets of Brother Polidor's black chest. They assumed not unnaturally that he was looking for the philosopher's stone.

He lived in an age when every landowner of pretension had his own shady alchemist charged with research into the transmutation of metals and the elixir of life.

Polidor has some success still recorded to his credit in the matter of plating metals, before plating as such was understood. He used saturated acid solutions, but his results were not permanent for nothing remains of them.

His local reputation was as the possessor of the evil eye.

Women lost unborn children, cattle died, and crops failed, so he was informed against, prosecuted, and sent to the burning. It is a grim but not uncommon story, for in those days the Devil danced one New Year's Eve in the very square that saw Polidor's farewell, and left footprints in the snow, upon pavements and roofs alike, to prove his presence. In the forests of Cacharel he frequently played the fiddle and was known to hold court with followers not of this world.

And of course he pulled down the *Tire-Bouchon*—the Twisted Tower of Cacharel.

He was here, there, and everywhere, and probably one man in three could swear to having met him face to face.

The whole story would not be of anything but antiquarian interest except for one item which gives rise to modern speculation. The municipal record again is the source.

"Paid to Master Hugh de Soissons, woodcarver and clerk, for the keep of two children, sons of Gaston de Charel, Executioner: two silver pieces. The father having been seized by the fiend on the feast of St Etienne, 1431, and the children starving."

It means in fact that within a fortnight of Brother Polidor's demise, the one man who was really close to him at that fatal moment took to his heels and was never seen again.

Brother Polidor, as I have said, has always been my favourite minor figure in the great tapestry of French history. He rates so few, so very few, personal stitches, but he has an individual look in his eye that promises excitement, could one but force him back as it were out of time and make him give up his secret.

He was never burnt, I decided, but escaped with the connivance of Gaston the Executioner: there must have been a pact between them, and pacts contain mutual considerations. The black chest of Brother Polidor must be the answer, and if one knew what it contained one would have the key to the mystery. The evil eye? The elixir of life? Perhaps they solved that ancient riddle and are still living, a couple of wandering Christians, travelling the face of the earth in an eternal search for death.

Only at Cacharel is there any real substance to the legend. The house of Gaston de Charel, the Executioner, still stands in the square, for his two boys, it seems, prospered as craftsmen and established a line running through many generations. They were workers in metal, making lanterns, sconces, and sometimes, in more delicate generations, jewellery.

Within living memory, my own for example, the old shop under the high grey stone house had a board which said:

BONNARD PERE ET FILS
Successors to Decharel Frères

and old Bonnard, a great-grandson of Bonnard fils, I believe, carried on a ramshackle business making heavy and peculiarly ugly costume jewellery until quite recently.

When I was last there, only two years ago, the shop had been sold to a chain of cheap jewellers who were gutting the ground floor in order to install an exotic bow window, complete with neon lights. It was a melancholy business for the shopfitters destroyed some fine stone mouldings, and nothing I could say was successful in rousing the conscience of the local authorities. I contented myself by making a friend of the foreman in charge and purchasing from him a couple of heavy carved stones.

He also brought me, secretly to my hotel, a piece of broken early eighteenth-century jewellery found under a floorboard. I paid over the odds for it in aid of our friendship and in the prudent hope of favours to come, and in this I was rewarded.

His name was Jean-Louis Poupart and he had a shambling walk almost like an ape's, which made him seem undersized, an effect increased by a very low forehead, cropped hair, and a perpetually secretive look. Despite this he was not entirely stupid and he had at least the sense to perceive in me a source of revenue. On this occasion he sidled up to me so furtively that he was sitting beside me at my cafe table in the square and pulling gently at my arm before I noticed him. It was late in the evening and I had started my final *fine à l'eau.*

"My friend," he said, "I think you should walk across to the shop. Not at this moment, but when you have finished your cognac. Come by the back in the Rue des Epiceries. I have found something."

He was shaking all over with excitement, even his face twitched.

"Be very careful," he whispered, "no one must see you. If you have a torch, bring it with you. Wait ten minutes to be sure you are alone. I have found treasure, great wealth without a doubt." His words were hissing out of his mouth like a faulty tap. "It will mean thousands of francs, a fortune—you'll see—you're an educated man, a scholar, you'll show me how to deal with this, how to keep it safe for me—when to sell it in the market. Don't make a sound—I'll let you in."

He shambled off with such an air of melodrama that had there been anyone interested at that hour they must have remarked his crablike scuffle into the shadows. All the same he vanished within seconds, having infected me with a great part of the excitement which was shaking him.

I paid my dues as casually as I might, collected a torch from my hotel, and did my best to walk unobtrusively.

Poupart was waiting for me, a shadow within a shade. He locked and bolted the door behind me, although the whole of the house stood open, a wilderness of planks, paint pots and scaffolding. We moved silently down a greasy passage which I could feel rather than see, and turned sharply through a door which my nose told me led to the cellars. Here I was allowed my torch and in the long vaulted room lanterns were burning.

Now I can give no valid reason for feeling frightened, except that the place was cold and the shadows in this incredible junk room were grotesque as if they were thrown by a dozen warring spiders suddenly immobilised. I remember a great collection of old travelling-trunks, heaps of bottles, a carpenter's bench, a lathe of sorts, and various pulleys, wheels, and decaying ropes.

We ploughed our way through this chaos to a wall where evidently the wine cellar had once been, for there were little arched caverns barely high enough to stand in. I could just detect that the last of these had been bricked up many years before, and it was to this far corner that Poupart was moving.

He picked up his two lanterns and stood for a moment with one in each hand, breathing heavily so that garlic mingled fiercely with the stink of decay. Then he placed them on the floor and began to move the packing-cases which stood against the far wall. They had been hiding a newly-made gap in the brickwork, a jagged black shape, which curiously enough resembled a question mark.

"It's inside there—the treasure—I've seen it," he muttered, and went to work with a crowbar.

The bricks prised away easily enough. Finally he stood back and let me flash my torch inside. It was a smelly dark cavity. I thought it empty, but Poupart's eyes were keener than mine.

"There it is," he said. "Just a few more bricks and I can get at it. Stand back."

There was certainly a box of some sort inside, but it was so grey with dust that I had mistaken it for a slab of stone. Within a minute he had wriggled half his torso into the hole and dragged it out. He pulled the box slowly towards him, gripped it, and with a final effort wriggled himself back as I pulled on his legs.

At last it lay on the floor between us. For a moment or two we eyed it warily as if it might bite us.

"There's nothing else inside the hole," said Poupart. "This is it—the treasure. Open it. Without doubt it is full of gold."

I did not answer him directly, but found a piece of sacking and began to clean it gently. There was no doubt in my mind that this was indeed Brother Polidor's black chest, but as I removed the centuries of dust certain peculiarities began to emerge.

In the first place it was not one wooden box but two, side by side, and they were clamped together by a flat rib of greenish black metal, probably brass or copper. On this strip was a handle rather like that of a modern petty cashbox. I lifted it cautiously, but it broke in my hand.

Poupart whispered, "Open it, open it."

"Not here," I said. "This must be done very carefully. Bring it to my room, and bring some tools, a chisel and so on."

He was in a cold sweat of excitement, suspicion and greed fighting for a decision. It was difficult to convince him that it would be criminal to smash the casing for its contents. But there was something very peculiar about the precise and careful clamping of the treasure that made me equally obstinate. In the end I won by promising to buy the boxes separately for myself regardless of what they might contain, provided they were intact.

We agreed after great argument to meet in my hotel room. At this point, for I had time to pause and consider, I blame myself bitterly for not solving the matter and so avoiding a tragic mistake, but like Poupart I was obsessed with preconceived ideas. Just as he was certain of finding gold, so was I confident of finding documents that would make footnotes to history. We were both, of course, completely wrong.

When the discovery at last was placed on my rickety hotel-bedroom table carefully covered with newspapers, Poupart reassured himself that the windows were shuttered and the door locked. He laid out a handful of tools and we considered the problem. It was not very intricate and with a little persuasion the tired metal was lifted away and I was able to look at the two boxes separately. They were of exactly the same size, made of ebony, but one had what looked like a glass boss sunk into the centre of the face which had been against its neighbour.

Poupart, his teeth chattering, said, "A jewel—a diamond!"

Even then I did not understand, except to suspect that this indeed was the evil eye of Brother Polidor.

My fellow conspirator was so anxious to pull the thing apart that, to divert him, I decided to concentrate on the second box which promised to be easier to open. It had a hinged lid, very beautifully fitted, and a brass catch on the protected face still in working order. With remarkably little persuasion it opened.

Inside were half a dozen thin flat metal oblongs fitted snugly into grooves which held them separate and rigid.

Poupart, seeing that they were not the treasure he was expecting, gave a hissing sigh of disgust; but I, like a fool, began to pry further. Gingerly I pulled at one of the metal rectangles and after some little difficulty I lifted it out.

It was dark and smooth and had the appearance of gun metal, but as I turned it to the light I saw that there was an impression on the surface. An engraving, I decided, or some form of mezzotint. By slanting it gently it was possible to see what it represented.

Here I got my first glimpse of the truth. The view, for that was what it undoubtedly was, showed the square of Cacharel dominated as ever by the Abbey. But this was Cacharel with a difference, it was Cacharel as it had appeared five centuries ago. Cacharel as seen by Brother Polidor himself. Here was the Abbey, still recognisable, but both towers were standing, and the higher of the two was the almost mythical Twisted Tower, the incredible *Tire-Bouchon* itself.

I held it closer and closer and suddenly realised that the image was fading. At last, too late, I had in my hand the secret of Brother Polidor.

He had made a camera.

What I was holding in my hand and destroying for all time was a sensitised photographic plate, which I was stupidly gawping at under a bright light.

It was too late to remedy matters. I switched off the light and put back the metal sheet as best I might, but the damage was done. No one apart from myself will ever be able to say, "I have seen the Twisted Tower—the incredible *Tire-Bouchon.*"

It was very difficult to explain to Poupart what I was up to, and just what our discovery might be worth.

Now, a full year after our adventure, Brother Polidor's evil eye has been officially examined and placed in the appropriate museum. The secret is out. It is a primitive but remarkably accurate camera invented centuries before its time, with a beautiful and accurate handmade lens. It is the forerunner of the daguerreotype, but it would seem that the little monk had not found how to preserve the plates against light, though he may possibly have known how to inspect them through red glass. This is technical speculation and I believe the experts are still working on it, for we do not know how he sensitised the metal.

No impression was found on the remaining plates and possibly some of them were never exposed, or perhaps—and I am haunted by this fear—I destroyed them by exposing them under that merciless bulb. This dreadful speculation occupies all my nightmares and I shall never be free of it.

That is why I must add a postscript, which is no sort of story for scientists. The truth is that Poupart also pulled out a plate that evening and was gaping at it just as stupidly as I, when I realised what we were doing. I snatched it out of his hand and had just one instant's glimpse of it before it vanished for ever.

It was a photograph, quite unmistakably, of the Devil. Of this I am sure, because it is not a thing about which to make a mistake. One cannot dilate upon evil, or even describe it: it is a matter for feeling and personal recognition.

You can if you wish take my word for it. It is no use asking the scientists, the historians, the theologians, or even Poupart himself. But it is certain that he was as shaken as I at the time by this frightening thing. They have all talked him out of it and he now agrees that it was a close-up of one of the gargoyles on the Tower of Cacharel.

But I, and Brother Polidor, know better than that.

Dead Ringer

You can't mistake an angry man for a human being in any other mood. This particular example was clearly just about to smash my jaw for me, which would be most unseemly conduct in the back office of an expensive art gallery, especially one which is only just off Bond Street.

Charles Wisbeck jutted his face much too close to mine, so that I could see he had all the signs - white nostrils, twitching muscles and two little spots of colour on his cheek bones. He is one of those artists with a "damn-you-get-out-of-my-way-I'm-special" look; a very attractive one to some women.

"Now just what in Hell do you think you're up to?" he said. "And the story had better be good."

This was the moment to play for extra time. He was beaded with cold sweat and there was a dribble of saliva at the corner of his mouth. I slid my chair back, beyond the reach of his fist and put on my best discreetly polished manner.

In my smoothest Bond Street voice I said, "What's the trouble, Charlie? It's two months since I've seen you. I've just sold four of your best canvases for a lot of money. Goldrophwasser is interested in you as a possible successor to Picasso and you come in here as if you were prepared to wreck the joint."

He lowered his head like a bull about to charge. "You know damn well what the trouble is. It's that canvas in the window. Here am I, just about to make your fortune and you have the blazing insolence to display a damned copy of my stuff."

"You're off the beam, you know," I said. "The man is an entirely separate painter - not an imitator, but a chap working along your line of thought, which is nobody's copyright. The painting has been in the window a fortnight and nobody - yet - has offered to smash valuable plate glass except you. What," I repeated, "is wrong with the painting?"

Charles drew a deep breath, like a man preparing to lift a ton of lead with his bare hands.

"I'll tell you - precisely - what is wrong with it," he said, and

153

the words came slowly in awkward jerks out of his mouth. "Look at this."

He had come in to my tiny office in such a flurry that I had not noticed the parcel under his arm. He now picked it up, smashing the brown paper away from its contents with an erratic hand.

It was a landscape in his best style, the paint still fresh and informing the nostrils with the tang of oil and studios which I still find exciting. He placed it very carefully on the chair bang in front of my desk.

There was a long pause: I, trying to think of a decent man-to-man escape route and he almost enjoying his own fury.

"Well, what about it?" he said at last, and in the tone of a strong man about to filch your last cigarette on a desert island.

The canvas on the chair, a typical Wisbeck study, was unfortunately almost identical with the painting which has been in my window for two whole weeks, signed 'Andrew MacDermot'. It was so like a Charlie Wisbeck (I admitted secretly) as to be asking for trouble. I must now make my own position clear, because I knew very well the kind of trouble to be expected.

Charles, I must explain, is one of our best new painters; a man who can mix this ultra modern abstract stuff - which I frankly don't understand - with strong factual representation. For example, if he were to paint Waterloo Bridge you would certainly recognise it, yet it would be so oddly presented that looked at from a purely outside viewpoint it might well be a pattern in oilpaint of the most advanced type - splashes and bicycle tyre prints and what are called 'incidentals' all over the place. Third programme stuff or the kind of thing you get every so often in the B.B.C.'s 'Monitor' series.

There it sat on my chair, blazing with half dry colour, the exact replica of the thing in the window.

Something had to be done to break the suffocating silence.

"Look, Charlie, "I said. "My partner, Robin, bought that thing in the window. I warned him that his discovery was a chap painting very much in your style."

I knew this was the understatement of the century but to my surprise Charles became almost human. With infinite care in the selection of words, coupled with the tolerance one sought to extend to a very stupid child (instead of hitting him sharply across the face) he spoke.

"Now listen to me, Philip. You know and I know that by some freak of chance you have displayed in your window a painting by a man who is copying my style to the last detail of thought. This stinking thief has so wormed himself into my mind that he has filched my unborn ideas. Now you have the proof in front of you.

This canvas of mine, painted only a week - two days - ago, was copied by a man stealing my ideas, my style, my whole thought process. And," here he thumped my beautiful desk very rudely, "before I'd even painted the damn picture myself. Now explain that to me, you oily commercial and illegitimate middleman."

There was no escape, particularly if I was to avoid a couple of black eyes and a broken jaw. I decided to play my hand (a pretty poor one) with as much bluff and bafflegas as I could command. I pressed the onyx bell on my desk and when little Elaine my secretary who is also a very fine 'front of house' girl appeared I said, with a splendidly casual air, "Miss Simpson, would you bring me that Andrew MacDermot landscape from the front window and also the two unframed canvases from the storeroom."

Neither Charles nor I spoke whilst she performed this job, and I was pretty glad of the pause, because it gave me time to think. At last the three canvases stood side by side against the wall whilst Charles' own new painting still squatted ominously on a chair. All four obviously (as it seemed) came from the same palette and two of them were as alike as a couple of peas. The situation called for very expert handling.

"Charles," I said at last. "I can't really explain this. I can only tell you the truth." This was the phrase I had thought out. Now came the difficult part. "This fellow MacDermot, showed his work to my partner Robin two months ago. They'd met at some pub in Chelsea, I think - the Lord Nelson if you must know. Robin brought one of two of them in to me the next morning and I of course said 'These aren't by MacDermot, whoever he may be, they're by Wisbeck or some fellow copying him so cleverly as makes no difference.'"

"And so?" said Charlie, flexing both fists in a most unpleasant manner and placing them upon my desk so that I should not lose the thread of the argument.

"And so," I continued, "I suggested we have nothing to do with this new chap who was clearly just a copyist. But Robin - and after all he is my partner - made me listen to him, just as you must, Charles. This man MacDermot has never seen a painting of yours in his life. He was born in Brussels of Scottish stock, his father was an international lawyer and he learned his painting in....."

But Charles was not listening. He was squatting on his haunches staring at one of the pictures signed MacDermot. Then he tipped it forward so that he could see the pegs stretching the canvas at the back.

"The bastard," he said. "The infernal fiend! This canvas has been cut down on two sides to make it compose better which is exactly what I did yesterday to the same painting which is now in my studio. But this is the damned part of it. You see that sort of whorl of loose paint in this corner? That's not in my canvas yet - but I made up my mind in bed last night to put it there. Damn it, I only thought it up in bed at two o'clock this morning. What the hell am I going to do, Philip? This is the straight road to lunacy."

Now that worry was replacing anger with Charles I felt safe enough to come out with the final piece of information.

"Robin says...." I began gingerly. "Mind you, I haven't seen this fellow myself....but Robin says that apart from his beard you're extremely like him. In fact he says he thought it was you playing a joke when he met him. If you and I hadn't been fishing in Scotland at the time I think he'd have believed he was being tricked somehow or other. Same voice, he says, same even temper, charm of manner, and so on. It was just at the end of last season. He was so rattled he rang me up and then insisted on talking to you on some footling pretext. You may remember it."

Charles straightened himself very slowly. Then he picked up his own canvas and held it above his head as if he were about to smash it. His arm stayed up a long time. Then, abruptly, he replaced it on the chair.

"No," he said, "that's not the way. I must see this fellow myself. You'd better take me to him. It's your problem as well as mine."

Now this sort of decision was more easily taken than carried out. Mr MacD. was, it proved, an elusive character and since Charles insisted on my presence a date had to be found when I could spare time away from the gallery. We had a card from North Wales saying only: 'Two canvases for you by rail. Moving on. J. McD.' which was no great help. A fortnight later he wrote, with no address, from Cheshire. At his Chelsea rooms there was no forwarding arrangement and a heap of mail accumulated - a fact I discovered for myself by hanging about the place for the best part of a day before I located an obliging charwoman.

By now it was late autumn and I hoped our man must be running out of money, for a quite respectable sum stood to his credit with us. Finally another postcard (he favoured the highly coloured photograph taken in 1910) arrived with the simple message: *I shall winter here——the Barn, Market Gedgeworth, Suffolk. Send me all you've collected in pound notes. J. McD.*

Charles and I left London the next afternoon, a Friday, in my car, which was uncomfortably small for a nervous driver and a gloomy man in a towering temper. He had changed quite a lot in the last two months, and worked hardly at all. My little Elaine, an openly adoring admirer, reported having seen him the worse for wear in several hostelries in her area and I knew she would be the last girl to let a situation like that go by without attempting some practical rescue work. Her own pert irritability in my office told me more about her failure than the occasional scraps of information she offered.

It was dark when we reached that large, straggling and hopelessly picturesque little Suffolk village, once an important centre in the Tudor wool industry and the one inn, the Woolpacker's Arms was clearly not used to casual trade at that season and not prepared to put itself out for our encouragement. There was only one guestroom we discovered, a fact the landlord had not mentioned in our telephone discussions, but it proved to be a large 'L' shaped room with a bath leading off - an apartment which also opened dangerously into the corridor - and two reasonably distant beds.

These domestic details increased Charles' lowering mood. He flung himself on the further bed and said "You suit yourself. I'll see you in the bar some time. We'll find this so-and-so in the morning."

It was about seven in the evening, chilly, with quite a thick mist building up outside. The house was warm enough but it was a nonentity of a hole, all varnish and Victoriana, 'ripe for development' as the advertisements say. There was no lounge: the staircase led into a largish hall with a bar in one corner. It was silent and poorly lit, but a man was standing by it with his back to me.

He did not move as I approached but stood unnervingly still against what light there was. I had to walk right round him, making it quite clear that I intended to see his face.

It was a very frightening minute before either of us spoke and I suppose I stared directly at him with my mouth wide open.

"I'm Andrew MacDermot" he said at last. "Have you brought the money?"

Even his voice was so like Charles that I think my face must have gone green with shock. My hair began to feel coarse and unnatural and I knew it was starting out of my head. The likeness was so horrible that I find difficulty in describing it. It was deeper than the likeness of twins, deeper than skin or superficialities of hair and colour. This was Charles all over again and in the same ominous mood that meant storms ahead.

"You - you've shaved off your beard," I muttered, knowing it made no sense. "I was told you were....."

"It's no business of yours," he said, "I haven't had a beard for six months. Just give me the cash and go to hell for all I care. Unless..." suddenly he turned full on me, the image of the furious

Charles in my office, "unless the fellow who came with you this evening is... well, who the Devil is he anyway?"

There was a pause, quite involuntary on my part because my mouth was so dry no sound came from it.

A voice in the shadows by the staircase said "His name is Wisbeck" and Charles came into the lamplight and stood between us.

I am a mild man, a timid man, and it is beyond me to describe this moment except from my own point of view. It was quite terrifyingly unpleasant. I remember looking at Charles and thinking 'he has beastly finger nails, they need cutting and the rims are full of paint' and turning to the other man whose hands were cast in that very mould - green paint on one thumb, red on the other: there was no difference.

With extraordinary mildness, for I had expected an explosion the man called MacDermot said: "By God, you're the man in my dream. I see you nearly every night, walking...walking...."

"In sand," said Charles in that even tone. "Walking across a desert. I walked from Benghazi to Tobruk. And you've not got away with it as easily as that, for I see you too. Sitting on your backside, day after day behind barbed wire. And there's nothing to draw on except the backs of prison orders; nothing to draw with except you make ink out of blood and brushes from human hair. Now will you please get to hell out of my life and out of my dreams."

With that he turned and almost ran out of the room, a sort of lumbering trot as if he were drunk. The landlord appeared from somewhere behind the scenes and without asking what the other man wanted I ordered two pints of bitter and two double whiskeys, Charles' invariable tipple. We drank in silence as if it were the most natural thing in the world, requiring no comment.

Finally he put his tankard down on the oaken bar and spoke as if it were a summing up.

"It's so damned insulting," he said. "All your life you have nothing really, but yourself. You are real. You are you. You are unique. You paint, write, compose or make little bits for motor cycles. It doesn't matter a damn because all the time you have the scant satisfaction of being you. And now quite suddenly you find you're not alone there's some other infernal stinker just like you, thinking your thoughts, painting your stuff - not anything better but just the same bloody stuff out of your own imagination. It's insulting. Do you see what I'm talking about, you filthy middleman?"

I had to say yes and I had no courage to argue or defend myself.

"I suppose," he said, speaking almost to himself, "that it was bound to happen. The Almighty - if there is one - is bound to repeat himself some time. How many codfish in a cod's row? Does every blasted cod fish think the same things, feel the same way? Doesn't the poor brute have any private entity of his own? I feel dirty - humiliated - useless. I won't stand for it. Do you understand that lot?"

"Yes," I said again.

"And I shall now get drunk," he finished. "But not in your infernal company."

With that he turned his back on me and walked out slamming the outer door. Only a wisp of mist that crept in as he went hovered around for a moment to show he had ever been there at all.

"A rum bloke," said the landlord. "Only been here a fortnight. Artist or something, they say. He put me in mind of your friend. Brothers perhaps?"

A storm got up in the night and rocked the old house as if it had been a ship. In the morning Charles and I drove back to town in teeming rain and barely spoke to each other. Nothing had been solved, nothing settled and it was quite beyond my thin store of courage to raise the subject at all. I dropped him very nearly without a word in St. John's Wood, just outside his studio.

A week went by, seven slow uneasy days which became increasingly sinister because nothing happened at all except the perpetual irritation of routine events.

Then one morning, unpleasantly early, two men appeared in my office.

"They're detectives," said the white faced Elaine. "C.I.D. - Scotland Yard, you know. They want to see you."

They were really remarkably human and very polite.

"We understand, sir," said the shorter of the two, "that you spent the night of the 13th - a Friday, oddly enough - at Market Gedgeworth in Suffolk." He looked and spoke like a high power insurance salesman, just missing the 'big executive' style.

I admitted the truth of it and enquired as mildly as I dared why he asked.

"Well of course you'll want to know that," he said, "of course. The facts are very simple and we usually say 'This is just a routine enquiry' but it's a little bit more than that to be honest. The fact is a man was found in a pond down there on Tuesday morning. At first they thought he'd fallen in after having a drink or two, but now it looks rather more serious. He was an artist, we understand, a Mr MacDermot. Did you know him?"

"Yes," I said, "I knew him. I saw him - in fact I went down to see him - on that Friday evening."

"Well now of course I must ask you why," said the policeman evenly.

I explained that we sold pictures and owed him money which I had gone down to pay in cash, £296 to be precise.

"Ah, yes indeed," said by smiling visitor. "No trouble there. We found it all on him. Now when did you see him last?"

I told him as near as I knew at about half past seven in the evening.

"And the man with you," said the policeman suddenly, pushing his face rather too close to mine, "what was he doing all this time?"

I did the best I could, speaking slowly but trying desperately to avoid sounding as if I was making a prepared statement.

"Charles Wisbeck," I explained, "is merely a friend who went down there with me. He happens to be a painter too, another artist whom we represent. He did not know Mr MacDermot before and even when they met they had less than ten minutes conversation. When MacDermot left Charles and I had dinner - a very poor dinner, by the way - and went to bed early. It was a noisy, stormy night."

The policeman looked at some notes in a folio.

"You shared the only guest room at the pub with Mr Wisbeck?"

"There was no alternative."

"Of course, of course. And neither of you went out that night?"

"Certainly not. It was a beastly night as I've just said."

He flung one of his quick ones at me.

"Sleep well?"

"I don't think I slept at all," I said. "That old pub is full of timber that creaks in the wind. I don't like strange beds and that one was damned uncomfortable."

"I see, I see," he said, tapping a pencil against his teeth. "And so very wisely neither of you went out and you spent the entire night within sight of each other. Couldn't have a better alibi even if you needed one, could you?" Almost to himself he went on. "Of course with a flat roof just outside that smaller window and only a six foot drop after that a man could...but that's nonsense, just plain nonsense, isn't it now?"

Turning directly to me again he said, "Now tell me about this poor fellow MacDermot, who was dead, by the way, before he got himself into that pond - fractured skull, you know. Quite a painter wasn't he? Make a lot of money for you?"

"He might have made us a very nice income for many years," I explained. "I scarcely knew him personally, but he'll be a pretty sharp loss."

"Well it looks as if that is just about that, eh?" said the

policeman. "Now I'll just take a formal statement from you if you don't mind and stop taking up your time and space."

Within a quarter of an hour the two of them were gone, and without so much as the lift of an eyebrow to suggest whether they believed me or no.

But whatever they thought privately it was the end of the trail for them. Andrew MacDermot had died, it was decided, by misadventure. Maybe he fell, banged his head and tripped into the pond. Or maybe not.

Whatever the truth, the fact is that I have a very nasty piece of perjury on my conscience, But what is a poor art dealer (with enormous overheads) to do? Must he lose one good painter by murder and another by imprisonment for life in one single evening? It is asking too much of any business man, especially when a little diplomacy will save at least half the cargo from the wreck.

For Charles did go out that night. He did go out by the window, when he thought I was asleep and he did come back in the very small hours soaked to the skin by the same odd route.

Or did he come back? I'm damned if I know. Certainly one of the two returned. The one thing I am certain about is that this world is too small to hold two such atoms without an explosion.

Elaine, I suspect, knows the answer, but we never refer to that sort of unpleasantness in the office.

The Thorns are Vicious

It is very kind of you, sir, to admire the roses.

They are the old fashioned blue roses which your grandfather had, I expect, in his garden - just the same - only these are enormous, as big as sunflowers.

I have one in the cellar where I live in the *Hügelstrasse* which I have measured. It is more than thirty centimetres across. *Es is ja ohne zweifel* - it is without doubt the largest rose in the world.

I do not wish to trade with you, sir, but perhaps if you had a cigarette...?

I have this from Trüblen, which was once a fine little town, maybe two thousand people, with a market place, three good bierkellers and an inn; everything very compact around the Rathaus which was too big for us but brought a few tourists because of some medieval wood carvings in the Mayor's parlour. Lately, I mean just before the war, some of the *Parteibonzen* - the bosses - would visit the place in their great cars to see the house where Kurt Lansburger was born. Perhaps you have heard of him. He was of the Party, the SS and I think not a very good man. Some dreadful things were said of him and it is best no doubt to hope he was mad, for he is dead, you know, and can trouble no one any more.

Trüblen was very pretty, stone and wood, with crazy red roofs like a fairy story illustration. Now it is gone and when there is a map of Germany again it will not be marked.

But it was not the bombs, nor the fighting which caused this matter; there were no soldiers there and no workshops. If the scientists and the professors had not been so busy at the war it would have been a sensation and a wonder for nine days as well as a great mystery. But no one could be spared and so the Gestapo put a fence around the place with a great deal of barbed wire and a new road was built which does not take you near to the mystery. Now the Gestapo has gone and the wire is rotting and broken. But nobody goes through: travel with us is nearly impossible nowadays, as you know, and who would go two hundred kilometres just to gaze at a mystery?

It may be that a few wandering people have trapped rabbits there, but the undergrowth is very thick, too thick to penetrate very far, and there are no roads any more. Nothing is there but trees and great briars which tear your clothes just as viciously as any barbed wire.

I know all this for a fact because I spent a day in the effort and failed. For my trouble I had a coat torn to ribbons - a bad thing for winter - some seeds and a few roots.

There was a time when I had a garden and could be interested in curiosities of this nature. Now I must content myself with a few cuttings which I can grow in the little patch of poor soil behind my cellar.

It is two years now since it happened. We have seen so many terrible events since then that this affair seems less peculiar than it should, but this is the way in Germany today.

Yet a great deal of it I saw for myself.

Even during the time of our victories Trüblen was not the easiest place to visit, but I was permitted to live there because of my mother who was very old and bedridden.

You see in the woods near the town there was a camp — a *Konzentrationslager.*

I do not defend this; for the most part we knew nothing of it, beyond seeing the Gestapo come and go, and it may well be that there were events occurring there which it is not good to think of. Certainly many people were sent there, packed in trucks, and nobody ever came out except for the guards, who drank all our good Trüblen beer so that there was nothing for us. Now our eyes are open and we can learn of these deeds, but even so we can only guess about the camp in the Trüblenwald. They say that Kurt Lansburger was interested in it and of him we knew that he did many most evil things. Certainly he came to the camp from time to time. But not at the end.

It is right to say that we in Trüblen were afraid, afraid to think or to speak of what might be happening. We suspected a little, for the guards were loose in their talk when they were full of liquor, but it has not been wise in Germany to think aloud in the last ten years.

That it was a bad place where wickedness was done every day I know from the talk of the guards, from what happened later, and most of all - *verstehen sie?* - from my heart, because I lived so near to something which I could only suspect.

We in Trüblen were uneasy about it, but in the war there was so much to trouble us. When the end came it was a matter for terror and not just for worry. Yet it started very quietly.

It began with the weeds in the market place.

163

There was always, of course, a little grass and some moss perhaps between the cobblestones. We noticed the change first in the late summer of '43. What little weeds there were should have been brown and dried-up. It was long after the hay crop and before the goodness returns to the soil. Yet suddenly the weeds began to flourish.

I knew old Shönemann, the Bürgermeister, well enough to chaff him. I told him his market place was beginning to look like an Austrian railway station before the Anschluss. He did not laugh about it and the next day some SS men - not the town officials - came and sprayed the cobblestones with chemicals.

It made no difference. By the end of the week the weeds came back and so strongly that they forced several stones out of place.

That evening I saw Shömemann again. We were in the big bierkeller next to the Rathaus. He was sitting alone at his *stammtisch*, which was unlike him, and looked worried, which would be nearly humorous if you knew his big, smiling face.

"The weeds are back, I notice, Herr Bürgermeister," I said.

For a long time he did not answer me. Then he turned round and looked at me straight in the face, his head very close to mine. "My eyesight is poor in these days, my friend," he said, "and I find it pays me to notice as little as I can. But do you see anything wrong with that wall?"

The *keller* was below the ground and the walls were of stone and very thick.

A great crack spread from the floor to the ceiling, like a river traced on a map. In the centre, almost like a human arm, there crept a root, a very strong brown root with young, white shoots.

"It's the ivy from the creeper outside," I said. "It's growing too fiercely. Perhaps it should be cut."

"Yes," he said, "it is growing. But it was cut at ground level four days ago by the SS. Tell me, have you been along the road to the camp lately?"

Now no one, except the camp officials, ever went that way. The road led only into the woods and to the camp and the SS did not encourage visitors. They also kept very bad-tempered dogs which were apt to stray.

"You should walk a little that way, my friend," he said. "You'll see a lot to surprise you. I wish you goodnight."

With that he left me and half his pot of beer too, which was most unlike him.

I was just going across to join some friends when something happened. I do not forget this, for it was the first real thunder-crack of the storm.

A great piece of plaster from the ceiling came crashing down on to a table and filled the whole room with dust. At first everyone was dumbfounded: then all the tongues began to wag together. "It's the bombing," said one, but there had been no bombing near us. "The earth beneath the foundations has moved," said another. And a third cried, "It's the roots of the ivy creeper — they're dangerous."

Next to me was Gottlieb Gross, a shifty old devil, but friendly, in his oily way, with all the Gestapo and the officials. A piece of the plaster had hit his shoulder and covered his hat with fine rubble.

As he shook it and blew the powder off he turned to me and said, "I'm getting out of here right away. Out of this town. If you take my advice you'll go too. I've seen things I don't like and this is the end for me. I'm going, if I have to walk as far as Göttingen."

We went up the stairs together. It was a fine, warm night with a big harvest moon as large as a ripe pumpkin.

"What have you seen?" I said. "Have you been down the road to the camp?"

He looked at me and nodded and winked. It was a trick of his, that wink, a nervous jerk he couldn't help, but it made him look confiding and sly.

"I've been right into the camp," he said. "I do a little business there now and again. I was there last night. And you mark my words. In a week's time there'll be no camp at all in Trüblen woods. They're frightened."

He began to giggle and I saw that he was not a little scared himself.

"They're frightened," he repeated, "and they'll clear out. You mark my words. They'll go, and I'm going too."

"What's the matter with the camp?" I asked.

"Plenty," he said. "You'll see - if you stay in Trüblen." With that he shambled off into the alley where he lived. I never saw him again.

The moonlight in the market square was very bright. At the corner I stumbled over a loose stone and paused a little to look round. There was no chink, of course, from any door or window. Nothing but the moon shining down on an empty market place. It was like a city of the dead, a city that had been dead a long time, with huge, rank weeds growing everywhere.

I walked home alone, twice alone, because my footsteps did not echo on the cobbles as they should have done: the moss and the grass made a carpet which absorbed even the noise of my wooden soles.

At the door of my mother's house I paused again because I thought I had been locked out. I banged and shouted and the old

165

lady called out to me. When I put my shoulder to the wood — the latch was up — it moved unwillingly.

The virginia creeper had thrown a net of shoots over it and it needed strength to force it open.

Mutti, my mother you know, was very old, over eighty. For all that she was sharp enough and with the aid of her maid Hilde she missed very little that passed in Trüblen. When she heard me enter the porch she called to me again.

"Come up, my son. It is late, but some events do not wait until the morning."

She was sitting up swathed in wool and old lace, with two candles on either table beside her bed.

"What are they saying in the town?" she demanded, and she looked at me very straight over the two pairs of glasses she wore for reading.

"They say, or rather, Gottlieb Gross says, that they are quitting Trübenwald camp. I don't know why — he wouldn't tell me."

"I can tell you," said the old lady. "They're leaving the camp because they can't stay there any longer. The trees, the briars and the weeds have invaded the place and taken possession. Every green thing is growing as if the soil had suddenly become as fertile as a jungle. They've tried everything and they can't stop it. The grass and the creepers have pulled down their huts. God himself knows what they've done to the soil, but it will take more than the Gestapo or the SS or Kurt Lansburger himself to put an end to it. You go to sleep now, if you can. When Hilde comes in the morning we'll speak of what's to be done."

On that she dismissed me. I slept very little, though I was tired enough, for the old house creaked and groaned as if all the winds in creation were tearing at it. But it was no storm which was grappling at the walls, but a green enemy, which was terrible because it was even less personal then a tempest.

It was a green dawn, too, when it came, for the light came dimly through my window, filtering through the creeper which nearly clogged it.

Hilde woke me. She looked more ill-tempered than usual and twice as fat, because, as I saw later, she was wearing nearly all the clothing she possessed.

"Get up," she said, "we're going. *Wir haben schon die nase voll.* We must get the horse into the waggon and make a bed of sorts for the Mistress. You will help me with her."

"Going, Hilde?" I said, and hardly dared to ask why.

"We're going," she said, "because if we don't we'll be eaten by the forest, just like the camp was. In two days there'll be no Trüblen. Listen, old Shönemann, the Bürgermeister, has called

166

a meeting for all able-bodied men - as if there were any in these days - to go out with him to fight the forest. But that's no good. With your limp you're useless, anyhow. Give me a hand with her, and quickly now."

I put on my clothes and went downstairs. She was right. The garden was a jungle. The flagstones in the hall were moving with grass bursting up between them.

In the cellar we kept a few valuables - most illegal, in those days, but one had to think for oneself - and I tried to retrieve them. But when I opened the door I saw it was useless. I descended a few steps and was forced back. The place was full of a fungus, bigger than anything I've ever seen. Somehow that frightened me even more; it was so obscene, so poisonous, so very malignant.

We boiled some water and got a little food together. Outside the sounds were not as they should have been. Instead of the rumble of the farm carts as they passed along the road there was a gentle rustling, like a loaded haywain passing down a narrow country lane. But the carts were going by and all in one direction — away from Trüblen, away from the camp and the woods which were suddenly swallowing everything with their now angry growth.

Nowadays we have seen so many people carrying everything they possessed on a handcart, but this for me was new and frightening. Our neighbours' waggons were the same, I suppose, as any others, but long tentacles of creeper and weed clung to them and trailed in the grass as they moved past our gate. The procession was doubly unnerving because it was so hushed, so carpeted.

Between us Hilde and I got the old horse hitched to the wagon and we spoke very little. I took a hedging knife and cut the cart clear of the wisteria which was twisting about it from the stable doors. We carried Mutti downstairs and lifted her into the bed we'd made for her.

"There's little enough worth taking with us," she said, "except the gold and my trinkets. You've got them safe?"

"They're still in the cellar," I muttered. "I can't get into it because of the fungus."

"Take an axe, boy, and try again."

I went back, but it was useless. I splintered the cellar door — it opened inwards, but the stone stairs and the walls were clogged with the filthy yellow growth and the stench as I tried to hack at it made me sick. Even Hilde admitted it was impossible. It was like cutting at a wall of billowing, reeking India rubber.

"When we've reached cousin Wilhelm's place and have found somewhere to live, I'll come back," I promised. "By winter a lot of this will have died off and I'll take the waggon and collect all I can find."

167

The old lady looked round for the last time.

"By winter," she said, "there'll be nothing left here. The weeds and the briars will have made Trüblen into a patch of rubble. It's a judgment on us. God knows what they've been doing in that camp of theirs. That's where it began."

We set off down the track which had been a tidy road only a few days before. At first it was difficult going, with Hilde leading the horse.

He was frightened, too, and kicked and plunged like a colt. Once a huge wolfhound - from the camp, I suppose - passed us going like a mad thing, and that set him rearing and tossing so that he nearly bolted with us. Only the undergrowth held him back.

The worst of the journey was over more quickly than I'd expected. Somehow one imagined that this revolt of green things was going on for ever and that the weeds would strangle every living thing in the countryside. But quite suddenly, at the crossroads, it stopped.

Behind us lay a jungle of briars, long grass and trees with their terrifying, unnatural burgeoning: ahead lay the good brown stubble waiting for the autumn ploughing, and the solid, civilised, metal road.

Mother was very ill all that winter and could not be left. They told me last Christmas that a great fence of wire had been put round Trüblen and that the road had been diverted, but I could not go back to find out what happened in the heart of it. In the spring the old lady died.

Things were bad for us here: it was months before I could make the trip. Then, when my chance came, I took a pruning hook and set off on my bicycle in search of the house and my little store of treasure.

It is a long ride from here, difficult for a cripple. I slept in ditches for two days and was very hungry when I reached the edge of the wild. It was not easy to find, even knowing the country as I do, for a new road had been built. But when I came to the boundary it was well enough marked by the barbed wire fence and the *Verboten* notices.

I chose an entrance where the briars seemed thinner, but the going was very difficult. Everything still grew in profusion and much bigger than is normal; the leaves, the fruit, the thorns were twice their rightful size. Where there had been, as I thought, good pastures in the old days there were young larches and silver birch, with bracken as high as my head.

It was like cutting a path through a jungle where no road has ever been.

For a day I struggled and hacked at it. I passed bricks and

stones and beams covered with lichen and moss where houses had once stood.

Then I gave up. I was frightened, I was hungry, I was dead with exhaustion and the thorns had torn my clothes and cut my skin cruelly. Moreover, my track seemed to be healing up behind me.

Though I was so beaten with weariness that it seemed I must drop dead, I ran and plunged and struggled until I reached the wire again. Then I fell down for the last time that day, sobbing and sweating, and slept until my own shivering woke me at dawn.

I knew then that everything was lost, that I would never see my mother's gold pieces or her rings and brooches and antique necklaces again. But because I was once fond of gardens, and these flowers were so big as to be a wonder for all gardeners, I took some roots and seeds and what cuttings I could without going back into that wild place.

These roses which you see are from there. I have also some wild strawberries, honeysuckle, blackberries, even a young cherry tree. They will make the wiseacres sit up when the time comes.

What the explanation may be for this strange happening I cannot say. My few old friends, who were my neighbours in Trüblen and who came this way, still talk of it, of course.

There are many theories. We can gossip freely now and there is little else one can do. It certainly began at the *Konzentrationslager* and some speak of the unnatural fertilisation of the soil at that place. But before the old lady, my mother, died she had some strange fancies, more terrible, I think, than these others.

She said that it was life itself which had revolted at what happened in the camp. She said that when Man did something that degraded him below the lowest spawning thing, then all the other teeming forms of growth on earth rose up and blotted him out, as if he had not been. Perhaps she was near the truth there. Certainly one sees something of the sort in little even among these bomb ruins.

A terrible fancy for an old woman to die with, but then she was educated in a convent and was very religious as a girl. We were strictly brought up.

These roses interest you? You English are sentimental I believe about your rose gardens. In Germany too there were many fine varieties before the war, famous all over the world.

You may have them if you so desire. They grow freely enough even in the little yard by my cellar.

Thank you, sir, thank you. It was not my desire to trade with you, but perhaps they remind you of better gardens than mine.

It is very kind of you, sir; very kind indeed. Be very careful with them, sir. They have vicious thorns.

169

One for the Record

(Pursuant to my duties as Rodent Officer)

To Arthur Gale,
Chief Inspector of Sanitation & Hygiene,
North Western Zone, London.

Private and Confidential

Dear A.G.,
Please forgive me for writing direct to you in the middle of your busy season, instead of going through Sewage (M) or Maintenance (M and P) but the enclosed report from one of my operatives seems to me to be something that ought to be examined within the next few weeks rather than waiting for Deferred Projects, et cetera, at the Annual General.

My regards to Mrs. G. and young Ron.
Yours truly,
Henry Dixon
Inspector, Sub Area B

[Enclosure:]
From The Rodent Officer, Sub Area B
Subject: RODENTS, MOVEMENT OF

1. Pursuant to my duties in this department, I have maintained a detailed record of the incidence of rodents and the numbers regularly exterminated in each division of the area. I now have to report that in Section 17 there is a pattern of increase occurring at regular intervals (see Appendix A) of up to 98%.
2. As you are aware, the movement of rodents has various basic causes, notably large scale rebuilding, destruction of slum properties, removal of dumps, modernisation of sewage systems, etc. These considerations do not apply within or near Section 17. Since no adjacent area has been affected on the occasions noted in Appendix A and there has been no deterioration in the sewage system (installed 1890, modernised 1927, 1954) the cause is considered to lie within the area itself or considerably further afield.
3. The centre of increase would appear to lie within the triangle

formed by Boundary Road, Marsham Street, and Upper Grange Avenue. These are well constructed semidetached houses, mainly erected in 1890, now sub-divided and accommodating units of personnel of an average income of £1,500 p.a. On the corner of Boundary Road and Marsham Street there is a group of shops comprising a fishmonger's, a grocery store, a newspaper /tob./conf. and Rampole's Miniature Theatre Shop. All of these establishments have been the subject of most careful examination and supervision. There is no ground for supposing any of the Hygiene Regulations have not been observed.

4. There has been a large number of complaints concerning the incidence of rodents from residents in the area defined and these have been investigated and found fully justified.

5. There is no animal dealer, pet shop, or private zoo within two miles of the area.

6. Considerable damage to property has occurred and it is feared that the Ratepayers' Association may take action and cause unfortunate publicity to be attracted to the matter.

7. Sanction for the addition of two Temporary Assistant Rodent Operatives to the normal quota of staff is requested. The M.O.H. (Dr Hubbard) is understood to support this suggestion.

Conclusion: This movement of rodents would appear to be caused by the change of direction of some underground stream or subterranean network. The advice of a geologist could be helpful. Perhaps Archives could assist in the question of obsolete drainage systems, though this officer can find no trace of any such stream or tunnel in the Borough Records.

R. Bates, Rodent Officer

* * *

From Arthur Gale to Henry Dixon

Dear Henry,

I don't like the sound of this at all. I've never had a Parliamentary Question yet and don't want to start. I take it you have waived any existing regulations about the keeping of domestic pets (i.e. cats and dogs) that may be in force?

As a first step I'm asking a friend of mine, Anthony Bodkin, Weights and Measures, who is a naturalist in his spare time, to investigate. Please help him all you can.

My best regards to Mrs. D. and the twins.

Yours, A.G.

*   *   *

To Arthur Gale from Anthony Bodkin

Dear Arthur,

About your rats in the Marsham Street area. It really is very odd. I have examined several specimens that young Bates, your "Rodent Officer", has trapped or poisoned and these include not only our old pals Rattus Rattus and R. Norvegicus but Phleomys, Uromys, Crateromys, Bandicota (1 only), Mesembriomys and Golunda. The latter hails from India. All are pretty rare over here.

There seems to be no pet dealer or brother naturalist in the area. I do not understand it at all.

The times of sudden infestation are interesting too. Early November, March, and late May seem to be the principal dates. This doesn't coincide with any cycle I know of, but I feel it ought to suggest something since it has been repeated now for five years.

I am still poking around and shall do a paper on it for my Society, but that will not help you much. Why not try an archaeologist to look up underground streams, secret passages, etc.? That is the other line of inquiry.

Yours,
Anthony

P.S. You might try J. W. Winkel of the Ministry of Works, who specialises in this sort of thing. He deals with subsidences, earth movements and so on. An eccentric chap, a teetotaller, unlike your Rodent Officer, but very knowledgeable. A.

*   *   *

To Arthur Gale from Jonathan W. Winkel

My dear Mr Gale,

Thank you for putting me on to the problem of the rats in Marsham Street and Boundary Road which I have found fascinating. I send you this account in some detail because I have been unofficially assisted by a friend, Alastair Redcar, the fifth Earl, who wishes no publicity. In any case you can put the affair into officialese, (omitting his Lordship) if you think fit. You are welcome to that side of the problem. I await the results with pleasure.

These are the facts. Firstly, there is no map of any age that

172

suggests an underground stream, and geologically it is most improbable. The present houses are the first ever built on this ground, which was open country of no significance prior to 1890. Underground passages are therefore also ruled out.

Rats as a community only move from A to B when there is a cause for migration. The rebuilding of the Bank of England for example in 1930 and the sewage changes in the city at that time is a case in point. Here there is no such cause.

We therefore decided to do some research on the ground itself, taking your ratcatcher Bates with us. By the way, what an odd job for a man of his education: he seems to enjoy it as if he were out for a day's hunting.

The focal point of the trouble he had thought at first was the row of shops, the fishmonger's naturally being the most suspect. He has by now dismissed this theory, and exonerated the grocer at the same time. We examined certain rat-routes between houses, all of which had been very expertly blocked.

Redcar, however, was fascinated by Rampole's Miniature Theatre Shop and, though Bates and I went all over the area, he was not to be shifted from this bright little junk hole. It seems that the place has a fair reputation among highbrows, specialising in Toy Theatres, puppets and Victorian toys, marbles, tops, skipping ropes, and so forth. Many of these are still in demand among the children of the neighbourhood.

In nosing around, Redcar unearthed the first clue, for he appears to have hit it off very well with old Rampole, who is a character and the last of a long line of toy theatre people. Asked when his slack seasons were, he said, "Well, the middle of term-time, of course. My younger customers are short of pocket money then and they feel the pinch. So do I."

The middle of term, you see. Mid-November, mid-March and the end of May.

Redcar asked what he did about it and Rampole - he really looks like the Wandering Jew in person - laughed and said, "I have a little remedy. Come back at half-past four, when the schools are closed for the day and I'll show you."

When the hour arrived, Redcar stood in the shop and watched. Rampole, it seems, has a private toy of his own, a remarkable curio. It is an old-fashioned musical box, not the tinkling cylinder variety, but the sort that gives out a species of organ music, rather like a minute fairground steam hurdy-gurdy. It plays two little tunes, one after the other, both very gay but difficult to remember, save that one is naive and the other sophisticated. They are repeated over and over again until the machine runs down.

The effect, which I have now observed for myself, is truly amazing. Within thirty seconds there were half a dozen children pressing against the window and before the performance was over the street was moderately full of young demons shouting and playing all over the place.

Several of them came inside rather sheepishly to listen and Rampole made a couple of sales: some marbles and a penny whistle, which now costs one and sixpence.

What is more extraordinary is the fact that whilst we watched three large black rats also scuttled across the floor, having come in by the door. The place is full of puppets and curios and the vermin disappeared like shadows.

If you do not believe me, go and check it for yourself. Redcar says they did a dance at the back of the shop but I didn't see it. The antique instrument I must add, (though you may have reached this conclusion for yourself by now) bears the label: *Speilman. Mfr. Hamelin, Brunswick.*

If you have your well thumbed copy of Browning to hand, it may refresh your memory.

Rampole tells me he doesn't use what he calls his Pied Piper tunes very often, since the instrument is old and rickety: he only has recourse to it when business is bad.

Thank you again for putting me on to this interesting inquiry. I don't see what your department can do about it, but I have found my adventure most stimulating.

Yours sincerely,

Jonathan Winkel.

* * *

To Arthur Gale from Edwin Rampole

Sir,

Reference your inquiry re miniature German pipe-organ.

I acquired this some years ago on the continent and I know of no law to prevent me from playing it. Many of my customers have expressed pleasure and I do not see on what grounds it can be called a nuisance. It is certainly not for sale to you or anybody else. Only last week Lord Redcar, who was sent to this shop by your department, or so he tells me, made me a very handsome offer for it, which I refused.

His Lordship did, however, with my permission, take a tape recording of the melodies and this, I understand, he intends marketing in the form of a gramophone record. If you want a copy it will be up to you to buy one, price will include a small royalty to this firm.

Thanking you in advance,
Yours respectfully,
Edwin Rampole,
Prop. Rampole's Toy Theatres Limited.

* * *

From: The Ministry of Health to the Dept. of Sanitation and Hygiene, N.W. Zone, London.

The Minister will receive the Chief Inspector concerned tomorrow, at 9.30 a.m. sharp.

Grand Seigneur

The most infuriating experience in the world from a journalist's point of view, is to sit on a story like a cork in a bottle of champagne and never to be able to loosen your own binding wires. In this case the cork is held in position by the suffocating wax of official statements about the event, by the golden foil which in terms of cash would make it unprofitable for any witness to open his mouth and by political wires which will be kept taut for a generation.

So, even today, I will not say "Now it can be told," because I am no expert in science or scientific jargon to make you simple explanations. But this was the experience and the adventure as it happened to me.

A decade ago I gained my living as the Paris correspondent for several English and American journals, covering not so much news as feature stories; a far more gentlemanly occupation for a naturally lazy man. My drinking pools were of course the Ritz and the Scribe, and it was in this last underground resort that Jean Louis Vertés tackled me. It was considered pretty certain he would be the next Minister for the Interior. They came and went at that time in weeks, sometimes in days. He was a little man, physically, with a grey parrot's quiff which he had allowed to grow rather long and artistic so that on great occasions it could be swept from his forehead when the gesture was required. He had the accent of Lyons, and a great deal of backing in that area, not only from the silk merchants.

We drank Ricard. After a decent interval, when he had cleaned a whole dish of the Scribe's delicious little biscuits, he said, "I think it might interest you to be present at an experiment which is going to be performed in Tourraine, at one of the Châteaux, the Seigneurie, in fact. It is at the moment very secret, very confidential, you understand? If it should not prove a success then absolute silence is essential."

"Why ask me?" I enquired. "Journalists aren't paid for keeping their traps shut. Quite the contrary."

"Because," he said, "this is a matter in which it is important to have an independent witness. We wish to have with us a foreigner who is not of the diplomatic corps, nor especially attached to a single press organisation. A discreet man, an intelligent man who can if need be hold his tongue. And someone who is not a scientist to be blinded by theories or details."

This was a good blatant line in flattery which went a long way with me - the length of two more Ricards. I hand it to Vertés, he was a very fine performer. *All* expenses, a point he emphasised with finesse, would be paid and the matter commenced itself with 'le Rolls Royce' which would call for me at my hotel on the afternoon of Friday next.

I was driven to the Château des Seigneurs, often called the Seigneurie, fifteen kilos out of Blois, with speed and pomp.

There were two uniformed men in front, my suitcase was handled as if it contained the Crown jewels and the car conveyed, though it did not say so in number plates, immense authority. There was a small flag, veiled, but implying great prestige and the gendarmerie saluted us on our way as if we were expected.

The Château itself is the oldest in that county of Châteaux yet the most mixed in architecture. The castle at Ghent is the nearest approach, though here the turrets and the banqueting hall belong to the age of elegance.

We did not sweep, as I would have wished, to the main doorway inside the courtyard because the cobbled area was already jammed. There were three big camions, a mobile power plant which might have been a dynamo or the energy unit for pile driving, a little crane and innumerable packing cases all over the place. At a guess one would have said a television unit was moving in or that a film was about to be shot on location. A splendid highly technical confusion reigned everywhere. In ten minutes, I thought, this will all be clear and Her Royal Highness will declare the exhibition open.

Vertés, in black and pin stripes but with a flowing tie to match his forelock, met me in the great hall.

"Precise to the moment," he said. "Perhaps you would agree that I should take you to taste an aperitif and to meet our colleagues on this occasion? My friend, this may prove a *very* great occasion. Let us be most discreet, and observe carefully all that occurs."

At this he took me by the elbow and pinched it so sharply that even I perceived that a couple of eye-openers would be quite enough. We proceeded through the stone hall bowed forward by a butler, a superior being with no roof to his mouth, to a smaller panelled room hung with very good tapestries. They are in fact the historic pre-Aubusson designs, showing Le Grand Seigneur greeting Annabelle of Lorraine, open to the public at visiting hours, 250 francs.

Here was a mixed bag of men, especially as to clothes, and Vertés introduced me in such a rush that they made only a blur. I sorted them out afterwards.

One I recognised: Henri Lafourchardiere, the historian, a member of the Académie who already looks like his own statue. He bowed from a great height and never spoke to me again.

Then there were M. le Prof. A., M. le Prof. B., le Comte de C., General P. de la D., and the Duc de Jenesaisquoi, who it seemed owned the place, and several others.

We all shook hands formally and nothing registered.

At the end of the row was a shabby little man still wearing a beret as if it were a skull cap. Michel Laborde, a wizened creature in a greasy grey suit with a none-too-clean shirt and a thin black tie. He had a little shaven moustache, hardly there at all, and a blue chin.

A drink was now in my hand and I was left standing beside him. There was a pause whilst he breathed a little garlic tinged with another indefinable odour across me. I opened with my usual gambit which rarely fails.

"Forgive my ignorance," I said, "but what do you do for a living?"

He cocked a bleary eye at me, a knowing eye that would have winked had it not been impeded by a nervous drag on the lower lid.

"Me?" he said. "I am the humble commercial figure here, not one of your eminent persons. Yet, you see, they cannot do without me. All of you come to me in the end - all of you - especially the great ones."

"You must be a debt collector," I suggested, "or a money lender?"

"Not far out," he admitted. "Not far out. I combine a little of both offices. I am in fact an embalmer, the President of the National Society of Reunited Embalmers of France, at your service."

He so shook me by this announcement that I said, rather abruptly, that I hoped never to have need of his skill, and took a second drink. He was still at my elbow, shorter and smaller than I had thought, looking up at me like a reproachful vinous-eyed gnome.

"If it wasn't for me," he said, "And for the records of my society, none of you would be here. None of you. It was through my researches that this place was discovered and selected."

"Discovered?" I asked, thinking that historians for some centuries were going for nothing according to his reckoning. "But this is one of the great Château of France, Le Grand Seigneur is buried here....didn't he build it? And Giles de Rey came here and Louis IX and the Eminence Gris and even the Marquis..."

"Oh yes," he said, "Precisely, precisely. We all know the history books. But it is I who did the research for this evening. It is I myself who have discovered the vital facts from my records about Le Grand Seigneur."

Vertés wafted me away. "That little horror," he said. "He was essential at the beginning, and now he must perforce be here tonight, for we may need him. Come and talk to our historian - no, not Lafourchardiere, but Beauregarde, the men who really knows the story."

He was a crisp young man with curly receding hair, an ex-Chief of Intelligence to one of the Resistance Generals, a bright boy of the new psychological school.

"You know all about Le Grand Seigneur of course," he said. "The chap I would like to know more about is L'Origon. Now there's a master whose life really is wrapped in mystery. Whatever happens tonight - and personally I expect nothing at all - L'Origon is the fascinating figure."

The superior butler brought me another drink which gave me the courage to admit I'd never heard of L'Origon.

"Well, he *is* obscure," admitted Beauregarde, very civilly, "probably right out of the normal orbit. Even in Russia they're not up to his standard. You've seen Lenin in his open mausoleum recently of course? No? Well, he's just a mess of pigmented wax, no real body at all. One good power failure in the refrigeration plant on a warm day and he'd melt away to nothing. Yet they employed the very latest methods. But L'Origon! Centuries before, and all the secrets lost! What a master!"

I was beginning to get the idea.

"He was an embalmer?"

Beauregarde elbowed me into a corner, as if I were a good student who deserves further confidential encouragement.

"L'Origon was another Leonardo da Vinci in his way" he said. "Not a charlatan, though he had very odd ideas about the transmutation of metals - and they may be sound, even now. He embalmed human bodies in a process of his own, God knows how, but it was perfect. The important thing is, *he preserved them intact.*"

The point of this was lost on me, so with considerable patience an explanation was made.

"Even the Egyptians only preserved the outer man - the insides were burned or buried separately. L'Origon took a complete human body, exactly as the man died, and preserved it, for all eternity - or at least until today. Very few examples of his work are

179

authenticated which is why we have that smelly little corpse fancier Laborde with us this evening. He has some early records. We had to find a specimen who had not died by poisoning, or wounds or anything of that sort, you see. The one perfect example is Le Grand Seigneur. Contrary to the legends you may have read, he was drowned here in the lake."

Le Grand Seigneur, King of France, of Acquitaine and Lorraine and of the Realms, heir to the spirit of Charlemagne, unique monarch of the civilized world. Here we were in his castle, standing, I calculated, almost directly above his tomb.

Beauregarde eyed me hopefully, clearly expecting a sound logical reaction from an apt pupil.

"Then tonight," I said, "we are going to see Le Grand Seigneur exactly as he was in life? These men are going to open his tomb? What a story! I hope there is a good photographer. My God, why didn't I bring a man of my own with me, instead of my third rate camera."

The young man - he was still very autumnal in colour from the deserts he had fought in - gave me a long straight look. He broke it only to empty his glass. Then he put his head closer to mine and dropped the professional air, becoming almost a fellow conspirator.

"Tonight, my friend," he said, "if these men do what they think they are going to do, we shall not only see Le Grand Seigneur but we shall talk to him."

"Messieurs" said the butler in the hollow exaggerated voice of an airport loud speaker, "Dinner is served."

We moved out in twos or threes to the main hall, which was chilly despite the early spring sunshine of the day. At one end, by the enormous stone fireplace which caught every draught in the room there was a long buffet table set with cold meats, salads and red wine. I found myself standing next to a gloomy middle aged man wearing the short trousers and correct grey suit of a civil servant. He looked like a walrus who was sad because some one had shaved off his moustaches: even his flapping hands suggested a melancholy chill.

I searched my memory for his name. "You are Professor Bezin, I believe? Forgive me for being so ignorant but what is your subject?"

He gave me a sad fishy look through old fashioned eye-glasses askew on his nose.

"I?" he said. "I'm of no importance here. Just a cipher in the proceedings, as usual, but I may as well boast to you, if you are to listen. I am Bezin, as you say. Henri Bezin of Grenoble. Ancient languages, you know, though I don't suppose you've ever heard of me. In this case I'm simply here as an interpreter if the need should arise - which I very much doubt. Archaic French is my particular study. They think it may be useful. My personal opinion is that they are all mad. But I receive a fee for my services. I hope you also have a commercial interest?"

I explained that I was a stranger here myself and had only the haziest ideas about what was going on.

"Ah," he said and filled his mouth with cold chicken. I had half expected him to toss the morsel into the air and catch it like a sardine, but he continued, "Then you don't know all these people?"

Vertés, I said deferentially, had asked me to come as an outside observer.

"That self-seeking ogre!" said my professor. "And what will he get out of it, you ask? I will tell you. Power, publicity, fame - perhaps the control of the Government. They will all get something for themselves, you'll see. Even the Duke himself who shows his chateau to tourists all day for pocket money. He is the most likely to win, should anything happen."

"Why the Duke?" I asked.

He looked at me pityingly with the cautious sadness of goldfish considering a cat. "There is publicity of course, which he will get in any case. But if there is something in all this scientific experimenting - if something really happens ... then, my friend, then..."

"Then what?"

"There is reputed to be great treasure here, probably in the lake. Legendary stuff, as one would expect, with very little foundation to it. Who ever heard of a king dying without a missing treasure? Ah, but here comes..."

Instinctively, almost magnetically, we had all turned our heads like a group of players at the entrance of the star. At the far end of the hall stood a man, consciously pausing for the perfect moment, who might well have been Hamlet himself.

He had a very large head crowned with untidy black locks, sunken eyes which burned, and two lines so deep beside his mouth that they resembled duelling scars. When he had our complete attention he nodded, a general bow to us all.

"In ten minutes" he said, "we will be ready."

His voice was as deep and as cold as a rock pool.

Then he strode over to the table, picked up some food in one hand and took Vertés by the other, moving him into a corner and whispering rapidly, privately. I watched him out of the corner of my eye, as we all did, and saw that his face was powder white, with two spots of colour in his cheeks, as bright as a clown's make up. He was shaking with controlled excitement.

Bezin said, "That, as you may know if you read scientific reviews - I don't myself, but they tell me of all this - is the great Auguste Janvier himself. He is the pet scientific wonder of the age. He has kept a dead ape in cold storage for a year and restored him to life. He has extended the lives of giant tropical moths by four mating seasons. They say he has bred an ant which is as big as a poodle. And rats which.... but doubtless you know the gossip. For myself I see him as unhuman and repulsive. I find that he resembles a snake."

The superior butler struck a small gong, a suburban anachronism in that setting, and there was immediate silence.

Janvier took two paces forward, his fists clenched at his side and his head lowered as if he were about to charge.

"This experiment," he said, "is delicate to a degree. I could have wished to be allowed to conduct it in privacy, for the results and not the subject are of importance from my viewpoint. Since this cannot be the case, you will all - all of you - remain absolutely still and silent, once you are in your places. Understand, please. No smoking, no movement, no talking. If you are ready, we will descend."

He led the way through a narrow door to a spiral stone staircase. We shuffled after him to the underground chapel of the Seigneurie, the tomb itself. It is of vaulted stone supported by thick columns, but at that moment it resembled nothing so much as a television studio. There were ropes between the columns us barriers and we stood sheepishly behind them.

There were arc lamps, coils of cable, and disembowelled pieces of machinery and apparatus everywhere, with the subdued hum of a dynamo. Two assistants were clearly mechanics, for they wore denims and stood by a panel of switches, and two were white robed and masked as for an operation. Janvier, now also in a white jacket stood apart.

But these were details which the eye took in at a sweep. In the centre of the room, raised upon trestles lay an enormous leaden coffin, very beautifully chased, its ponderous grandeur enhanced by mould and white lichen. It had clearly been lifted from the vault beneath, which was covered by planks, and the lid had already been loosened.

Janvier waited again for the moment of absolute silence. The two mechanics moved forward armed with metal levers and raised the crusted lid. It was immensely heavy, so that they slid it carefully to one side before carrying it away altogether.

Inside lay the body of a King, an undoubted monarch who was also a giant.

I cannot tell how best to grip this moment to the paper in words to be read in easy relaxation. It was a moment of awe in which no one drew breath.

Le Grand Seigneur lay in his coffin as lonely and as remote as a dead planet in space. His hands, yellow as old ivory were clasped over the hilt of a naked sword, the tip of which rested between his feet. His robes were still white, his eyes were closed and his great grey beard flowed from his jaws over his chest. He could have been sleeping a day or a thousand years.

Even Janvier stood beside him as if petrified and the two mechanics became rigid and grotesque, their backs half straightened after the weight of the lid, as if a film had suddenly stopped in the middle of a scene. Only the dynamos maintained their throb like a long inevitable headache.

Finally Janvier made a gesture and little Laborde the embalmer teetered forward. He stood for some time giving the body a long professional stare. Then he bent over the coffin and touched the forehead, the hair and the hands. The spell was broken but a sense of unease had me in a cold vice. Apart from the protagonists we all stood motionless.

The whole scene was enacted in silence and it was clear it had been carefully discussed beforehand. Laborde, satisfied that some particular requirement of his trade had been fulfilled stood back. Four pairs of hands raised the upper part of the rigid figure and slid a board beneath the body so that it lay tilted, three parts out of the sarcophagus. A piece of fragile drapery broke off and fell to the floor and some yellow fragments of twigs dropped to nothing, revealing a stain on the white robes, the imprint of a withered funeral wreath.

Now it was Janvier's turn to satisfy himself. The others stood apart as he lowered his head. In just such a way I have seen a pianist bow over a key board before striking the first chord. Then he spread out his arms and snapped his fingers, the first sound in the vault to rise above the muffled rhythm of the dynamos.

His two white coated assistants now brought him belts of grey flexible material to which wire cables were attached. These he wound round the forehead, the hands, the feet and the chest and as he did so the burial clothes broke into frail cobwebs. The massive dignity of that gigantic figure survived these insults.

When it was all done he made a sign and a man at the switchboard turned a dial. The throb of the dynamos rose by a semitone. Needles on the board began to flicker. To the layman it was like watching the cockpit of an airliner when the pilot is engaged in a tricky manoeuvre.

Janvier stood for several minutes beside him, one hand on the man's shoulder. Then he returned to the body. The rhythm became intolerable with dull urgency.

Beauregarde, the historian, was standing beside me, though until this moment I had not noticed him. In all this suspense no one had stirred, but suddenly he leaned forward and crossed himself, a reflex gesture which was involuntary.

"Mother of Heaven," he said, "he....it....Le Seigneur...is sweating."

It was true. A waxen surface on the body was melting. A deeper colour had returned to the ivory face and with it, moisture trickled from the forehead.

Janvier, his hands gripping the leaden edge of the coffin, drew to his full height. He made a swift gesture to the white coated men with him and they laid their hands upon the body in unison. Artificial respiration.

To and fro, on and on. Pieces of white burial cloth began to float like feathers to the stone floor.

At last they stopped and the two with him stood back. The whirr of dynamos, still a pain rather than a sound, rose again.

Then it happened. We all saw it, all of us, and it was a terrible moment.

The body shuddered. The great chest with its mat of grey hair, now three parts bare in its feathery rags, gave an enormous convulsive heave. It was alive.

Again Janvier gestured to the switches: and the throb rose almost out of earshot.

Another breath, and another. The whole carcass writhed. If there is feeling in this frightening moving creature, I thought, it can only be intense pain. This is torture in a modern clinical hygienic pit of Acheron, an eighth circle undreamed of by Dante.

We who watched made a strange animal noise between us, a compound of 'No' and 'Enough' and 'Spare us all for the love of God.'

The two spots of colour on Janvier's checks burned bright as paint and his eye sockets might have been dark glasses with polished jet boot buttons in the centre. For the first time he spoke to the man at the controls.

"Group Two to five thousand," he said, "and all you can make on three and four."

To me he seemed the incarnation of merciless power and obscene curiosity, driving into a secret beyond human acceptance.

Slowly, jerkily, like an enormous marionette, Le Grand Seigneur arched his back and the huge chest, every rib and muscle quivering, expanded to its zenith. Now he was bolt upright on his haunches, the sword still between his hands.

And now his eyes were open. They were china blue, without focus, staring straight ahead like the eyes of a doll.

From his forehead, his chest and his hands the dangling wires drummed their infernal life force into him. An intensity of pain wracked me as if the currents were passing through my own body.

His brows contracted and his eyes darkened as if he were staring directly into the sun. He can see, I thought. Now he can see us all, in the miserable shame of our puerile curiosity.

He did not turn his head but his eyes moved. Yet he was still unreal and the suggestion of a great marionette was enhanced by the trailing wires.

I saw his hands tighten and change their grip on the sword and slowly, jerkily, he raised it in a long arc until it was held directly above his head.

Then he spoke.

It was a deep rasping voice like a gramophone record played too slowly through an echo chamber, each particle of sound separated from its fellow. I did not need Bezin's gift of tongues to understand.

"*Who breaks my dream?*"

There was complete silence. None of us dared answer. But Janvier took a half pace forward, one arm outstretched to the instrument panel, like a conductor sustaining a single note.

The flash of blue lightening followed by utter darkness came almost as a relief. It etched the scene on our blinded eyes for a long moment and indeed for a lifetime.

At last one of the engineers shouted.

"Master switch! Quick, the battery set!" There was scuffling and voices crying "Candles!", "New Fuses" "Everyone still, please."

A pocket lighter made a pinpoint, then the beam of a torch swept the stone columns and finally a single naked bulb in the roof moved coldly into being.

It was the last tableau in the whole nightmare and again every movement was arrested as the picture cleared, sharp and chill, on cobweb and stone, black silhouette, tangled wire and moulded lead.

The Seigneur lay inert half in and half out of the sarcophagus. He had returned to his long sleep and this time it would surely be for all eternity. The skin was parchment stretched over bone, taut and rigid as a winter leaf which would soon be dust.

Only the sword between his hands retained its reality, blackened silver and tarnished steel. But it was still a sword and the blade was crimson bright with blood. From the black shadows on the flagstones into the central pool of light and into darkness again there was a slow glimmering stream which found the crevices, absorbed them, and flowed on.

Janvier. Not the scientist, the brain which was mastering the secrets of time, but a crumpled hulk in a white coat blotched with dust and spattered scarlet, with ridiculous patent leather shoes and a sagging black sock, an enemy killed by the single sweep of a sword on a battlefield of his own choosing.

We reached the upper room with what dignity was left to us. Our cheeks were grey and each man stood apart from his neighbour, glancing covertly, trying to read if his own face was as scared and shriveled as those about him.

Vertés moved to the table like a sleepwalker and poured cognac, spilling half of it over the cloth. One by one we followed him.

Beauregarde, standing nearest to me, mumbled out of a dream which was glazing his eyes.

"He said 'None shall pass.' His motto, you know. His rallying cry. It is on the coat of arms."

Bezin heard him and shook his head. "No," he said. "The words were quite distinct. What he said was 'I am not mocked', or something very like it."

None of us have ever been disposed to argue the point.

The Seeds of Time

Young Foster ran down the Quadrangle through the cloisters and then slap into a brick wall. Wallop. Just like that.

He bashed his head, spilt a lot of blood, knocked himself out and was carted off to the Sanitarium where he stayed, pretty dizzy, I suppose, for the best part of a week.

This is the vividest memory of all my school days because I was one of the chaps who caused the trouble. It was 12.15 p.m. end of morning lessons and in those days the fashionable rag was to belt the man ahead of you, preferably someone who was wandering out of a class alone, smartly across the backside and cry "I'm after you!"

The man thus struck ran like a stag until he could find some other person similarly placed, whom he could strike in turn. And so on. It seemed to us wildly funny and the chase led, by unwritten law to any latrine, which was an agreed sanctuary.

It was I who hit Foster across his rump and he set off at speed clearly knowing what it was all about, and enjoying the rag. But he ran straight into the wall, and that was the start of it. I felt pretty guilty because of the accident, though there was no sort of bullying involved. He was quite good at games and might easily have got clear away. I didn't know him at all well although he was in my own form and my own house. Even so, conscience nagged at me and I went down to the San to see him. It was the beginning of a year long friendship.

He was a very odd fellow, small and shy, with big dark eyes and the kind of nose that earned him the nickname 'Beaky'.

The first time I really noticed anything strange about him was during an English lesson under old Mothballs, not a natural schoolmaster but a dull dog who got by with uninspired efficiency. The subject was John Fairclough, the poet, a minor light of the late eighteenth century, but one of our more illustrious old boys. Indeed, there is a Fairclough Memorial Fountain in the Quad which had just been cleaned and refurbished for this was his bi-centenary year.

Mothballs was talking about the Fairclough biography, re-issued and re-edited for the celebration. It is the standard work, by a man called Ramsden, also a son of the school, a contemporary of the poet's. The old man was rambling along, almost intoning his remarks, when he perceived that Foster was asleep. Always a fine shot with a piece of chalk he caught the boy right on the bridge of his nose. There was some applause for the feat, which he followed up by remarking:

"Perhaps Foster, you would care to give us some of your personal impressions of Fairclough, a few nuts from your squirrel's hoard of information? Some private morsel already in store, since you are clearly not in need of anything which can be gained by paying attention."

Foster was rubbing his nose, which was apparently pretty painful. Everyone was laughing at him; he was hurt and very angry. He stood up.

"Yes sir," he said, "I can. Fairclough had ginger hair and a stammer. His eyes used to water a lot, particularly when he was being ragged. And he was a dirty little sneak when he had half the chance. He sneaked on Ramsden once for breaking bounds and got him a birching."

Old Mothballs was taken out of his stride by this but he came back acidly. Sarcasm was his speciality.

"Indeed Foster? How remarkable then that Ramsden never mentions this incident, though he gives us a wealth of other information about their school days - in this very classroom, my boy, possibly just where you are now idling - and when he speaks of Fairclough's hair he says it was golden as a cornfield."

Foster was so angry that he did not see the trap being baited. He went on, still rubbing his nose: "Fairclough sat in the front sir, because he was jolly short-sighted. Not in my seat, sir, but where Forsdyke is sitting now. Ramsden sat at the back with the rest of the bullies. He wasn't a friend of Fairclough's at all. He only said that later, years afterwards, when he wanted to make himself out to be important. He was just a common toady. Even the masters didn't like him."

By now Foster had made rather an effect. He spoke as if it had been only the term before and he really did know what he was talking about.

Even Mothballs paused before he remarked: "But this is fascinating. I never credited you with possessing either erudition or imagination. Perhaps you can enlighten us all about the incident of the flying pork pie? Was there injustice in those days, Foster?"

He was referring to the one good piece of gossip in the schooldays chapter, a passage which describes how the poet was accused of throwing a pork pie through the headmaster's dining room window thereby disrupting the meal which was in progress (for it struck an open soup tureen) and bringing down a fearful vengeance on the young poet who had always protested his innocence.

"Oh, he did it all right," said Foster, "but it was a mistake. He was sweet on the Head's daughter, Dorothea. He was trying to chuck it up into her bedroom, just above. He was always a rotten shot, being so boss-eyed."

We were all listening now. Mothballs was in some danger of losing control of things. Finally he said: "And how are you so certain of all this, Master Foster? Were you a spectral visitor at the scene? Speak up, boy."

Foster lost his nerve. His face went from red to white and he shook himself, a twitch as if he were a wet dog.

"I'm sorry, sir," he said at last. "I made it all up. It was a.....a sort of daydream I had. I beg your pardon."

He sat down; or rather he crumpled up as if he'd been winded.

"In that case you will confine your dreaming to the proper place in future. You will also write out Ramsden's excellent chapter 'Our Happiest Days' in a fair copperplate hand and bring it to me by Wednesday morning. Without fail. It should cure you of the modern tendency to sneer and to denigrate the heroes of old."

That was the end of the incident. It might have been worse, I decided, if poor Foster had not looked so ill at the end. Most of us thought he was going to faint. I gave him a hand with his copying, for we were now regular friends and whilst we sat at it in the dayroom I asked him what on earth had come over him.

"I don't know," he said. "He riled me, hitting me on the nose like that. I ought to have shut up about all that tripe of Ramsden's. He was a greasy swine, anyhow."

"How on earth do you know?" I said. "Been swotting it up in some other book?"

"No," he said. "I'm not a swot. It's just that I....oh, forget it. I'll tell you some other time. I promise." Then he turned to his lines and muttered "Carroty-headed little stinker."

I tried again but he just clammed up and we finished the job in silence.

The second odd thing happened on a Tuesday in June. I remember it very well because it was the eve of Derby Day, and the maths master had been encouraging us to take an interest in simple arithmetic by calculating odds and running an imaginary book in class. He was one of those 'with-it' types, very rare in those days.

Just before afternoon school Foster dashed up to me in the changing room where I was oiling a bat. He was very excited.

"I say," he whispered. "Do you have any money you can lay your hands on? I've just remembered...that is, it's just occurred to me...we can do ourselves, proud. Coronach's the name for tomorrow. We can't go wrong."

Now even at that tender age I had heard that once before and pocket money was precious. But Foster was so excited and so persuasive that he whisked my objections away. In all, we scraped five pounds together and in the late afternoon we found old Pudney the groundsman and cricket pro at the nets. He was our strictly illegal bookie, though it was an open secret, for the masters also used him freely.

We won £25, a great fortune.

As we were counting our hoard for the sixth time behind the pavilion - it was towards tea time on the Saturday evening and the first eleven were dragging out their game for a draw - I raised the matter which had been bothering me for three days.

"Look here, Foster," I said. "When you first thought of this effort of ours you said 'I've just remembered' about Coronach. Then you backed out of it and said 'It's just occurred to me', as if someone had given you a tip out of the air or something. Now you jolly well own up and tell me how you knew."

He looked away from me and began to mumble.

"It was just a hunch. I didn't really know. Honestly, I simply guessed it." He brightened. "But it came off, didn't it?"

"Bosh," I said. "You knew about it somehow and you won't admit it. I think it's something to do with that bang on the head you got when you ran into the wall. I think you see visions and you just won't own up to it. Look, if you do, why don't we go into partnership on bets and things and become millionaires? You might even be able to see what things to bone up on for the exams."

He shook his head. "No, old boy," he said. "It isn't a bit like that. That bang on the head was only a silly mistake. I...I thought I could...well, never mind what I thought. I forgot something, if you must know."

He shut up for a bit as if he'd been about to confide in me but had thought better of it, but then went on, rather red in the face. "Look, about this twenty five quid. I'd rather you had it. None of it really belongs to me and you could get a motor bike for that if your old man would stand for it. You keep it. I can't use it anyway. Pity to waste it. Please hang on to it, well, at least to the end of term. You'll see what I mean then."

I told him bosh and rubbish but he was so solemn and so insistent that I agreed to hold our loot until the hols when we'd have our share-out whether he liked it or not.

In a way, a rather miserable way, it was just as well. About three weeks before the end of term Foster killed himself. He blew himself up one afternoon in one of the science labs, where he had no business anyhow, for it was a half hol and stinks wasn't his subject. There was one hell of an explosion, all the electric circuits in the school went haywire, there was a hole in the wall of the physics lab you could have driven a cart through, a considerable fire and a mess which stank the place out for days.

But no Foster. Not a rag nor a bone, except for what they thought might have been his cap, but could just as well have been anyone's from the state it was in. We only knew it was Foster because a cleaner actually saw him there mucking about with some wires.

Well, of course there was the most awful row you can imagine. He had an old uncle with whom he lived, who naturally came roaring down from Northumberland where he was supposed to own a great castle (sometimes it was a haunted grange, according to rumour) together with dozens of officials and policemen and journalists. Nothing came of it, although uncle and his friends poked about in the remains for weeks, even after the school broke up. No one ever discovered what Foster had been doing and no trace of him was ever found. Death by misadventure they said and added a lot of tripe about adequate precautions being taken with dangerous equipment.

I was more cut up about it than anyone, certainly than his uncle who seemed, I thought, curious and excited rather than sad, as any decent guardian ought to have been. He ransacked Foster's locker and took all his kit away, even his schoolbooks which weren't his anyhow.

This matter of fact, clinical attitude made me so angry and so sad that I moped all through the summer hols and never told anyone about the one bit of Foster that remained, apart from his share of the twenty five pounds.

This was his folio, a sort of stout cardboard file with flaps which you tied with black tapes and kept exercise paper and note books and letters in. We all had one, for they were issued to us, but Foster had managed to wangle two.

The second one was what he called his secret file and he never showed it to anyone, not even to me.

The day after the explosion I found it right at the back of my own locker and I knew he must have put it there himself just before the accident. I guarded my secret at first with a miserable resentment against fate, which had removed my friend so suddenly, then as a sentimental relic of my schooldays.

Finally, of course, I forgot all about it.

Foster, having disappeared or disintegrated or been blown to atoms, lived on only as a nine days wonder to be discussed at Old Boys' gatherings, along with Watson's stupendous six over the Chapel right into the Quad, Entwhistle's try against Charterhouse and Fat Potter getting six of the best in the dining hall for amateur ventriloquism.

It was at one of these gatherings that the subject inevitably arose again. Old Boys' Day was wet that year and we gathered gloomily in the Big School after lunch for there was no cricket to watch. In its place was an exhibition of old prints and maps of the school going back over four hundred years.

The man standing next to me said, "That's odd. Do you remember poor old Beaky Foster running into the wall of the cloisters and nearly braining himself?"

I agreed that I did and asked what was odd about it.

"Look at this map," said the man. "Drawn in 1790, before the library was built. If Foster had been dashing down the quad then, he'd have been able to turn sharp left and had a clear run as far as the Head's yard. I always thought he was odd even before that bang on the head. Never quite with it, you know. Remember that day he lectured Mothballs about Fairclough's red hair?"

The whole thing came back to me so vividly that I felt quite sick with a sudden surge of forgotten emotion. When I got home I rummaged around for Foster's secret folio which I found after a long search at the back of a drawer full of theatre programmes. It must be thirty years since I last turned over the contents. In to-day's light they are an extraordinary collection.

There is a photograph cut out of a Rugger group of John Pilchard who I am very much afraid may be our next Prime Minister but one, and a complete essay - rather a good one - in a round schoolboy hand, a set piece for prep, signed by the late Charles Winters the dramatist, which must be quite valuable now. Then there are three separate signatures, pinned together, of Sir James Purdee the atomic wizard, who is the biggest name in the business today, and an amateurish snap of Wagstaff the composer, aged about fourteen, holding a fiddle. An old fashioned fountain pen has a label "Lauderdale's pen, which he gave me when it went wrong" and this is almost too valuable a trophy to keep these days, when every scrap connected with that immortal hero is a collector's item.

There is a sketch of an aeroplane, remarkably modern, signed and dated 1926, by Bradley who is the greatest of living designers, but showed no sign of talent at school and finally a whole collection of signatures and bits of writing, together with a button and a very scruffy school tie, marked as belonging to Adam Makepeace, aged 13, Lower IV B, whom I don't remember and have never heard of since. There is nothing, I regret to say, of my own.

There were about seven hundred of us there in 1926 and out of those boys Foster had collected souvenirs of our six famous men, and with one exception, nothing else.

You must admit that wherever he came from or wherever he went to, there was something very odd about Foster. Odd, you know, because he wasn't weird at all - just an ordinary rather nice shy chap who always seemed on the verge of confiding something but never did.

I often had the feeling he might turn up again, though I don't see how. In the meantime I watch the papers for news of Adam Makepeace and I advise you all to do the same.

The Last of General Trotter

War Office files of the 'Most Secret: Burn-Before-Reading' type are always mystifying and sometimes, infuriating. The diligent student is often driven to the fringe of madness in his efforts to disentangle them. It is a matter of speculation whether an astute spy would make anything of a Top Secret folder which began with four separate schemes, each ponderously documented and ended, as they almost invariably do, with a scribbled postcard bearing an illegibly stamped crest and the words: "This is all very fine in its way, but on reflection I think we'll proceed on the lines you and I discussed with Bertie on Tuesday. J."

Even the masters of espionage must be foxed by such superb feeling for security. Probably this is all for the best, provided the V.I.P.'s really know what is afoot and the underlings are left with what the Pentagon rightly calls The Bafflegab.

Sometimes of course it deepens a mystery.

In the personal file of the erstwhile Commander in Chief of the Imperial General Staff, the War Office, the late Lt. General Sir Hector Drummond-Trotter, K.C.B., D.S.O., etc. etc., there was once a letter, again identifiable only by an initial and an obsolete crest, which held the key to what might have made a seven days wonder for the world, had the world ever known about it.

The document is preserved in the great room overlooking Whitehall, with its dignified portraits of King and Field Marshals, where the mystery occurred. It is preserved, like a glove once worn by a hero's mistress, but never referred to. On the single sheet of very expensive paper is inscribed in precise Oxford script, these words:

I am so glad you will see the old boy. I feel sure he has something, but he is too vague and irascible to get past your barrage of experts. In any case he may amuse you for half an hour. I have told him Tuesday a.m. Yrs. A.

At the bottom is scribbled in the C.I.G.S's own green pencil, "Earling? Irving? 11.30."

The only other clue to the mystery is a curiously shaped piece of bone or ivory which is now housed in the desolate darkness of what is called "The Trophy Store (Room 6)".

Ex-R.S.M. Ransome of the Coldstreams, two security scrutineers and Capt. Betty Tripp W.R.A.C. who would hate to be described as an usherette or even a receptionist, all on duty on that fatal Tuesday in the War Office, have roughly the same story.

"He was an old man. Looked vaguely like Augustus John or Bernard Shaw. Had a beard and a biggish hat, which he took off very politely. He wore one of those cloak style overcoats which old men sometimes wear and are now affected by very young men from the Varsities to attend race meetings or rugger matches. He came to the front entrance at 11.30. and was not seen to leave."

Capt. the Hon. Robert Van Tiffin, the P.A. to the C.I.G.S. is a little more precise.

"I think he was very old," his statement runs. "About 80 or possibly more, but reasonably spry. His hair was still strong but quite white. He had a slightly trimmed beard and a big head with a beaky nose. Not Jewish, but sort of patriarchal. He also had freckles which I've never seen on an old man before.

"The only really odd thing I noticed about him was that he appeared to be smoking. I mean that in the lift I nearly ticked him off for it, since he blew a cloud of smoke out of his mouth, but did not do so because I could see no pipe nor cigarette. He had very old black ammunition boots and his coat was some sort of green tweed. I left him with the C.I.G.S. at 11.35. and did not see him go out."

The old man in fact stood still just inside the tall double doors which the Hon. Robert had closed discreetly behind him, and gazed around with slow almost awestruck curiosity upon Haig, Wellington, Kitchener, King William (of William and Mary) and F.M. the Earl of Kirkintulloch, of whom history records practically nothing.

Sir Hector Drummond-Trotter had kept his desk in the same place as many of his predecessors, with his back to the domed central window, so that on a fine morning he was practically invisible or at best a silhouette confronting the visitor. This gave him what he called a strategic advantage, for he was never a man to coin a phrase.

After a decent pause in which he summed up the situation with what must be considered masterly ineptitude, he picked up one of his four telephones and said "Ah, Bobby. Let me know, will you?" which was a private signal meaning: "Come in and get rid of this fellow just as soon as I press the bell under my desk."

To the visitor he said, "Well, come in, come in. Sit down, will you? Make yourself comfortable, eh? Now, Sir Arthur has told me a lot about you in a roundabout kind of way. He seems to think you may be useful. I'm afraid I haven't a lot of time, so let's get to the point, eh?"

As Generals go, Sir Hector was a fair specimen. He was not an intellectual, but he had a phenomenal memory for facts and data. His mind was a first class filing system, perpetually and rapidly producing sound answers. He was short, square, handsome in a heavy middle-aged English style and he had the trick of looking indomitable. As the stranger put on a pair of pebble thick glasses to peer at him he donned this protective expression. The old man clearly fell into the category of 'Lunatics; harmless.'

"I was told, sir," said the stranger, "that you might be interested to see my Dragon's Teeth." He rummaged slowly within hidden pockets and finally produced a leather bag or purse with a drawstring. "This one, for example."

"Don't follow you," said the General. "Some sort of anti-tank device? These ideas are a bit out of date, you know - war's more mobile now. Concrete and all that has gone by the board; takes too long to fix."

"This," said the old man, displaying a yellow object which might have been a small ivory paper knife, "is very rapid. Do you possess earth here?"

His magnified myopic eyes, like a bullfrog's behind the lenses, searched the room and fixed upon a decorative pot containing ivy on the great desk, standing next to a silver-framed photograph of its donor, the Lady Drummond-Trotter.

"This will serve," he said, and pushed the curious fang into the soil at the base of the ivy. His voice had a rumbling rheumy quality as if someone was playing a record too slowly through a railway station loud speaker.

"*Yakavit. Evabo. Lembia,*" he said and struck the palms of his hands together. There appeared between them a small cloud which might have been dust.

"Look here, be careful," said Sir Hector. "My wife gave me that damned thing and if anything happened......"

But it had begun to happen.

The jagged ivory object in the flower pot was growing like an Indian fakir's seed. It expanded in a series of grotesque jerks to the size of a respectable elephant's tusk. The pot shivered and smashed to fragments, earth was spread all over the desk, the telephones, the in-tray and its neighbours. The silver frame fell flat on its face and a single ominous creak from the desk showed that whatever was growing had roots which were strong and deep.

196

The tusk itself branched into a dozen vicious forks with knife edges, quivered for a fraction of time and was still.

Sir Hector's voice became shrill with fury.

"What the devil do you think you're up to?" he shouted. "Stop it, I say, stop it! Put it all back!"

The visitor spread out his hand in a gesture which took in the terrifying growth which now had a rigid permanence about it and indicated his leather purse.

"With one of these," he said, "a man could stop an army. It is a deep secret, but very simple in operation. A peasant could use it, or if you prefer it so, a resistance fighter."

"Damn your conjuring trick," said the General. "You seem to have smashed my desk."

"True," replied the old man, "but this specific of mine has broken stouter tables than that in its time. Now Sir General, may I show you my Simple whereby a man may make himself invulnerable against all enemies however powerful?"

"No, dammit, you may not," said Sir Hector, who was now displaying all those warning signals which had frightened more than one Army Corps into discipline.

"You'll clean up this infernal mess you've made, with your own two hands. You'll look sharp about it and then you'll get out. I've got work to do."

He paused for breath and was once again confronted by the defiant object, larger than himself, which resembled an enormous yellow claw placed between him and the stranger. It really was beyond a joke.

"Now look here," he said. "I don't know who the devil you are, but we're not interested in conjuring tricks here. Go and play your damn games in a music hall. You don't suppose this blasted growth would stop a tank, do you?"

The old man regarded his handiwork above his thick horn glasses. It was the affectionate glance of a craftsman.

"A handful of them once held up an avalanche," he said. "Your toys would break before them. Now here, sir, is a little powder. Sprinkle it upon the air....thus and thus......"

Sir Hector would have stopped him forcibly, and made to do so, but the claw had branched to that side of the desk which it was his habit to pass and he had to turn right and so negotiate telephone cords and a wastepaper basket.

He was too late. There were tiny particles of gold floating in dusty air about the old man.

"And I turn," said his caller, pivoting slowly, "I turn three times and I blow upon this dust. *Yakavit* I say...and *Yakavit* again. *Poste, Poste numah* and thrice *Yakavit.*"

As he spoke the floating golden fragments exploded into little flames and vanished leaving wisps of smoke about the tweedy old figure which were slightly scented like oriental tobacco.

"You get out of here," said the General, advancing upon him. "Get out of here now, before I throw you out."

"That is impossible," said the visitor. "It is beyond your powers. But pray make the attempt. Strike me, for example. Strike with that black rod upon your table. If you are a fool you must learn the fool's way."

Upon the desk lay an ebony ruler; an impressive but useless object, part of the ponderous furnishings. It was within arm's length and the General seized it almost as if to arm himself with a baton of office.

"I've a damn good mind to," he said, "if you don't get out of here now - and at the double."

"I shall not move," said the old man. "Strike and perceive a wonder. Strike at the air about me if you feel some trifling respect for my years. Strike, I say."

The General was in no mood for trifling. He took a step and a step and swung the ruler, not so much to hit as to threaten. It snapped in two and the thin smoke eddied in the air about the jagged stump still clutched in his hand.

There was a long pause whilst neither man moved a muscle. Finally Sir Hector, with an effort which deepened the colour in his face and thickened his neck perceptibly, replaced the broken symbol on the edge of the desk. He straightened himself, clasped his hands firmly behind his back in a final effort to keep his temper, cleared his throat and spoke.

"Who ever you are," he said, "understand this. Neither I nor any of my colleagues want any part of this ridiculous mumbo-jumbo monkey business. We do not deal in tricks, understand? I don't pretend to see how you've achieved all this nonsense and I don't particularly want to. I'm neither Maskelyne nor Devant, sir - I'm not even Barnum and Bailey and I want no part of your tomfooling. Now get, get out quickly before I have you flung into Whitehall."

Sir Hector was a man, who, in an emergency, could make a point clearly and finally. Having delivered himself he returned to his desk not altogether without dignity, sat down, picked up some papers and half swung his chair towards the light.

Without the ignominy of ringing for aid it was the best that could be made of the situation. He was not a negligible figure and he managed to convey very precisely the degree of insult he intended. So far as he was concerned, from that moment on the visitor was a vulgar nuisance, utterly without significance.

After a while the old man made a pass in the air about him and took a pace forward very delicately as a man might in stepping over a trip wire. He peered at Sir Hector with concentration.

His voice was a deep and angry rumble.

"You are a fool," he said, "and an ass. But now that I see you clearly your face is more like that of a pig. Not a wild boar, for you have not his crafty cunning, but a pig. And by all the powers within me, a pig you shall be."

He raised both hands above his head.

"A pig," he said again. "*Yakavit. Demnos. Yakavit hoie demnos demnos yakavit.* A pig."

* * * * * * *

Captain the Hon. Robert Van Tiffin's glance passed idly from his wristwatch to the wall clock in his office and thence to Captain Betty Tripp's new hair-do.

"The Governor's a long time with that old boy," he said. "Think I'd better go and break up the party?"

"I wouldn't risk it, Bobby," said his sister officer. "They might be talking very important stuff - racing, agriculture, grandchildren. Vital War Office business, you know. Dangerous to put your nose in to that. Who is he, anyhow - the old boy, I mean?"

The Hon. Bobby glanced at his memo pad.

"Haven't a clue," he said. "Never heard of him. Somebody A. King sent, I believe. All the same, it's after twelve and I think I'll go and see. He's lunching in ten minutes."

He moved over to the door, opened it for a couple of inches and peered through the crack. There was no sign of the visitor but he was greeted by a most peculiar succession of sounds.

"I say," he said. "There's something pretty queer going on here. You'd better come with me."

They entered the room on tiptoe, Bobby a pace ahead, but they were hand in hand before the strange growth on the General's desk had made its first impact. Behind it was an even greater shock.

Sir Hector was still in his chair and was indeed rotating it slowly from side to side. His collar had burst wide open and his suit, for mercifully he was not in uniform, was parting at every seam. He was making a noise which can only be described as a series of very angry grunts.

"Oh, I say, Sir!" said his aide. "Are you alright? I mean to say.....that is.....your ears, sir...oh, sir, have you looked at yourself in a mirror?"

"Hurrumph!" said Sir Hector with menacing ferocity.

The Hon. Bobby tightened his grip on Capt. Tripp's hand. He appeared to be thoroughly scared.

"We'd better get out," he said under his breath. "We must have help."

To Sir Hector he spoke aloud. "I'll come back in a moment, sir. I'll get someone. Don't worry, it'll be alright. I'll come straight back."

He heard his own voice using a tone of that reassurance more suited to an animal than to a human being.

"Gerrumph! Gerrumph!" reported Sir Hector and he turned in his chair towards them.

Hand in hand they retreated before the malice in his eyes. Outside they turned to face each other, the flush which had begun as embarrassment draining slowly out of their cheeks, leaving them pale with fright.

"What the Hell do we do now?" said the Hon. Bobby. "I mean - I don't think the M.O. quite.....do you?"

Capt. Tripp was leaning against the door, with her back to it.

"Before we do anything, Bobby," she said, "We must *think*. Who *was* that last caller? Haven't you any sort of record?"

He swung away from her and searched the memo pad on his desk; he was frowning with concentration.

"Can't read my own writing," he muttered. "I wrote it in a hurry. The name seems to be Irving or Earling. *Or* it might even be Merlin. That name rings some sort of bell with me. How about you?"

Capt. Tripp regarded him steadily with beautiful but deeply horrified eyes.

"Merlin?" she said bleakly. "*Merlin.* My goodness, d'you think we ought to call a Vet?"

The Hon. Bobbie, an astute and resourceful young officer, moved towards the telephone.

"I shall get on to this chap Arhur King himself," he said. "All explanations - and there'll have to be some, pretty damn quick - should be conducted on the very highest level, I feel. This is right out of our innocent class, old girl."

Editorial Notes

Although he began writing short stories whilst a serving officer in the British army in the North African desert campaign, Youngman Carter's most prolific period was 1959–1962 when he was a regular contributor to Argosy in the UK with many of his stories reprinted in Ellery Queen's Mystery Magazine (EQMM) in the USA, often with a change of title.

From papers now lodged in the Margery Allingham Archive at Essex University, it is clear that around 1965 he was preparing his own anthology, rewriting and editing published stories and adding previously unpublished material, under the title *Tales on the Off-Beat*. After the death of his wife, Margery Allingham, in 1966, Carter concentrated on completing the unfinished *Cargo of Eagles* (published in 1968) and then further novels featuring her famous detective Albert Campion.

Where no publishing history is known, some stories in this collection – taken from typed manuscripts in the Allingham Archive – are presumed to be published here for the first time.

Humble's Box: First published in *John Bull* in October 1959.

[*John Bull* was an illustrated weekly magazine, the British equivalent of the *Saturday Evening Post* in America. Its heyday was the late 1940s and '50s and featured short fiction (or extracts from novels) by popular authors of the day including Agatha Christie, Alistair Maclean, Victor Canning and Gerald Kersh. In 1960 it was relaunched as *Today – The New John Bull*.]

The Trivial Round: First published in *Argosy (UK)* in February 1962.

Means of Escape: First published in *Today* in September 1962. Retitled ***The Most Wanted Man in the World*** for *EQMM* in November 1962 and collected in *Ellery Queen's Mystery Mix #18* in 1963.

[Possibly Youngman Carter's most successful short story, which went on to be published in Australia, Sweden, Denmark, Finland and twice in Holland.]

Old Soldiers Never Lie: First published in *London Mystery Magazine #52* in 1962.

[Published from 1949–1982, *London Mystery Magazine* was a quarterly publication offering the "Best Crime, Mystery and Detective Fact and Fiction".]

The Trouble with Locksmiths: First published in *Argosy (UK)* in June 1960.

The Proper Charley: First published in *Argosy (UK)* in August 1961.

Uneasy Lies: First published in *Today* in 1961.

[The weekly *Today* magazine (not to be confused with the daily newspaper published 1986-1995) was the successor to *John Bull* and in 1964 merged with *Weekend* to aim more at the growing teenage market.]

Collector's Item: First published in *Argosy (UK)* in May 1959.

Peter the Blind: First known publication as **London Night's Entertainment** in *EQMM* in February 1954.

[At one point in the story, a portrait painting is described as "like Irving trying to play Hannen Swaffer". Frederick Charles Hannen Swaffer (1879–1962) was one of the most popular journalists in Britain between the wars. Known by his peers as 'The Pope of Fleet Street' he was also a committed socialist and also a leading spiritualist.]

Alias Mr Manchester: First published in *EQMM* in September 1967.

The Last Hangman: No known publishing history.

The Second Saint: First published in the *Edgar Wallace Mystery Magazine* in July 1966.

A for Assassins: No known publishing history.

Kane's Doll: First published in *Gen* in May 1943. Reprinted in *Argosy (UK)* in July 1945.

[The revised and retyped manuscript of *Kane's Doll* in the Allingham Archives bears a hand written note by Youngman Carter indicating that the story was originally written (or conceived) in 'September 1941, south of Matruh' – a reference to Mersa Matruh in Egypt, an important strategic point for British and Commonwealth troops fighting in the Western Desert campaign. In this and other 'Army Stories' reference is made to an A.B.64 which was the soldier's Service Record and Pay Book and functioned as an identity card.]

Mr Healy's Day: First published in *Gen* in June 1943. Reprinted in *Strand* magazine in July 1944.

[Described as 'The Services' Fortnightly' *Gen* was an illustrated magazine published in Baghdad (?), circulated to the British and Commonwealth forces serving in the Middle- East and Persia-Iraq Commands, 1943–45.]

The Green Box: No known publishing history.

[Possibly written originally for the Army magazine *Gen* but certainly revised by Youngman Carter in the 1960s, the story's punchline has echoes of Margery Allingham's *Traitor's Purse*, published in early 1941. The song referred to in the story, *We Are the Wanderers of the Wasteland*, came from a popular Gene Autry cowboy film of 1937.]

The Genuine Article: First published in *Gen* Issue 51 in January 1944.

[Published in the army magazine *Gen* during the war, the story references the BBC's *Café Continental*, presumably a radio programme as the BBC Television variety show of that name was not broadcast until 1947. The expression *Safragi* is an old Egyptian Arabic term for 'waiter'.]

Old School Type: First known publication in *EQMM* in November 1946.

[Possibly Youngman Carter's first story to be published in America, which mentions – in passing – Guffy Randall, a familiar character to readers of Margery Allingham's *Sweet Danger* (1933). The setting is again the Western Desert, shortly after the 'Msus Stakes' – a reference to a rolling, disorganised battle (sometimes called 'The Second Benghazi Handicap') which took place around Msus in Libya in January 1942.]

The Evil Eye of Brother Polidor: First published in *Argosy (UK)* in May 1961.

[Youngman Carter changed the title to **Brother Polidor's Eye** when he revised this story in 1965(?). He also altered the names of some characters and of the town from Cacharel to Moulin La Vièrge, possibly because of the establishment of the French fashion and perfume company Cacharel in 1962. His name for the ill-fated twisted tower of '*Tire- Bouchon*' is almost certainly a private joke from his days as a writer on wine.]

Dead Ringer: First published in *Argosy* in September 1960.

The Thorns Are Vicious: First published in *Argosy (UK)* in May 1946.
[This story, which evokes something of the Brothers Grimm, was possibly Youngman Carter's first post-war attempt at fiction, clearly influenced by revelations about Nazi concentration camps at the Nuremberg Trials.]

One For The Record: First published in *Argosy (UK)* in July 1964.
[Also known as ***Pursuant to my Duties as a Rodent Officer***.]

Grand Seigneur: First published in *Argosy (UK)* in September 1959.
[Retitled ***Leave Legends Alone*** by Youngman Carter c.1965, but without significant revisions.]

The Seeds of Time: First published in *Argosy (UK)* in July 1965. Reprinted in *EQMM* in December 1966.

The Last of General Trotter: First published as ***The Last of General Chitterling*** in *Argosy (UK)* in January 1961.
[This version retitled – substituting one pork based dish for another! – with minor revisions by Youngman Carter c.1965. At one point, the exasperated General Trotter refers to 'Maskelyne and Devant' in the same breath as 'Barnum and Bailey'. John Neville Maskelyne and David Devant were two of the foremost stage magicians in Britain, forming a partnership in 1905 and achieving international fame eclipsed only by Harry Houdini. Maskelyne's grandson Jasper, also a flamboyant stage magician, served, like Youngman Carter, in the Western Desert during World War II, supposedly employing stage magic (!) to help camouflage British positions and tanks.
The mysterious 'old man' of the story refers to 'my Simple' to make him invulnerable. A 'Simple' in this sense refers back to the Physic Gardens of Apothecaries' Gardens of the Middle Ages where plants were grown for their medicinal (or "magical") properties. A Simple was a single herb or flower which was used as a basic ingredient for ointments, potions and perhaps even spells...]

**Mike Ripley,
Colchester, 2015.**

www.ingramcontent.com/pod-product-compliance
Lightning Source LLC
Chambersburg PA
CBHW070115030726
47506CB00002B/751